Other books by the author:

Absolution, winner Novello Prize

A STONE FOR BREAD

Miriam Herin

Livingston Press

The University of West Alabama

ISBN 13: 978-1-60489-156-0, trade paper
ISBN 13: 978-1-60489-157-7, hardcover
ISBN: 1-60489-156-4, trade paper
ISBN: 1-60489-157-2, hardcover
Library of Congress Control Number: 2015941914
Printed on acid-free paper.
Printed in the United States of America,
Publishers Graphics
Hardcover binding by: Heckman Bindery
Typesetting and page layout: Angela Brown, Joe Taylor, Amanda Nolin
Proofreading: Teresa Boykin, Joe Taylor, Amanda Nolin
Cover design: Amanda Nolin
cover photo, courtesy of:
Bundesarchiv_Bild_192-210,_KZ, Mauthausen,_Hinrichtung,_Bonarewitz

No novel is brought into being solely by its author,
so there are those I need to thank:
—my friend of many years, Manuel Wortman, who grew up in Cleveland County,
N.C., and was invaluable in helping me understand what Henry Beam's childhood
might have been like;
—two exceptional proofreaders: my niece Rebecca Lanning, who's fashioned an
outstanding career as an editor, and who meticulously went over an earlier version
of the *A Stone for Bread* manuscript; and my neighbor and friend, Liz Pinson,
a former editor with the *Charlotte Observer*, who thoroughly and painstakingly
proofed the galleys;
—Ian Keith, a gifted young writer, who provided excellent feedback on the manuscript;
—my fiction workshop colleagues Hannah Logan Morris, Jeffrey Sykes, Jennifer
Ray and Roger Robbins, who helped me rethink the novel's opening chapters;
—Dr. Joe Taylor, professor, poet and editor extraordinaire of UWA's Livingston
Press and his wonderful staff, who have created a press of literary excellence;
—my children, Carol Herin Jordan and John Herin, both writers and literary readers, whose many critiques were essential in the writing of the novel, and whose
belief in it after I had abandoned it sent me back for another look;
—my husband Tom, my first reader and foremost encourager, who took me to Paris on our honeymoon and several times since, who's read every draft of A Stone
for Bread, and without whom, my ambition to write fiction would not have been
possible.

first edition

6 5 4 3 3 2 1

For

John Herin

&

Carol Herin Jordan

A STONE
FOR
BREAD

The ash wagon
carries its load to the river,
gray residue of souls,
hanks of hair,
fingernails, teeth,
shoveled on blue water.

The men scattering the refuse
talk of football,
how in '34,
the Jew Sindelar failed to score,
how it might have come down
had Guaita not scrambled the goal
off the post.

"A cheat,"
one says,
leaning on his shovel.
"Guaita wasn't Italian, you know."

"The mud won it,"
argues the other.
"If it hadn't rained.
It's a thing like that sometimes,
no more than a thing like that."

Work done,
they climb in the truck,
voices drifting away
like ashes on the Danube.

> —*author unknown*
> —*translated from the French*
> *by Henry Beam*

ONE

René was four years old when he buried a grenade in the garden behind his house. It was the summer of 1917 and there was war in France. Months before, soldiers had bivouacked in the village. When they moved on, René's father went to join the fighting farther north. The boy's grandparents spoke in hushed tones about *Les Boches* and guns with names, Big Bertha and Albrecht and one called the Distant Princess. René heard the booms from his bedroom window. He watched the sky flare with light. One morning a line of French soldiers passed through the village. That afternoon, his grandfather buried a tin box in a corner of the barn. The box held coins, a silver vanity set, two gold watches, a jeweled brooch belonging to a grandmother generations back, medals won by his great-uncle Albert in the war with Prussia. René held the small box while his grandfather dug. He watched him place the box in the hole, tamp down the dirt and cover it with straw and hay bales. The next day, René buried his treasures, bits of metal and colored rock scavenged from the woods. His twelve-year-old brother Étienne found them in the garden a week later when his hoe sliced into the grenade. Étienne's arms were blown from his body and he bled to death quickly.

Of course, it was an accident. The notary who investigated sadly shook his head and reminded the family it was wartime. A dog could have dragged it in. René wasn't told the notary's explanation. He was, after all, a child and did not understand why his brother had died, what evil thing waited in ambush among the leafy turnips. Did it too have a name? Realization came to him only gradually, the way one's hands go slowly numb with cold.

TWO

Rachel Singer was brought up to honor two primal verities: respectability and caution. The respectability was a rather thin distillation of southern Calvinism—chastity before marriage and an unspoken prohibition against embarrassing the family, in her case, her mother. The caution was more complicated, but understandable, and it embodied both verities. Her mother had lost her first child, a son, from a tumble on basement stairs before Rachel was born. When Rachel was three, her father died in Vietnam, not in combat but when his jeep collided with a truck. From an early age, Rachel was inoculated against risk by her mother's fears: the dangers of straying from the yard, talking to strangers (which included anyone her mother didn't approve of, like some of their neighbors), crossing streets, riding bikes and roller skating, petting dogs, sunbathing (from which one got skin cancer) and, of course, stairs. As she neared adolescence, particular attention was paid to the catastrophic consequences of sex: VD, herpes, AIDS, illegitimate babies, a ruined reputation and shame. But by eleventh grade, Rachel had decided not to be constrained by someone else's tragedies and began ignoring a number of these injunctions, although she did so with caution.

She wasn't a rebel in the classic sense, was never arrested or publicly drunk. Her friends' teenage limit-testing was confined primarily to passing around joints at parties, a few beers, parking with their dates behind the abandoned barn a mile from the high school. Besides, Rachel—who preferred to shut her bedroom door and study rather than answer a dozen who, what and where questions—was an exemplary student. She finished near the top of her high school class and attended the University of North Carolina at Chapel Hill on merit scholarships. It was only when she married Randy soon after graduation that her mother let her know, well before she walked down the aisle, that she had transgressed the first hallowed verity—or as her mother put it in her southern idiom, Rachel had "thrown it all away." What "it" was, Rachel understood, wasn't some fine ambition that she didn't then possess, but a respectable marriage. Randy was Catholic. Rachel grew up southern Presbyterian. When the marriage foundered five years later, her mother seemed almost gleeful to have her only child slouch home to Charlotte, wounded and depressed.

Which was why Rachel chose soon afterwards to take herself off to Chapel Hill, where she found a job as assistant to the Operations Manager at the local PBS station. She left that position two years later to enter an M.A. program at the university in English Lit—why, she wasn't certain, other than the need at thirty to be aimed in some direction. But she liked her professors, was stimulated intellectually by the reading and enjoyed the freshman comp classes she taught as a T.A. Yet there were days she worried she was merely treading water. Where was that fine ambition she seemed to have missed out on? Could it truly be found through an English master's degree in this decade of burgeoning dot-coms?

It was on one of these days that she ran into Scott Trevelian at the circulation desk at Davis Library.

"You're taking classes?" she asked, noting the vinyl portfolio in his hand.

He shook his head. "Just looking up some things."

Scott was a producer at the PBS station. They'd known each other there and had even gone out a few times. She hadn't seen him in months though, long enough for his sandy hair to drift over his ears and down his neck. He'd also grown a beard that unlike his shaggy hair was neatly trimmed.

"I like your beard," said Rachel, as they were leaving the library.

"Likewise your hair," he said. "Auburn looks great on you."

"Probably because it's the real me." After her divorce, she'd tried life as a brunette but reverted to natural when she left the station.

"Well, I like it." Despite the alterations to his appearance, Scott's skewed grin was engagingly the same.

They exited the library into a dreary November rain. She had an umbrella but Scott didn't, so they shared hers as they crossed the campus. When they reached Franklin Street, he suggested coffee, and they headed for a small café a half-block from campus. It was there Rachel first heard the name *Henry Beam*.

"He was a poet?" she asked after Scott explained he was researching Beam for a thirty-minute documentary.

"Still is. Sort of. But here, check this out." He took a yellow legal pad from the vinyl portfolio and slid from it a single-page photocopy, handing it to her. "Ever hear about any of this?"

The photocopy was of a newspaper clipping headlined "Professor Accused of Literary Lie." The article was short, more a notice than an in-depth piece, four column inches in length. She scanned it quickly. The professor, Henry Beam, was on the English faculty at Duke University and had published a book of poems by an anonymous prisoner in a World War II Nazi concentration camp. Following the book's release, questions were raised about the poems' authenticity. There were even accusations Beam had written the poems himself and tried to pass them off as genuine. Penned in the photocopy's margin was the article's date: May 3, 1963.

"Thirty-four years ago," Rachel noted, returning the photocopy. "I wasn't even born then, and no, I've never heard about this."

Scott shrugged. "I guess no one's teaching Beam's poetry at Carolina these days."

"Not in the English Department. So why a documentary about the guy now?"

Rachel brushed back a strand of hair that was about to dip into her coffee cup, while Scott flipped pages of the legal pad.

"The man's an interesting story in his own right. It seems he emerged from the North Carolina backwoods in the early 40s to attend Duke, a rural, up-from-poverty prodigy. He earned B.A. and Master's degrees at Duke and published a volume of poetry before he was 23. Which landed him a fellowship for a year's study in Paris. When he came back to the States, Duke offered him a teaching position." Scott flipped another page. "He wasn't a professor, just an instructor in English lit. But that's when he brought out the so-called concentration camp poems. He claimed they were given to him by a man he'd met in France, someone he called René in the book's preface, no last name, just René. Probably a pseudonym. If he even existed."

"But people thought Henry Beam wrote the poems himself?"

Scott scratched through his beard. "Nothing was proved one way or the other. I've heard there was talk he stole the poems, you know, plagiarized them. The accuser may have been a Duke grad student. There were rumors about an affair, scorned lover kind of thing. As for Beam, he denied the accusations but never took any legal action in his defense. Interestingly, the controversy sent book sales soaring, apparently rare for poetry, but it may have made the guy a chunk of change. It probably helped that he chose not to come clean. But soon after the uproar, he was gone from Duke and pretty much dropped off the planet. Until recently."

"So what happened recently?"

"He's back living here and just published a new collection of poems, the first since the controversy. The critics, the ones who've noticed, seem pretty lukewarm." He gulped a swallow of coffee. "I'm not much into poetry, Rachel, but I don't find these poems to be particularly terrific. The story's more that the man's surfaced after thirty-plus years."

"So now you want to unearth the truth about the poems."

He frowned. "I wish. But that's not what the station wants. They have this sponsor, a local guy who was a student of Beam's years ago at Duke. He's personally funding the show, but he's certainly not interested in any exposé. Says he just wants to see Beam's reputation restored."

"Pretty dull for you, I guess."

"Yeah."

Rachel glanced at her watch. 19th Century American Novel met in twenty minutes. She reached for the book bag by her feet.

Scott stuck the legal pad and photocopy in his portfolio. "Maybe you should do it."

"Do what?"

"Dig into the controversy. Don't you have to write a thesis or something?"

"Yes, but I doubt this Henry Beam guy would be considered significant enough for Chapel Hill."

Scott laid a couple of dollar bills on the table. "Well, why don't you at least go with me out to his house Saturday and maybe meet the guy."

"Maybe?"

"Well ..." He drummed his fingers on the table. "It's complicated. I haven't been able to get up with him. He's kind of a recluse who doesn't like to be bothered."

"You haven't contacted him?"

"Tried. His phone's unlisted and I've written him twice, but he's never responded."

"And you're just going to go knock on his door?"

"Last resort. But you'd be a real help, Rachel. You're into literature. If he's home, you can speak his language." He leaned toward her. "And maybe help me get in the door. Hopefully, the two of us won't seem threatening."

"He's going to feel threatened?" she asked, startled. "What does that mean?"

"Not much, but okay, there's a story he scared off some UNC students a year ago with a shotgun. Richard Squires, the man funding the show, just laughed at that, called it a rural legend, thought the kids had probably been smoking something." Scott grinned. "Look, even if Henry Beam finds me threatening, I doubt he'd feel that way about you."

Rachel took that as a compliment, even as her mother warned in her mind: *All those innocent girls who trusted that horrible Ted Bundy.* But it was the rebel who answered. "Okay, tell me what time and where." She knew she would have her qualms about this afterwards but decided she needed a break from classes and study. There were still two weeks until Thanksgiving. A literary mystery sounded like R & R.

Saturday morning on the street in front of Rachel's apartment, Scott raised the hatchback of his Chevy Sprint and handed her a cream-colored chapbook from a stack of folders. "Take a look at this on the way out," he said. "Beam's latest."

Henry Beam's name was embossed on the cover, the book's title *First Things Last.* At least the man was actually a published poet.

Rachel fingered the pages and saw twenty or so fairly short poems printed on quality bond. With lots of white space. Beam lived near Durham, a thirty-minute drive from Chapel Hill, which took longer because Scott had to find the place. So she had time to read all the poems twice. Beam's poetry was competent but not extraordinary. Perhaps the man was rusty if he hadn't published in thirty-four years. Yet there was a poignancy to several poems that felt authentic, particularly "Going Gentle," Beam's rejoinder to Dylan Thomas' famous poem, "Do Not Go Gentle Into That Good Night." She read through that poem a third time.

Life is not reckoned
by the dance of deeds
however bright.
Our lightning words
fork empty skies.
Few meteors blaze
beyond sad heights.

Who flies with angels,
wrestles Grendel to sleep
near ancient keeps?
We are mortal,
only that,
thrust from the first wet
whimpered breath
toward death.

What use our rage at dying light?
There's no reprieve.

There's nothing we can do
but draw the shades
recheck the locks,
and with our griefs and losses packed,
await the porter's knock.

"Have you read 'Going Gentle'?" she asked Scott.

"I've read everything Beam's written, plus the concentration camp poems."

"What's your take on 'Going Gentle'?"

"It's okay, but I'm no expert. Never read much poetry, except when I had to for school." He swerved the Sprint onto a curvy dirt lane. "This should be Beam's road."

She had seen no sign, no mailbox at the turn, nothing to identify it as such. She glanced through the windshield. The sky had turned gloomy. The trees along the road were stark, bare, their fallen leaves piling in drifts through the woods. She was glad she'd worn her black wool slacks and brought along a heavy sweater. The road snaked through at least a mile of desolate woodlands until they rounded a bend and saw the house, two-storied, old, wind-swept and bleak, its pine siding in need of paint. It sat back from the road in a clearing surrounded by pine woods. Henry Beam had described the house in a poem titled "Master," indicating it was pre-Civil War. It certainly could be, thought Rachel. Behind it, toward the woods, were a barn and sheds and an empty paddock. An old blue pickup was parked by a stack of cut firewood. Two brindled basset hounds roused themselves from the porch to bark at them, then trotted amicably into the dusty yard. No smoke came from the stone chimney, but a thin vapory spiral rose from a metal flue in the roof.

"You want to stay in the car?" asked Scott.

A Stone for Bread

"From the poems, I don't think Henry Beam seems particularly scary."

As they opened the car doors, one of the dogs ambled toward them. It licked her shoe, wagging a canine welcome.

"Not exactly ferocious," she noted.

"We haven't seen the shotgun yet."

They walked onto the low porch. Scott knocked. The boards underfoot had been recently replaced, unlike the house's pine siding with its flaking paint. When there was no sound from inside, Scott knocked again. Rachel turned from the door. Henry Beam stood at the edge of the woods across the dirt road, some twenty yards away, as if trying to decide about them, whether to advance or flee—or make a run for the shotgun. She recognized him from the black and white photo on the frontispiece of *First Things Last*. He was heavy-set, mid-sixtyish with gray curls brushed across his scalp to camouflage, with little success, a receding hairline. The curls refused to stay put in the November wind, springing from his head in coils. He wore faded jeans, running shoes and a red plaid lumberjack shirt under an old bomber jacket. A tin bucket dangled from his left hand. She nudged Scott. Turning, he stepped off the porch and hailed the man. Beam walked slowly toward them, his stride heavy-footed. He paused at the Sprint.

"Yeah?"

"Mr. Beam?"

"Yeah."

The tone of his voice was wary, as if they'd come selling encyclopedias.

"I'm Scott Trevelian and this is my friend Rachel Singer. I wrote to you. A couple of times, in fact."

Beam stared at them from under wiry eyebrows that met at the bridge of his nose. He seemed to be weighing his options.

"I wrote you," Scott said again, "about a PBS documentary."

Beam glanced toward the barn. Rachel followed his gaze and saw nothing there to distract him.

"This is a project I'd really like to do," Scott continued, "a short piece, a profile on you. Twenty-eight minutes max. Most of it would be interview."

"I don't give interviews."

"Is that a definite *no* or can I try to talk you into it?" Scott flashed his most ingratiating smile.

Beam's mouth twitched. He set the pail on the ground and wiped his hands on his jeans. When he looked up, his eyes shifted from Scott to Rachel as if to solicit her help in the matter. Surprised, Rachel looked away.

"And how do you propose to talk me into it, Mr. Trevelian?"

"Look, there's no money involved. At least not much. I'm a producer for UNC-TV in Chapel Hill. My operations manager wants me to do this, and I want to do it. Your work deserves a hearing. The documentary would give you a forum to respond to your critics, let people know about your work. The critics, as you know, get free rein in the media to tell their side."

Scott seemed to be warming to Henry Beam's frosty challenge. But Beam wasn't having it. He picked up the pail and moved closer to the porch. "You think critics are all that important in the cosmic scheme of things, Mr. Trevelian?"

"Damn right they are. They're the gatekeepers. They prevent people from bothering to find out whether an artistic work is good or not."

Beam shrugged. "Perhaps."

He stepped onto the porch, Scott trailing after him. Rachel glanced into the pail. It was filled with green leaves.

"Creasies, Miss," said Beam, as if anticipating a question.

"Creasies?" asked Scott.

"Creasy greens," Rachel explained. "You eat them, like mustard greens. I picked them at my uncle's farm when I was a child."

"The ignorance of a city boy," Scott quipped.

Beam waited in front of his door like a stranger wondering whether to knock. It was obvious he didn't know what to do with them.

"You care for tea? Coffee?" he said finally.

"Coffee would be great." Scott gave Rachel a quick thumbs up behind his back as Beam ushered them through a hallway, past a stairwell and into a high-ceilinged living room. There was an uncomfortable moment, the three of them stalled mid-center in the room, while Beam decided his next move. Rachel looked around, noted a table by the front window for an electric typewriter (no computer), a ream of paper beside it. The one tidy spot. Otherwise the room was a clutter of books and papers, empty Coke bottles, beer cans, dirty dishes. A pan of kitty litter sat near a wood stove. The yellow cat slept on a crumpled flannel shirt on the floor. The place smelled musty. She caught a whiff of sour milk. For the cat? A massive stone fireplace covered much of the far wall, two logs but no fire on the hearth. The other walls were lined with metal hardware-store shelves crammed with books, some flopping on their sides, others stuck haphazardly on top. Hung above the fireplace was a faded green Mexican serape. Below it on the mantel sat the most fascinating object in the room, a carved rosewood lion. Rachel walked over for a closer look while Scott attempted small talk, asking Beam if he did any farming. The lion's head was larger than its body and distorted as if viewed through a fisheye lens. Its mane, which stuck out wildly, looked to have been zapped by lightning. It was a magnificent carving.

"I guess everyone asks about this," she said, when Scott had given up on farming.

"Yes," said Beam, and stopped there, as if nothing more needed saying about the lion, then realized she *was* asking. "From France. Brought it back years ago. The artist, I don't know what became of him. He was a young man, not French but an Iranian immigrant living in a squalid project outside Paris. I found him quite by accident. Sometimes I wonder if this is the only piece he ever carved, or if no one else ever came on him like I did. I've never heard of him again." He shook his head. "I mean that's an imaginative fancy of mine, I guess."

"Did you ever go back, try to buy something else?" Scott picked up on Rachel's lead, obviously pleased to find a subject that evoked a response.

"No. I sent friends to him but they said he was no longer there. An Eritrean family was living in the flat. Maybe the poor fellow needed someone to make a documentary about him, so people would find him."

Beam's tone was a surprise, its bite. Scott frowned and moved to the wood stove to warm his hands. Beam gestured them towards the couch, excused himself and disappeared through a door, presumably to a kitchen. Scott stayed by the stove. Rachel sank into nervous couch springs, surveying the room for further clues to this reticent man. Beam wasn't neat. He read a lot. Those two things were obvious. Definitely bachelor's quarters. No womanly touches here. The yellow cat uncurled itself from the floor and joined Rachel on the couch.

"Coffee's on," said Beam, emerging from the back. "I have nothing but Instant, I'm afraid."

Scott nodded. "Instant's fine."

Anything hot sounded good to her. The room was drafty. Beam must have felt it too for he tossed a chunk of wood in the stove and poked around the grate with a long barbecue fork.

"You've read some of my work?" he said to neither of them in particular, although he glanced toward Rachel.

Scott answered in the affirmative.

Beam turned slightly, offering him a solemn, inscrutable face. "What do you think of *First Things Last*?"

"I like it, particularly 'Going Gentle.'"

"Ah."

Rachel wondered what *ah* meant. "I liked that poem too," she added, "although I'm curious about such a passive acceptance of aging and death."

Beam wiped a hand across his face. "I guess that's just the way I felt when I was writing it."

Scott tried a different tack. "This is another beef I have with your critics. The ones I've read go after you for taking on a poet like Dylan Thomas, like Dylan's some holy relic. But why shouldn't poets take each other on the way scholars and scientists do? I mean, look how the guy died. It may not have been gentle, but doing yourself in with acute alcohol poisoning isn't exactly noble."

"You speak well, Mr. Trevelian."

"Scott, call me Scott."

"You drink your coffee black? Milk or sugar?"

He left them again. Scott settled himself into a bentwood rocker near the fireplace. Henry returned with a tray of mugs and handed them around, then perched on the edge of a wooden straight-back chair by the door to the kitchen. He looked like an oversized stuffed bear about to topple forward onto the floor—a very ill at ease stuffed bear. There was a quality of disconnection about the man, as if what his body did or mouth said were separate from the simultaneous working of his mind. Robotic, Rachel thought. Or perhaps he was merely bored, hoping they'd leave. She wondered how often anyone came down that dirt road.

"What would you do in this documentary, Mr. Trevelian?" Beam asked, his eyes cutting toward Rachel. "What would you expect of me?"

"I'd bother you," said Scott, who seemed somewhat bothered himself. "I mean that's a given. I'd follow you around for a day or two. I promise to make it short and sweet, just enough to let my camera record your daily routines. Not anything you don't want me to see. You'd have control. And you'd get used to me, I hope you would, forget I was here except when I tape a direct interview."

"See the poet brush his teeth, is that it?"

Rachel smiled. Beam didn't. Neither did Scott.

"I don't own a television," he said. "It's banal, don't you think, television?"

Scott perked up. Beam had handed him a topic on which to soar. "But it doesn't have to be. Who says television has to be the medium of American mediocrity? TV can be as significant a channel of culture and information as we choose to make it. Look what Ken Burns does. I do quality work, Mr. Beam, about things and people that matter."

This last statement seemed to affect the man, for he visibly softened. Scott saw his advantage and kept going.

"I'm not interested in PR pieces, fluff. This is my art."

"I'm a private man, Mr. Trevelian."

"But your poetry isn't private."

"Yes, yes, I know, a work once made has a life of its own and ceases to be the property of the maker. I assume that's what you mean."

"Not exactly. It's more like if you publish your work, you expect others to read it, want them to read it. Simple as that. Which means there's no advantage to hiding away from the very people you want to buy your book. You can't have it both ways."

A Stone for Bread

"Unfortunately." Beam shifted on the chair and tilted it backward against the wall, its front legs several inches off the floor. He was silent, as if considering Scott's argument. "You think people really read my poems?"

Rachel heard the plaint of appeal in his voice.

"I have," said Scott. "Rachel's read your latest book. I know others who've read *A Stone for Bread*. Those poems definitely capture the—"

Beam thumped the chair's front legs down hard on the plank floor, waving Scott off with a swipe of his hand.

Scott flinched but quickly recovered. "Okay, so that was over thirty years ago. I've read about the controversy. But that's what makes those poems so damn interesting. That and the back story. They're good work. You may want to believe only your latest poems matter, but the others are important. Hell, there're actually people out there who think the Holocaust never happened."

"Maybe it didn't."

"Huh?"

"Well, I wasn't there." Beam twitched his shoulders as if to shrug off a fly or something equally distasteful. "I wasn't a witness."

"So when does an artist have to be a witness? Tolstoy wasn't born until after the time frame of *War and Peace*."

Rachel was surprised. Scott was more literary than he'd let on.

Beam ignored Tolstoy. "You seem to think I wrote those poems, Mr. Trevelian."

Scott leaned back in the rocker. She saw his knuckles whiten as he gripped the chair arms. He'd obviously seen enough of Henry Beam. If the man was so stiff and defensive in casual conversation, how would he be with a camera in his face? Scott started up from the rocker.

"When do you want to begin?" Beam asked.

"Begin?"

"The documentary, Mr. Trevelian. Isn't that what we've been talking about?"

Scott was visibly rattled. Beam remained seated, offering no hint why he'd agreed to the project. He wouldn't look at either of them but seemed to fix his gaze at a spot on the floor.

"Uh, well," Scott stuttered, "I've got a few days after December 7th. Rachel, how about you?"

"What do you mean about—"

"We'll compare our calendars," said Scott quickly, his eyes sending her an explain-later message.

"Yes, uh, yes, sure, it's Christmas break."

"I have no commitments then," said Beam, rather mournfully.

Rachel wondered whether the man had anyone in his life.

They made arrangements to be in touch and left. Scott shut his car door and stared through the windshield, hand thumping on the steering wheel. "Damn it to hell, what a goddamned disaster."

"Come on, Scott, so he's stiff and defensive. He'll probably loosen up when you get into it. I'd be stiff too if I thought you were going to follow me around with a video camera."

Scott snorted. "Stiff? How about catatonic? Particularly his face. Like a man at a funeral. And the weight on him. He's going to look really, really bad. Video adds pounds. Plus he's terminally boring. I can see him looking into the lens with those hooded eyes and saying, 'Well, I'm a private man.' Shit, they'll laugh me out of the station."

"Okay, whatever," she conceded, "but what's this about comparing our calendars?"

He hesitated before he answered. "If I can just get him to talk about the controversy, the concentration camp poems. You could help with that, Rachel."

A Stone for Bread

"I don't have time, Scott. My exams are right after Thanksgiving."

"What about over your Christmas break? They know you at the station. Maybe we can make it a temp job, get you paid for a few days of research. Or just come, at least the first day, just to keep Beam happy and relaxed."

"What's that supposed to mean?"

"No no, you can't tell me you didn't notice the guy spent the whole time looking at you. My bet is he doesn't give a damn about the documentary."

Her face warmed. She'd noticed, how could she not have. But she had chalked it up to the man's anxiety. He seemed such a shy man, whose privacy they were proposing to invade.

"This isn't just about me, Scott. You were quite persuasive. After all that talk about not being literary, you knew how Dylan Thomas died."

He grinned. "Freshman English at State. Our T.A. was obsessed with that poem."

"And Tolstoy?"

"I think I made that up." He started the Sprint. "So how about it, Rachel? Two days, that's all."

"Okay," she said, and wondered how much she'd regret this later. But Henry Beam intrigued her, the old house, the poems she'd read on the way, the controversy over *A Stone for Bread*. A boring man would never have bought that rosewood lion.

THREE

*W*hen he first saw her standing on the porch, a shudder went through his body like a train passing. "Someone just walked over your grave," his grandmother would have said, reaching into her gunny of folk aphorisms. And she would have been right, for at that instant, something in the young woman's pretty face, the play of light off her auburn hair, had awakened him from a death of spirit darker than death itself. It was as if he believed, at least in that moment, that one day he might enter her with his terrible secrets. There was so much to tell. That needed telling. The year in Paris. Eugénie. René. And there were other stories too, stories of his childhood, that he guessed he might not tell her, tell anyone, stories he told only himself in his solitude, his thoughts like a wind-up toy car running in circles. Sometimes he caught himself repeating them out loud to the cat, the furniture, the rosewood lion. The run-down cropper cabin, his bullying brothers and schoolmates, the impoverished childhood with its litany of absences—of food and protection, encouragement or love. He could even re-create the gnawing in his gut, the hunger for something beyond food and nourishment, an insatiable craving of mind—as if God the maker had left out an essential nutrient of his being. Like the split bodies of Aristophanes' lovers, the boy he once was had lusted after a lost mirror image. It was this, he believed, that urged him upward from poverty toward a dimly perceived vision of his true self.

He was born in the Great Depression. Hard times in a land of hard times. In Cleveland County, North Carolina, where a single cash

A Stone for Bread

crop, cotton, kept the proverbial wolf from the door. Cotton had made a comeback in Cleveland County in the twentieth century after the desolation of the War Between the States. Henry's father was a tenant cotton farmer with five rented acres and a house—no, Henry wouldn't call it a house—it was a shack with tar-paper siding and a tin roof, hardly worth the $20 cash his father paid each month in rent. It too was a place of absences, absent plumbing and electricity, absent screens in the windows. When it rained the ceiling dripped water, the ping-pings of rainwater into a No. 10 can, the music of his childhood. The place was dark and foul, smelling of smoke and rancid grease, a dreary shelter for the two adults and five children crammed in like immigrants in steerage. Dirt poor. Owners of nothing. Not an icebox or a radio or living room furniture. The bathroom a stinking privy. Their personal possessions a few cracked dishes and cast-off pots, a large iron skillet, wood stove, mattresses on the floor for beds and home-stitched clothes ill-fitted to their bodies. Henry's father rented or begged a plow and mule to sow his acres. He borrowed seed money and fertilizer, borrowed a truck to haul the fat burlap gunnies to the gin. And when the cotton was finally baled, he bartered most of it for ginning fees. The land gave back little or nothing, despite the tortured backs, scarred fingers and burned faces earned working the fields, all of them working, the children too, from as far back as he could remember.

Cleveland County lay seventy miles west of Charlotte in the shadow of the Southern mountains. Shelby, the county's one town of size, had a population then of about 15,000. But for the boy, Shelby was city. He didn't get there often, except on rare days when his mother left him at his Uncle Tyler's Esso station on Dixon Street. Those were looked-forward-to days, when he felt himself thrust into the midst of life, real life, Fords and Plymouths rolling across the pavement, nosing up to gas pumps, the honk of horns, screech of tires, people waving and calling, houses, stores, electric lights, Uncle Tyler's telephone chirping like a catbird. Where Henry lived, in the north of the county, there was little but unrelieved stretches of country, small farms planted in cotton, and acres and acres of pinewoods. Some things were universal, though, he learned early, particularly in matters of privilege. Even in the worst of times, some people had more: more land, more cash under the mattress, more clout with the local banker.

The place of Henry's family in this rural hierarchy—it shamed him to remember—was the bottom of the ditch. His father, Jared Beam, the son of sharecroppers who were sons of sharecroppers and on back to the Revolution and the first indentured member of the Beam family, was a rather indolent farmer who lived from one credit slip to the next, feeding his children off a plot of corn and vegetables. Having despaired of farming's futility by the time Henry was in school, Jared left most of the field work to his children and hired himself out to guard the Busby brothers' whiskey still, tucked in a copse of pine woods a mile from their house. A simple task, suitable for a man of languid disposition. The only skills required were an alert eye and a quick finger on the trigger to scare off animals and snooping kids and to fire off a warning to the still's custodians when the rare revenuer found his way to it. Even as a boy, Henry understood that his father must have spent as much time boozing as protecting the brew. Sober, Jared Beam was a quiet man, but fired by Pop-Skull, he underwent a dramatic transformation. Henry learned early to avoid Jared until he'd had his supper, when enough beans and corn bread had filled his belly and quieted the whiskey demons. But more than once Henry felt the bite of "Jared's wand," the flat chair stave used as a doorstop, which in his father's hand became a weapon of abuse.

Henry was the third son, born between two sisters and christened Orville Henry, names he hated throughout his childhood. But when he got to high school, he found pride in his middle name from Henry Adams, after reading Adams' book on Chartres and Mont St. Michel, a book that awakened him to an aesthetic that astounded him and taught him a poignant truth: there were worlds beyond Cleveland County, beyond even North Carolina and America. The hunger in his soul took aim, sighted toward a more exalted ambition to one day seek out these worlds and find his place in them. He quietly dropped the *Orville* and afterwards answered only to Henry. When he was old enough, he took summer and after-school jobs in a nearby cotton mill, saving what money he could to feed this now obsessive ambition—to get as far from Cleveland County as possible. It helped that Henry had a talent for school. By sixth grade he was top of his class in reading and social studies. This precocity startled his teachers, even as it riled his class-mates. Jared Beam's boy? The old sot. There was the usual tongue wagging about alien roosters in the hen house, or what his mother might have been doing before Henry was born when she waited tables at the Fireside Restaurant in Shelby. Henry ignored the gossip. He had more important battles to fight.

His classmates, his brothers among them, resented how teach-ers fawned over him and taunted him for it. They followed behind some days after school to chuck rocks at him and shout out names, accuse him of fucking teachers for grades. They kept their distance and seldom tried to scrap with him. Henry was a muscular boy. He'd worked his share of acres and hefted heavy bales at the mill. Though gaunt from poor diet, he was big-boned with thick hands and arms that seemed too long for his torso. His wide face, when he glimpsed himself in a school mirror, was somber and impassive. He didn't think much of his appearance, and from the reactions he got from those who didn't know him, he sensed they saw in him little more than a supreme dullness. But his mind wasn't dull. He finished high school first in his class of 200, a light-year beyond the girl who was second.

But no matter that he was first in his class, or the brightest student to come out of Cleveland County anyone could remember, he never felt free of assault, even at school, assault not by bullies but by daily and unremitting indignities. "White bread" indignities, he called them. In Cleveland County, schoolchildren brought their lunches from home. Those whose fathers perched comfortably atop the Cleveland County social ladder, the ones with large farms or small businesses, brought lunches to school in shiny painted boxes with clasps and metal hinges. Henry's lunch was wrapped in newspaper or gunny cloth. The children of privilege unfolded squares of wax paper and munched on sandwiches made of white bread, store-bought bread that oozed peanut butter and fruit preserves. The poor kids, their status for all to see, ate hard biscuits left over from supper the night before, a slab of fatty ham in the middle. As he grew older, this affront to his pride grew so intense, he refused to eat with the other students, enduring his cramped gut until, alone on the path home, he wolfed the offensive food.

That's why Paris was so special. That's why years later, when he arrived in Paris, he wrote in his journal three words in big printed letters and twice underlined: <u>white bread time</u>. The ultimate. Triumph. The long-deferred feast of entitlement. Yes, he'd won a scholarship to Duke and done well there. And two years after graduating, he'd earned his Master's and published a collection of poems. But he had been miserable most of those years. College came with its own weapons of humiliation. The day he moved his few possessions into Double H on West Campus, his freshman roommate, a boy named Keener from Richmond, eyed the new brown sport coat that hung on Henry like burlap on a scarecrow and mumbled, "Kinda narrow in the lapels, eh buddy?"

Henry didn't know what to answer.

He almost never knew what to answer. There was so much he didn't know, things his classmates took for granted. Like clothes, what was in style and what wasn't. Besides the sport coat, he had one suit, purchased from his earnings at the mill, and an extra pair of trousers. He'd brought with him no footlockers filled with checked jackets and striped neckties and dozens of shirts. He didn't own tennis whites or a dinner jacket or golf shoes. Didn't even know where to buy these things. His fellow students weren't unfriendly to him; they just came from worlds he barely imagined, casually bantering with each other about New York and Europe, "Yardbird" Parker, rhythm and blues, sports, movie stars, cars. Henry felt himself on an island, marooned by his ignorance.

To protect himself, he went into hiding, spent most hours when he wasn't in class in the library or studying in his room. He made few friends, but his diligence rewarded him: he finished his degree in three years, graduated Magna Cum in Literature and French, then spent another two years in the graduate school. During his last year, at age twenty-two, he published *Nightshade*, a collection of 17 poems. For this, he was briefly touted and toasted, patted on the back by English Department professors and a few classmates. There were some half dozen letters from readers, and the slim volume won two awards: a prize for most promising new work by a young poet from some publication he'd never heard of and a small stipend from Duke. But the job offers and reading invitations never materialized. Sales of the book were predictably dismal, not unusual, he was told, for a first volume of poetry. But the brief congratulatory letter from his New York editor contained a P.S. at the bottom that chilled him. "What's next?"

What next but more work? There was no end to it. Like hard biscuits, work was a function of class. He'd spent his life, all twenty-two years of it, working. Working to get out, away, escape, and in a boy's kind of idyll, working so that one day he could cease working altogether. But the letter from his editor brought home the awful truth: nothing was enough, nothing was ever enough. He grew so despondent that in his worst moments he imagined a leap into oblivion from the high gothic tower of the Duke Chapel. Yet what frightened him even more was that he might be forced back to Cleveland County, to apply for a job there in the executive offices of the cotton mill, or to teach in the high school. During those last miserable weeks at the university, weeks when he hardly left his room, he understood another truth that had eluded him in his dogged pursuit of that mirror image: he didn't belong anywhere. Certainly not at Duke. He had come far, yes, but for what?

He was saved by a letter. *Nightshade* earned him a fellowship for a year's study abroad and sent his dejected spirits soaring. His hopes for the future restored, Henry Beam, at the ripe age of 23, embarked by ship for Paris. Everything in his life, he believed, the long hours of study and work, the insults borne, the poverty of his childhood, had ripened into this one gloried triumph. <u>WHITE BREAD TIME!</u>

FOUR

In the year following Étienne's death, René had bad dreams. He heard his brother beckon him from the garden, saw him standing like a scarecrow, blood spewing from empty shoulder sockets. Sometimes in these dreams, his father called from the battlefield and begged to be taken away from the booming guns. One day, René's grandfather found the child in the barn, crouched near the hay bales where they had buried the family treasures. René's arms were locked about his knees and he was rocking on his heels. When his grandfather spoke to him, René didn't answer. His mother consulted the curé. The priest came to the house and spoke with René in his grandparents' sitting room. He assured the boy Étienne was safe in heaven. Although we can never understand such a tragedy, we must accept it as God's will, he told René. You must trust the Resurrection when Étienne will embrace you with both arms. Until then, be a good Christian boy and pray daily for your brother's soul.

René did what the priest said. Each night, he knelt by his bed to pray for Étienne. He prayed for him again at Sunday Mass. By the time he was six, he could walk the short block to the village church several afternoons a week to pray for Etienne there. But the bad dreams did not go away. Soon the boy refused to leave the house except to go to the church. Even then, he raced through the streets as if pursued, racing quickly home after a quick genuflect and prayer at the altar. The war was not over. Guns could still be heard near the village. René's mother took the boy away from the war to her cousins in Orleans. She and René and his sister, Magdelena, packed their belongings in an old trunk and left, traveling by train.

When the war ended, René's father joined them. Although he had been a farmer, the war had taken a generation of young men and he easily found work loading freight on the shipping quays of the Loire. His mind was as strong as his arms and within a few years, he was supervisor of a large warehouse.

The move to Orleans seemed providential for René. Though he still had bad dreams, they came less frequently. Etienne and the village where he was born faded from memory. Sometimes he could not remember the house, or the barn, or the bent figure of his grandfather. As he grew older, it was as if the world of his earliest years was a story told to him by his parents. It helped that Etienne's name was seldom mentioned and René had started school and could no longer hide in the house. Even so, he lacked the natural spontaneity of childhood. He rarely smiled or laughed. His most striking physical feature—deep-set, cobalt eyes both brilliant and cold—did not invite camaraderie. How could one ever know what he was thinking? Or if he were thinking? At school, his classmates were puzzled by him. His teachers watched him closely. Yet René did well in school. He was an intelligent boy who spent time away from class in study and reading. He did not waste his afternoons on games. Once, when the other boys coaxed him to play football, they discovered an odd quirk in the boy. If someone pushed or bumped him in the heat of a game, René would shriek and furiously lash out, so that his classmates learned to leave him alone. Their only nod to his existence was the nickname they whispered among themselves—Twitch, for the odd facial movements that marred his face when he was nervous or angry.

For René, school was merely the next stage in the long slow forgetting of his first four years of life. Study was respite. When he read a book, he didn't think, was not possessed by fantasies and terrifying images. He read whatever books he could find, stayed up late into the night reading book after book. This industry pleased his parents. They were proud of his good marks in school, believed him fully recovered from the nervous illness brought on by the war. They let him study in the parlor after everyone was in bed, found him books and encouraged him, though sometimes the intensity of his study habits worried them. It wasn't unusual for René to work himself to exhaustion, when he would grow irritable and whiny, scornful of his parents' lack of education. His father's family had been farmers, savvy, intelligent men who made the land prosper. His mother came from different stock, descended from an old Burgundian family with at least one army major among her ancestors and a great-grandfather who had studied law before the family fortunes disappeared in the wars of the 19th century. This ancestry did not appear to have left its mark on her. With no more education than her husband, she seemed perfectly satisfied to wrap her life around home and family.

As long as René sustained his energies, he managed school well, but when his body tired, he succumbed to a debilitating despair, what he secretly called a visitation from the *ange noir*, the dark angel. These periods of the *ange noir* terrified him. He felt surrounded by a smothering darkness, which might at any moment consume him. To ward off this despair, he fled into his books and studied harder. As he grew older, he considered the *ange noir* a kind of possession, as if the dark angel released in him a fury of winged creatures that dug their teeth and talons into his soul. When the despair was severe, René feigned illness and stayed home, allowing his mother to tend and comfort him with her quiet hands.

In his *lycée* years, when he was fourteen, René began a new subject of inquiry. He grew preoccupied with the phenomenon of death. His science teacher, M. Durand, saw promise in the boy and encouraged him. René went about this inquiry in a quite rational manner. He read every book he could find on the subject and asked if he might study anatomy and vivisection by initiating his own experiments. Pleased, M. Durand provided him chemicals and implements. René scoured the countryside around Orleans, returning with jars of grasshoppers and caterpillars, later traps with mice and rabbits from the fields. Carefully, in a makeshift laboratory in the *lycée* set up for him by M. Durand and under the teacher's friendly guidance, René learned to chloroform small animals and cut through their flesh, isolating the tiny, still functioning organs, peeling back membranes and muscles so as to observe death at its onset, as the organs shut down one by one, the brain swelling with fluid. He was not a cruel boy, one who killed mercilessly. He was quite gentle with these creatures, concerned to make their dying peaceful. And the experiments were performed after school with M. Durand in attendance. The teacher wrote a note to René's father to report on the boy's remarkable skills, suggesting René had a great future as a surgeon or scientist.

His parents were happy for their son. Étienne's death had caused them such deep anguish that the fear they might lose a second son to an undiagnosed illness had weighed on them since. Of course, they had set about their own recovery from the tragedy. Two more children were born after the move to Orleans, another daughter, and at last, a son. They named the son Michel Étienne to honor the dead boy but called him Michel. René doted on his younger sister but was never fond of Michel. After Michel's birth, René's father enclosed a section of the attic to create a room for René, where he could pursue his studies in peace. The family lived in a small house with two bedrooms, one for the parents, the other shared by the children. Now René had his own room, a privilege bestowed on him for his hard work at school. René seemed content with the small attic dormer from which he could see across the rooftops of Orleans, watch the smoke curl from chimney pots in winter, be warmed by the glint of sunshine off roof tiles in spring and summer.

In 1930, when René was seventeen, M. Durand again spoke with his parents about René's future studies. He was certain, M. Durand told them, that the boy would do well enough on the national baccalauréat exam to attend a university. Perhaps he might even try for the prestigious école normale. As the examinations approached, M. Durand gave René lists of questions and problems that might appear on the test. René worked exceedingly hard. He stayed up even later at night. When did he sleep? his parents asked, proud of his industry, but concerned about his health, the incessant twitch in his left cheek. The baccalauréat was two weeks away when the *ange noir* visited René, more vengeful than before. He felt himself swimming in blackness and was unable to study, unwilling even to open a book. When he did try to read, he experienced an insatiable urge to take a knife and cut away the book's pages, slice through the binding to the table, to the floor, to his feet, his legs, cut everything away within the arc of his slashing arm.

He shut himself in the attic room, lying to his parents that it was so he could better concentrate. His parents brought food and left it outside the door. He barely touched it. Had this been an ordinary few weeks in René's life, his mother would have grown alarmed at the sight of his blanched face and glistening eyes, the constant pace of footsteps in the attic. One night after what seemed hours of pacing, when his mind tried without success to throw off the darkness, René fell into an exhausted sleep. He dreamed of dismembered bodies and bloody legs and arms, some bodies human, some field mice and rabbits. He was smothered in limbs, drowning in the stink of chloroform. He awoke terrified. Outside the attic window lay true darkness, for it was late into the night. He left his room, his steps soft on the stairs so not to arouse his parents, and slipped from the house. Once on the street, he ran the five blocks to the parish church. Opening the side door that was usually left open, he entered the nave. In the dark and empty sanctuary, he flung himself on the altar, his body trembling with panic. He tried to sob, but nothing except loud gasps came from his throat. He beat his fists against the stone altar and prayed for help.

Moonlight through a high window of the church splashed his face. He raised his eyes to the bronze crucifix above the altar, Christ, his hands nailed to the crossbeam, bathed in light. As René stared at the crucifix, he imagined, or perhaps saw, the arms of Christ disengage from the bronze nails in the beam and reach toward him. René shut his eyes, crossed himself and prayed the *Pater Noster*. The wings of the *ange noir* lifted from his heart. He prayed at the altar a long time, lit a candle for Etienne and went home.

He took the *baccalauréat*, but the day after the examination, he informed his parents he had decided to become a priest. This came as a shock. Though religious in a nominal way, they could not understand why their brilliant son would want to be a priest. What about the *école normale*? M. Durand, on the other hand, was furious. He took René's decision as a personal affront. After all I have done for you, he shouted at the young man. You give it all up for … for a dead theology! He dismissed René from his classroom, followed him shouting down the hall. Days later, M. Durand met with the *Proviseur* of the school. He had grave concerns, he told him, about the young man's baccalauréat. No one at the *lycée* needed to be convinced. The other teachers had always had doubts. There was something not right about René. They had never understood M. Durand's interest in the student, explaining it among themselves as the teacher's suspected proclivities for boys.

One afternoon, the Censor stopped René in the school hallway. Had he seen any baccalauréat questions beforehand? he asked casually, before he took the exams. René nodded. Yes, he had a list from M. Du— He was not allowed to finish. The Academy Inspector was summoned. He personally took the problem to the Academic Council. The matter went all the way to Paris to the office of the Minister of Public Instruction. When the baccalauréat marks were posted, René had failed.

Sunday afternoon, Rachel stopped by Davis Library. She found Henry Beam's two books shelved with American poets, the recently published *First Things Last* and his early poems, *Nightshade. A Stone for Bread* was among a special collection of Holocaust poems. When she went to check out the three books, she asked how often they'd circulated. *First Things Last* twice in the last month, the young man told her, *A Stone for Bread* once. There was no record for the first one. "Which probably means not in years," he said. That night, she read all three, beginning with *Nightshade*, published when Beam was twenty-two. She saw in *Nightshade* a precocious talent with sparks of the potential that had brought him notice and publication. Certainly, they revealed a more gifted poet than *First Things Last*. There was a photo of Beam on the back cover of *Nightshade*, a young man with a pudgy face and thick curls windblown onto his forehead above wide, sad eyes. An attractive man, she thought, although there seemed a diffidence about him as if he weren't quite sure where to focus his eyes. The poems in *A Stone for Bread*, however, were not at all like Beam's two collections. Perhaps it was the subject matter, the horrors of the Nazi death camp in stark and ironic images that settled into her psyche like the acrid smoke they described, haunting her long after she had read them. But if Henry Beam had written them himself, he would have intended to make them different.

The day after her last exam, she met Scott for lunch. She had declined the research offer and any stipend from the station. She had no time in her life for this now. But she agreed to return to Beam's house for the two days of shooting in December.

"Maybe you could come up with a few questions I could ask him," Scott said.

"I'll give it some thought."

Scott seemed to have resigned himself to the video's original purpose. "If it's to be a puff piece, I'll puff it the best I can. Frankly, I'm not sure I give a damn."

Two days later, the weather cold, sky overcast, they drove to Beam's farmhouse, three people and equipment stuffed into the Chevy Sprint. Scott had brought along a station intern, Adrian Phillips, a sophomore at Chapel Hill. Skinny to the point of emaciated with lank brown hair and a quiet manner, Adrian's job was to haul equipment and monitor audio. Beam met them on the porch, sleepy-eyed and fidgety, as if he might be ready to nix the whole deal. But he ushered them in, and the guys set up the camera and two lights in his living room. Scott pulled the bentwood rocker near the wood stove and positioned the camera in front of it. On Scott's instructions, Beam had dressed casually in pressed jeans and a white shirt. Scott wasn't happy with the shirt and had him change it. They settled on blue plaid flannel, much like the red shirt he'd worn the day they'd met him. Satisfied with clothing and equipment, Scott motioned Beam into the rocker. The poet positioned himself uneasily on the chair's edge as Scott clipped a small microphone to his shirt just below the open neck. Scott stepped back and switched on the lights and camera. Startled, the yellow cat leaped onto Beam's lap. Scott wanted to shoo the animal away, but Rachel suggested the cat provided a homey touch and Scott agreed— her first contribution to the morning's work. Most of the time, she stood near the monitor, which Adrian had placed on a small folding table, and watched.

The ambiance in the monitor looked good, the rug and chair, the walls appearing more intimate than they actually were. The colors were bright. Beam, however, was stiff. Scott shot forty-five minutes of tape, his questions asked from off-camera, several she had suggested. Each question received a thoughtful answer, though the lights bothered the man, so that he bent his head downward and never quite looked directly into the lens. Henry Beam was as dull as Scott had feared. Head drooping, eyes squinted, he seemed unable to discern the questions and kept tilting forward, as if to see Scott beyond the hot lights.

Question: Which poets most influenced you in your work?

Answer: Yeats, I guess. Wilfred Owen too, maybe. Many poets really.

Question: What is it about Yeats' work that most appeals to you?

Answer: The naturalness of line in his later work.

Question: Can you elaborate on how that's reflected in your own poems?

Answer: Well, I think the modern poet is forced to a natural line and cadence. We can't follow the Tennysons and Wordsworths here. The modern ear won't allow for it. So I've tried to keep that in mind. Is that what you want, Mr. Trevelian? [Beam leans forward, head filling the frame. He looks like he's about to swallow the camera.]

Question: A reviewer of *First Things Last* says, and I'm quoting here, "Beam's new poems seem to be two-dimensional, half-grown from a soulless intellect."

Would you like to respond to that? [This was Scott's question. Rachel would never have asked it.]

Answer: Well, I don't agree. No, I, uh, no I really don't agree.

It's easy for critics, you see. They have only to respond to a work, not produce it *ex nihilo*. So they jump on what they can. Sometimes the two-dimensionality of a work, its simplicity, so to speak, becomes its own metaphor. I think I'd respond with something like that.

Scott got more from him when he turned to Beam's childhood, what it was like growing up in rural North Carolina.

"My father was a dirt farmer, sharecropper, you understand, but I had an uncle who worked in town. In Shelby. Ran a filling station. Didn't own it. Didn't own anything, just ran it. As a boy, I thought that was the best job a man could have, running a filling station. He always let me help, not really help, pretend to help, like holding on to the hose while he pumped gas. When I was small, I used to wonder what he was always looking at under car hoods. I wasn't tall enough to see for myself, so I used to imagine it was the car's mouth, you know, that he was looking down its throat, at big teeth and the car's tongue. Then I grew taller and was disappointed to learn it was just hoses and belts and greasy metal."

After a few more similarly tedious answers, Scott paused the interview and stretched. Beam headed off to the back of the house for a quick break. When he returned, Scott moved behind the camera and motioned Beam to the rocker.

"Just a couple more questions, Mr. Beam. You're doing great." He lobbed Beam two softball questions about sites referenced in *First Things Last*. After Beam had answered both, Scott stepped back from the camera as if ready to announce a wrap. He stroked his beard with both hands, somewhat nervously, Rachel thought.

"Something I'm curious about," Scott said quietly, hardly glancing at Beam. "Who was René?"

The question obviously caught Beam off guard. He jerked forward, squinting at Scott as if he had misheard him. "What? What did you say?"

"René, the man who gave you the poems in *A Stone for Bread*. I'm really curious about him."

Beam gripped the chair arms, blinking rapidly and shaking his head. "But there's nothing to know. I mean he was just a man, a Frenchman." His face reddened.

Rachel held her breath, wondering what Scott would ask next. He moved a step closer to Beam. Was the camera on?

The next questions came quickly, with barely a pause in which Beam might answer. "Can you tell me something about René? How old he was? Where he lived? Just something. Anything."

"Well, I was in Paris," Henry stuttered. He straightened and suddenly lashed out with his voice. "And no I won't tell you any more! You'll have to wait! I'm writing about him! I can't talk about it now!"

Scott smiled. "That's great! So you'll actually tell us the real story behind the poems. That's a book I definitely want to read."

Beam shot Rachel a frenzied look. Fear? Or was it anger? Or an attempt to gauge her complicity in Scott's questions? She shrugged and opened her palms toward him with an I-haven't-a-clue gesture.

Henry Beam came up from the chair. "No, that's not what I'm doing, Mr. Trevelian!" he snapped. He unclipped the microphone from his shirt and tossed it on the rocker seat. "We're done here. Pack up your things and leave my house." He pivoted and nearly sprinted across the room to the door at the back and was gone.

Scott hadn't moved.

"Scott, what was that?" asked Rachel.

He shook his head, chagrined and penitent. "I just wanted some reaction from the guy, something real. Which I guess I got, but I'm sorry. I didn't mean to make him mad."

Rachel went to the door through which Henry Beam had just

disappeared. "Mr. Beam," she called. "We're sorry. We didn't mean to upset you. Scott really didn't."

There was no answer from the back. Scott and Adrian began packing the equipment.

"What now?" she asked as they drove to Chapel Hill.

"Damn if I know," said Scott. "I at least have his phone number. I'll call and apologize. If I can't finish this thing, I'll get hell from the station."

"Well, he told you he didn't want to talk about those poems."

"Probably because they're a fraud, like the man himself. He's probably making up some story about René to justify what he did when he published *A Stone for Bread*."

It was almost midnight when Scott's phone call woke her.

"We're going back tomorrow."

"That's great. I'm glad he accepted your apology."

"Actually he didn't. I couldn't get up with him. His goddamned phone rang and rang. But then he called me. Just a few minutes ago. He's some strange dude, Rachel. He apologized to *me*. Like he'd done this awful thing. Sounded like a kid. Really upset. My bet is he was drinking. But we're back in. We need to be out there in the early afternoon. Can you do it?"

"Yes." She yawned. "At least I can sleep late."

There were only the two of them. Adrian had a job interview. Beam seemed little different from the man Scott had been interviewing before the René questions provoked his outburst. Like that had never happened. Yet it had happened, and that it remained unacknowledged kept her uneasy through the first hour. Scott seemed to acknowledge it only when he told him he had finished interviewing him. But he still had Beam wear the same clothes as the day before, sit in the rocker and read several poems from *Nightshade* and *First Things Last*. Beam selected the poems, some of which he called favorites, though he read them with little emotion, his voice a nasal drone. That done, Scott shot video of the room's interior, the framed certificates and awards above Beam's writing table, the table itself, with its neat ream of paper and electric typewriter, and of course, the carved lion. He asked Beam to sit at his writing table so he could film him at work, or at least at the pretense of work.

Scott showed Rachel how to monitor the audio for the ambient sound he wanted, the click of typewriter keys, the clock bonging the hour, an occasional canine yelp from the porch. She listened through a headset and kept her eyes on the red recorder needle for too much gain. She was familiar with the rudiments of videotaping after working at UNC-TV, although she'd been mainly in the office. Scott instructed Beam to behave normally and imagine the camera didn't exist. He couldn't, of course, and glanced around often, sometimes throwing questions at Scott: had he seen any Carolina basketball games this year? What did he think about the accusations over Princess Di's death?

Scott was patient. He had no choice. He explained in simple terms what he wanted, took shots from different angles, often several times, and repeated his suggestion that Beam pretend he was alone in the room. But the man seemed incapable of shedding his discomfort. When he sat at his writing table, he kept pulling books from a stack beside him, leafing through them almost mindlessly. When he went off to the bathroom, Rachel glanced at the titles. A somber collection: the Holocaust, a biography of Stalin, a slim paperback about the Cambodian killing fields, *The Death and Life of Dith Pran,* and two books on the Rwandan genocide. Beam obviously relished slaughter. She wondered if he was writing poems about these atrocities. For the camera, he typed a few lines on a clean sheet of paper but would not allow Scott to see them.

Mid-afternoon, when Scott filmed outside, Rachel sensed a decided shift in Beam's manner. He seemed to relax. He called them by their first names and expected to be called Henry. The day was cold but the sky was crystalline blue. "Perfect," Scott had exulted on the way over. He had Henry walk through the woods, accompanied by his dogs, lean against a fence rail and even pick creasy greens. The poet himself suggested a shot of him seated on an old pine stump.

"This is where I come to think," he said, lowering himself onto the stump. "Men speak of journeys," he began, a line Rachel didn't recognize from either of his books, "oceans dared, Everest, the stars, for what? God, gold, the cities of Cibola, pale Nirvana and that fragile icon love? I take my journeys here, in dawn-lit forest, gold monarch's wing, ragwort, pulp of acorn presaging oak." He sighed. "Well, I wrote that a long time ago. A bit adolescent, I'm afraid."

"I haven't read that one," she said, when Scott turned off the camera.

He smiled. "I was sixteen." He seemed to hesitate before he asked, "You've read my first book?"

"I've read both published collections."

She sensed he wanted to ask something further, her opinion of them most likely, but he frowned and stared past her, a gloomy expression settling on his face. He rose from the stump and headed toward the house. Scott raised his eyebrows in a question. What had she said to make him walk away? She shrugged and they traipsed after him. When Henry reached the porch, he turned back to them.

"Dinner?"

Scott seemed uncertain, then asked, "That's an invitation?"

"Why not? I'm not such a bad cook, you know. And I owe you, Scott." His first acknowledgment of yesterday's anger.

"Okay, we accept."

"One condition."

"Sure."

"No camera."

Scott gave him a thumbs up.

Once in the house, Henry went off to the kitchen while Scott packed up the equipment and loaded it into his car. Rachel joined Henry to rinse salad greens. He seemed loose, almost jovial, his gloom having dissipated between the woods and kitchen. He took Scott off somewhere in the house to fetch a small round table, which they set up near the fireplace. They hauled in logs from outside and built a fire. The evening turned cozy, even friendly. Henry *was* a good cook. It was a simple meal, green salad and made-from-scratch marinara sauce over rice, but it was excellent. The wine too. The conversation, however, proved less successful. When Scott seemed to run out of ideas, Rachel plunged in.

"In 'Going Gentle,' you seem to say death's inevitability is a reason to passively await death, to, in other words, go gentle. But to me that seems like surrender."

"Wait until you're older," he said, his voice edged with the bitterness they'd heard before.

"But I don't agree," she protested. "Why surrender to death? Particularly if you're not dying. And you're not that old, Henry."

He flashed what for him was possibly a smile, though it had the character of a smirk. "Well, Rachel, we can't fight it. There's not a damn thing to be done. Nothing."

"Stating the obvious," Scott added, cheerfully.

"Of course, it's the obvious," Rachel responded. "But not going gentle has more to do with the way we live than how we die. Like Andrew Marvell's lover—if we can't make the sun stand still, we can make it run." She caught Scott rolling his eyes and got his message. Please, Rachel, not poetry. But Beam's hospitality had heartened her. She wasn't ready to back off poetry. "I mean, isn't that really all Dylan Thomas is saying, that we should live our lives fully to the end, a rage to live, you might say?"

Beam sent a sly glance her way. "I might contend that Andrew Marvell only wanted to get the lady in bed, but that's not your point. My point is what does fighting old age and dying gain us? Ulcers? Or drinking one's self to death like Dylan did? What kind of life is that? Hardly worth it, I'd think." He leaned forward. "Life is a crock, Rachel. That's all there is to it, to be endured. We come into the world with nothing, go out with nothing, all that's in between is a tiny asterisk, our Kilroy was Here."

"But it's what the asterisk connotes that matters," she countered.

"Well, popular culture has its expressions about that. You do your thing, I do mine. Or maybe more enticingly put, I'm into poetry, you're into film. So the asterisk is a culmination of 'things' or 'intos'."

"Pretty bleak, Henry," chimed in Scott. "So what's your purpose for writing poetry or should I say being into poetry?" Scott had apparently decided if he couldn't stop them, he'd join them.

"As I noted this afternoon, I don't write much poetry." Again the bitterness.

Scott seemed not to notice. "What are you working on now?"

"Is this off or on the record?"

"I'm not a reporter. And the camera's packed up."

"I never trust a journalist of any kind. Particularly you, Scott." He attempted a weak smile. "But your question ... sometimes I think I'm not working at all, on anything. True confession time, right? Sometimes like today, I just walk in the woods and think. Many days, I don't even do that. What I do most is read. I'm taking a survey, you might say. The crimes of the twentieth century. Not petty crimes, like murder or rape. But crimes on a grand scale, those committed by civilizations and governments, with the aim of eradicating an entire race or nation or class, crimes that require the complicity of thousands, maybe millions, Auschwitz, the Gulag, the killing fields of Cambodia, Sukarno, the Chinese cultural revolution, Rwanda and et cetera, et cetera, et cetera. This enlightened, technological age of ours is as red with blood as any in history, possibly redder. Our technology is so wondrously efficient. I don't know where we get the notion we've progressed. Damn stupid conclusion if you ask me." His face flushed with anger.

She should have stopped then, but her curiosity about the man goaded her to another question. "When you published the death camp poems—" she started, but he cut her off.

"I'm not talking about those!" he snapped. "The Nazis weren't the only murderers in the twentieth century." He brought his fist down on the table, hard enough to rattle the dishes. She feared his fury about to erupt again. Scott raised his eyes, looked quizzically in her direction. But Beam's anger died as quickly as it had come. Embarrassed, he apologized. "I'm sorry. I just, well, I'm so sorry."

There ensued an awkward silence, until Scott broke it. "So what's your plan for this research, Henry? Future poems maybe?"

"No particular poems. I have a title. Maybe that's where we writers begin, with titles. Do you know how difficult it is to write sometimes? Not the creation, but to actually force oneself to put words on a page. I can think of a thousand things I'd rather do. A thousand things."

"What's the title?" she asked, wondering what thousand things Henry Beam found to do every day.

"*Danse Macabre*, The Dance of Death, it's a medieval phrase. Here I'll show you, Rachel."

He got up, went to a pile of books by the writing table and retrieved a large volume. "Reproductions of early woodcuts," he explained, "done by the sixteenth century Parisian printer, Guyot Marchant. They ornamented a book called *Danse Macabre*. Marchant was inspired by paintings covering the walls of the cloister of the Cemetery of the Innocents in Paris. Where the dead of Paris were buried back then. You see, death was perceived as a grim dance, despite their Christian notions of heaven. There're all kinds of paintings in which death personified carries off people—kings, peasants, even printers with their books, God forbid. Unfortunately they didn't have critics in that day." He smiled at his little joke. "The Cemetery of the Innocents became a popular spot in Paris, a place of rendezvous and friendly gatherings. People even had what might be called parties among the dead. The bones, you see, were disinterred after a time and stacked up, neatly, even aesthetically stacked, I might add, in a charnel house, and people would picnic nearby, probably tossing their fish bones in among the human bones. Delightful, yes?" He paused, his face more animated than she had seen it. "You can get a sense of this in the Paris catacombs."

"And what do you intend to do with this image?" asked Scott.

"It's a symbol really, the living picnicking by the bones of the dead. Because we still do it. We may look around and see progress, space stations, computers, medical miracles, while the bones pile up in this so-called progressive century, 6 million Jews, 3 million non-Jews under the Nazis, 2 million Cambodians, 800,000 Rwandans, and these are only a portion of the slaughtered. We're the picnickers, the revelers, dancing on the bones of the dead. But Death has the last dance, as in Marchand's woodcuts. A dance to which we're all invited and will one day be forced to attend. You see, that's what my poem 'Going Gentle' is about. The fight is futile."

Beam's passive acceptance annoyed Rachel. "Well, maybe against death, yes. But what about how we're to live? We do have choices there."

"I don't know if that matters."

"Hell," Scott cried, "I don't concede that!" Eyes lit, he straightened, no, stiffened, geared for battle. "We don't have to be picnickers, as you put it. To fight against genocide is purpose in itself. It doesn't mean we'll beat death, but we can sure work to improve life on this planet. Our little asterisk can represent more than a footnote. It can be a bit of starburst, our moment of fire."

Henry smiled. "Very nice, Scott, very nice."

"You like my image?" Scott returned the smile. He seemed pleased Henry had finally turned from her and given him his due.

Beam sighed. "Well, I guess I'm just getting old and probably not going as gentle as one should."

In that moment, he looked old, his face pale, fleshy, eyes bruised. Rachel felt sad for him. He had allowed them a peek behind the façade. She remembered something she had wanted to ask about *A Stone for Bread*. "Henry, there's a line in one of the death camp poems, the one about—"

"I don't want to talk about those." He scowled and pushed back from the table. He had slammed the gate.

Scott thanked him profusely for the excellent meal and stood up. "We're pretty much finished the shooting part of this, Henry. I'll be editing over the holidays. If I need to re-shoot something, I'll call you."

Henry rose more slowly. "You're finished with me?" he asked.

His wistful regret surprised Rachel. "Today was fun, Henry," she said. "I've enjoyed the time."

They said their thank-yous and moved to the door. Henry trailed them.

"Scott, I've had an idea," he said rather hastily. "Maybe a gathering here, you know, a party, a few of my friends, writers. You could film that, add some human interest."

Scott appeared befuddled. It took him a moment before he brightened. "Sure, sure that's a great idea. What about after Christmas? That'll give me time to look at the footage and see what we need."

"You really think that's a good idea?" she asked as they started toward Chapel Hill.

"Well, it would give me editing options, which I sure as hell may need. Who knows, after Christmas, he'll probably have forgotten he suggested this."

"I doubt it."

Scott sighed. "You're probably right. Because it's still about you, you know. He's got this thing about you, Rachel. He'll probably keep trying to figure out ways to prolong the whole damn project. But hell if I will."

SIX

*W*hy had he gotten himself into this? How could he have been so stupid? All that blather about *Danse Macabre*. A man in his dotage wanting to impress an attractive young woman. Of course, he'd been flattered by her interest in his work. But she had motives for that interest. She was, after all, working with a filmmaker. Why wouldn't she try to wheedle information from him? That's what Scott wanted her to do, what Scott had tried to do himself. Had the young man thought him a fool when he threw those questions at him, as if he might confess the whole sordid thing? But as Henry knew, he was his own worst enemy. He had actually invited them back when he could have been done with the both of them. And now this stupid suggestion for a dinner party. When had he last had a dinner party? He couldn't remember.

Much too restless to sleep, Henry sat at his writing table, opening books and closing them again. When nothing fixed his attention, he wandered the living room, searching his bookshelves for something to read. He didn't find anything and instead opened a bottle of wine. Not bothering with a glass, he uncorked the bottle and drank straight from it, letting the wine's warmth spread through his gut. It was well past three o'clock when, groggy from downing the bottle, he sat again at his writing table, pulled out his dictionary and scribbled notes on the pad by his typewriter. Sometimes he mumbled to himself and once or twice even chuckled. Gray light was seeping through his windows when he rolled a clean white sheet into the typewriter and began to type.

Etymology

Nice started as stupid.
Cardinal meant hinge,
before a Pope unhinged it,
in red-vested men.

Sinister's left-handed,
like the dark lord of hell,
Pencil? Came from *penis*,
in turn derived from *tail*.

But *auburn*, lovely auburn,
white from first accounts,
until they spelled it
and turned it to *abrown*.

But *beauty*'s never altered,
remained the same through time,
while Rachel, lovely Rachel —
with auburn hair,
beside my door, standing there,
remains yet undefined.

He read back through his night's work and smiled. Silly doggerel
yes, and nothing that approached poetry. He had never written whim-
sy, too serious a man to bother. Yet somehow the poem pleased him
and he laughed to himself. Still not wanting to sleep, he left the house

and walked a ways down his road, briskly walked, as if he were actually going somewhere. The cold air sobered him. When his legs trembled from the exertion and his breath came in gasps, he returned to the house. He picked up the newly typed poem and read through it again. "Foolish, horny old man," he muttered, crumpling the page between his fingers.

Seven

René never understood why he had failed the baccalauréat. Perhaps God had chosen to more compellingly ratify his vocation. The next month, he left Orleans to enter a *petite seminaire* near Rouen. As at the *lycée*, he was an exemplary student. Despite this, his counseling priest, Father Armand, doubted almost from the beginning that the young man had a true heart for God. Yes, he grasped Latin and the essentials of *The Summa* with astonishing facility. But charity and piety—well, these were different matters altogether. He was much too aloof and somber, his eyes cold as the stone of the chapel. Though he did everything properly, observed the rules of the seminary, it was without the slightest joy, or even remorse for his joylessness. When Father Armand asked him about these things, René replied only that he had entered the seminary to learn about God. This answer troubled Father Armand, as if God could be found in a work of theology. More troubling was the recognition that he did not like René. He prayed about this dislike, discussed René often with his superiors. Why was the young man so relentless in his studies, yet so unmoved by worship and prayer? What lay behind the sterile eyes, the arduous hours of reading and study? One venerable priest—granted, he was a rather senile man—suggested they might have a demon among them. Others of the faculty dismissed this as overwrought, but certainly René's presence in the seminary discomforted them. When asked about his sense of vocation, René refused to defend himself. He needed time, he responded, to discover what he had come to find. The fathers shook their heads wonderingly, but decided that if this brilliant young man needed time, they could at least give him that, although no one at the seminary expected he would ever become a priest.

René believed he had responded truthfully to the fathers' questions. He had certainly come to the seminary to find God. His experience before the bronze crucifix that night in Orleans had deeply affected him, even if he had not understood it. What he did understand was the phenomenon of death. He had seen organs of small creatures quiver and grow cold, but then what? He recalled that a priest once told him about the Resurrection, how the dead would live again. René had never quite believed him, although for years he had prayed for the soul of a brother who was now nearly forgotten. But in his study of science at the *lycée*, he had abandoned those prayers. He did not think decaying organs could be regenerated into ones that pulsed with life, that dust could become flesh. But neither could he explain the shimmering cross that night in the Orleans church, the bronze Jesus that appeared to move. At the seminary, he set about to recreate that miracle so he might affirm with authority that God could alter the natural world. He began slipping into the chapel at night when the others were asleep. But here the windows did not admit moonlight in the same way as at Orleans. Here Jesus did not shimmer or stretch his arms to him.

Though this deeply disappointed him, René's bitterest experience at the seminary was not his failure to find God. It was his discovery of evil, the truth of which he discovered in a place difficult to eradicate— in his own heart. The evil presented itself in the form of Georges, a fellow seminarian. As René was darkness, Georges was light, a blond youth from the Saône whose disposition matched his fair hair and skin. Georges laughed merrily and often, found goodness everywhere, even in René. He was one of the few students who was kind to René.

Most, like his fellows in the *lycée*, found René odd and unnerving and tended to keep a distance from him. But Georges spoke to René as if he were truly interested in him. He asked about his classes, told René about his home and life before entering the seminary.

They shared a room in the dormitory with six others, Georges' bed hardly four steps from René's. At night, he listened to Georges' little snorts and rhythmic breaths as images of the sleeping seminarian warmed his thoughts. He observed him in the chapel, saw how his head bent in prayer, how the shaggy blonde hair fell on his forehead, his lower lip protruding slightly when he prayed. Sometimes René followed him along the corridors of the seminary, at a discreet distance, of course, noting how he greeted the other students and patted their shoulders in camaraderie. Whenever that same gesture came René's way, he ducked to hide his burning cheeks.

But René burned with more than passion. He burned with shame. What tumultuous obsession had taken hold of him? He fought against it, established rules by which to avoid Georges. At Mass, he closed his eyes tightly. In the classroom, he sat several seats in front of Georges to avoid seeing him. At night, well, night was difficult. He could not avoid the young man's breathing, the occasional word muttered in his sleep. He could not avoid Georges' smell, the dusky male scent of him. And no matter the rules René made to keep his aberration in check, they were quickly broken. Powerless, he buried himself in his studies and prayed more fervently. But each night, Georges was there, four paces away, breathing. René knew his breath the way a mother knows her baby's cry. He knew its distinct rhythms, could isolate it from Maxime's nasal sniffs, the slow inhalations of Jean, the slightly erratic rhythm from Jean-Paul.

Sometimes, awake in the darkness, he imagined himself inhaling the air Georges exhaled, timing this so they breathed in tandem as a single pair of lungs, sharing in the only consummation allowed him. At the latrine, he could never resist a furtive glance as the students lined up before the urinal. The spraying penis, Georges' hands cupped lightly, almost joyously, about it. René saved these images for his night thoughts, the movement of Georges' hands in the latrine, the flair of his blonde hair, his innocent, manly smile. René imagined studying with Georges in the library, shoulder to shoulder, encouraged by Georges' pats on his back, the two of them in one bed, body beside body, or on the floor before the altar in the chapel. These fantasies tormented René and were in no way relieved by his own furtive touchings under the bedcovers at night of himself, his penis, his body.

At Mass the next morning, he would pray for deliverance. But the one act that might have saved him, he could not bring himself to: he could not confess this sin to Father Armand. To do so would cause him to be sent from the seminary. He studied harder, so much so that the *ange noir* soon visited him. He reported sick to the infirmary, stayed several days, although the priest in charge pronounced him a malingerer and insisted he return to classes. He grew even more aloof, retreating into his fantasies of Georges. Whenever the seminary faculty met, René's name was usually mentioned, followed by worried discussions among the professors. He was brilliant, yes, top in all his classes. But a priest? How would this strange young man ever become a priest?

Eight months into the term, there occurred a shocking incident. Silver was taken from the refectory. When several days later the Superior's gold crucifix turned up missing, the senior faculty convened to discuss the possible thefts. That night they sent two priests through the dormitory after midnight on a surprise search of the students' rooms. The priest who entered René's room, Father Rémy, approached René first, reached down and shook the young man's shoulder. René

A Stone for Bread

did not stir. When the priest slapped him, René came up shrieking, fists flying. The priest fell back against a table. The next day, when a report of the search was made, it was René who received the most attention, despite that the missing crucifix was found in the room next to his, hidden in the back of a cupboard.

Of course, no thief would be so stupid as to hide his treachery where suspicion would fall on him, suggested one of the professors.

A good point, Father, said another. Why would the young man have attacked Father Rémy if his conscience were clear?

That in itself was grounds for dismissal, the professors decided.

René was called before the faculty and questioned about the attack on Father Rémy.

I was startled from sleep, he said.

Particular note was made of the fact that René twisted his hands in his lap during their inquiry and an odd twitch appeared in his face. Although he apologized to Father Rémy, it was in a cold voice. Surely, no true remorse resided in the heart of this seminarian, the priests murmured afterwards. When asked about the missing crucifix, he had replied in the same icy voice, I know nothing about it.

The interview only intensified the faculty's suspicions. They watched René more closely. Though nothing else was found missing in the next few weeks, they decided the young man perceived he was being watched. One night, a priest saw René slip into the chapel when everyone was in bed. He watched through a crack in the door as René approached the altar. The priest stepped into the church and switched on the electric lights. René jerked around.

Is it the candlesticks? the priest cried.

What?

Going for the candlesticks, eh?

René squinted at him across the small nave, his hands twisting nervously. I came to pray, he said.

The priest reprimanded René for being out after hours. He was called before a committee of the faculty.

Is there not time in the day for your prayers? he was asked.

Yes.

Then why do you break the rules and enter the chapel at night?

René did not answer, was unable to answer. He had left his room because he believed he could no longer control his urge to leave his bed and lie next to Georges, pressed against the seminarian's body. In the chapel, he had prayed for absolution, and if not for that, for the will to end his misery by taking his life, though he knew that too was a sin.

You won't speak? Father Armand asked.

René's face twitched.

One of the others, a kindly man who had no taste for inquisitions, tried a different approach.

Do you believe, René, he said gently, that you possess a vocation for the priesthood?

René was trapped. He briskly rubbed the palms of his hands together and stared at the priests. Would God damn him if he lied? He remained silent.

The man asked the question again.

René's tongue swelled to clog his mouth. He dipped his head. The professors noted this slight movement, an almost imperceptible genuflect and each in his own way decided René had nodded *no*. They dismissed him from the room and met briefly afterwards. There was nothing further to be done. The young man, however brilliant, could not remain at the seminary. His removal was a quiet matter. René gathered his few belongings from the dormitory and left the next day. Father Armand gave him train fare to Orleans.

EIGHT
Eight

*T*he party at Henry's farmhouse was scheduled and rescheduled three times. Rachel wondered whether the man had trouble unearthing a few friends. The date was set finally for the week after Christmas. She was at her mother's house Christmas Eve when Scott reached her there by phone.

"Rachel, I can't do Beam's party."

"Why not?"

"I've been pulled off it that night for a special New Year's show the station wants. The Beam documentary's on hold at the moment." He sounded happy.

"But after all it took to schedule the thing," she protested.

"Well, I don't know." He hesitated then said, "Maybe Adrian can do it. In fact, I'll call him. The two of you tape the party and I'll put the show together when I get a chance."

From the way he said it, she wondered if Scott would ever find that chance.

But Adrian was available, so when Rachel returned to Chapel Hill after Christmas, she met the intern at the station where he was viewing the raw footage. It took only a few minutes of Henry's first interview to understand why Scott seemed eager to postpone the project. The outdoor shots were fine—stark bare trees against the blue sky, the old farmhouse, the dogs on the porch. The interiors of Beam's house weren't bad either. But when Henry faced the camera, he stiffened and was not merely dull but protective, as if he needed to ponder every word before he let it be snared by Scott's camera. Why would anyone care about Henry Beam? Even if Scott took the time, she doubted he would be able to edit the show into something watchable.

But there was no canceling the party.

The evening before it, she again read through *A Stone for Bread*. She could understand why Henry might not want to discuss the poems. Their publication had sabotaged his career, despite the money Scott said he'd made from them. And they were bleak, painful poems, rendered in ironic images accentuating the human depravity of that horrendous epoch. More difficult to understand was Henry's obsession with that same depravity, the crimes of the twentieth century as he put it. She noted again the inscription on the book's title page. *For René*, and underneath it the Latin words *Cui bono?* She had looked up the Latin at the university library. *To what end?* or *For what good?* The tone of the question was cynical. For what ulterior motive? Who *was* René really? Did he actually exist or had Henry invented him? She wondered what Henry was writing in the book he mentioned, the one he said was about René. Would it reveal the truth about *A Stone for Bread*?

She met Adrian at the farmhouse, arriving a few minutes before he did and two hours before the party. Henry greeted them with a smile, a genuine smile. He was dressed in something other than his usual checkered shirt and jeans—a tweed jacket and beige shirt, tieless, shiny brown western boots in place of the Reeboks. When he took the time, shaved carefully and combed his stiff gray curls over the bald spots, he was a handsome man, despite his age and weight. As Henry helped them set up, he appeared nervous, continually shifting things about, moving the table close to the crackling fire, then farther away. The room was less cluttered and he now tried, unsuccessfully, to straighten the stacks of books. Finally, he gave up and ambled off to the kitchen. Adrian fastened the camera onto a wheeled tripod so it could be moved around the table. He laughed and joked with Henry, seemingly thrilled to sub for Scott, as if he'd been handed the reins to a Ken Burns documentary. Once again Rachel would monitor the audio. Otherwise, she seemed completely superfluous. She suspected Adrian would have preferred she wasn't along. But Henry wanted her here and she sensed Adrian might even be relieved Scott hadn't come, that this was now *his* project.

There were four guests: Abe Wisner, a poet of some local interest, Dr. Ralph Smith, retired English professor, and a couple probably in their fifties, Wallace and Helen Martin. Wallace Martin was an insurance executive. Helen, a small, chirpy woman, wrote self-help books, their titles unfamiliar to Rachel, but then, she didn't read self-help books. During the dinner, which Adrian filmed until he seemed bored with it, the woman chattered about her books, mostly guides for tapping into one's spiritual self or finding perfect love. Fortunately, after a few glasses of wine, she retreated into a sleepy silence. Maybe husband Wallace had kicked her under the table. Ralph Smith, on the other hand, was delightful. He told witty stories about students and historical personages in early North Carolina history. Abe Wisner, an elderly wizened man with heavy glasses, looked like a tired rabbi, but after a few drinks, his mood shifted in a direction opposite that of Helen Martin, soaring while she sank with a hilarious story about a walking tour years ago through Ireland where he was mistaken for a member of the IRA.

Henry seemed almost relaxed with these people and their easy conversation. The meal, she knew, was wonderful, though she spent it monitoring the audio. But Henry had let her sample his cooking earlier in the kitchen. The Cabernet, which the professor proclaimed excellent, flowed freely. Rachel imagined a well-stocked wine cellar under the house. But for whom? The more Henry's guests drank, the louder they talked, possibly too loud. Rachel watched the red recorder needle take precipitous jumps. She was an amateur here. What if the audio turned out garbled or distorted? She hoped Adrian would decide to pack it up before the voices got louder. They already had good footage: Professor Smith's stories, Wisner's trek through Ireland, even a few beatific expressions from Henry.

But then Wisner said something about a guitar. "Go on, Henry," he coaxed, "I brought my harmonica." He whipped the small silver instrument from his jacket pocket and blew a note.

Henry seemed genuinely pleased. He left the room and returned with an old and somewhat battered acoustic guitar. Pushing his chair from the table, he fiddled with its pegs to tune it as Wisner's harmonica whined out "Saint Louis Blues." The recorder's red needle fluttered. Adrian checked the video tape and decided to change it out. He had just loaded a new tape when things took off. Beam and Wisner started with blues and moved to bluegrass, vibrant, foot-stomping bluegrass. The music thumped and moaned and trembled the old wood boards of the floor. Helen Martin, who had said little over the last hour, woke up. She tapped her hand flat on the table and when she knew the song clapped and sang along. Wisner soon tired of the harmonica, his breath coming in wheezes. On his own now, Henry shifted from bluegrass to poetry, accompanied by guitar strum. He began with sonnets of Dante in the original Italian, segued to Baudelaire in French. He'd had his share of wine too, but his voice was clear and surprisingly dramatic, keeping his guests enthralled even when they didn't know the languages. Everyone was quite loose now. They laughed and applauded, and inwardly Rachel joined them. Henry was terrific! Scott should see this. Something special was happening and she knew from Adrian's hunched shoulders against the camera he knew it too. He moved the camera slowly and carefully, panning it to catch every face at the table. Henry's face was red and shiny, charged. Then without so much as a skipped beat, he shifted from French to English, not Dante this time, but *A Stone for Bread*:

> The mad Jew of Gusen
> sings of the Alsace,
> summer and green wheat,
> new vines on ancient hills,
> a dirge for the corpses
> he rolls into furrows,
> covers with dirt.

> The guards taunt him,
> mimic his singing.
> One tosses something his way,
> "Bread," the guard calls.
> "My wife baked it this morning."

> The Jew lunges, pirouettes,
> a bony dervish,
> hunger-mad,
> the guard's offering
> inches beyond his reach.
> The Jew stumbles,
> sprawls on putrefying flesh,
> his own body
> indistinguishable

from the newly dead.

The guard tosses another.
His comrades join the game,
sailing small rounds
above the prisoner's splayed fingers.

The frenzied man leaps higher,
until at last snags down his prize
and falls again to earth.
Laughing, he stuffs it in his mouth
and breaks his teeth on stone.

Henry's face changed once again, the pain real, as if he had been there, known Gusen, witnessed the Jewish prisoner and his tormentors. Rachel forgot about the red needle and fought back tears. The room hushed, the only sound Henry's voice. He recited several more of the concentration camp poems, then choked on a line and stopped. Adrian kept the camera running, pointed directly at him. There was a flicker of recognition in Beam's face, like that of a man waking from a trance. He blinked and laid the guitar on the floor.

"It's late."

His guests roused themselves, mumbled a few thank-yous and goodbyes and left. Rachel helped Adrian wrap cables and pack the equipment. Neither spoke. Henry began carrying dishes off to the kitchen. The equipment loaded into his car, Adrian headed home. Rachel went back inside the house to find Henry. He was seated at the kitchen table, head propped on his hands.

"Henry?"

He offered her a bleary look.

"I'm going now, but I wanted to thank you. For the evening."

He slowly raised his head. "You have to go?" The tone in his voice was sad, almost pleading.

"No, I can stay a while longer."

He lurched from the chair. "I'll get you something to eat. You only snacked."

She wasn't hungry but didn't want to offend him. She knew how Henry reacted when he was unhappy about something. She sat down at the kitchen table while he fetched a plate and spooned leftovers onto it, a slice of beef, a bit of salad. He set a glass of Cabernet in front of her, poured himself another glass and returned to the table. There was an awkward silence. She tried to eat but felt exposed, every bite sounding like the crunch of feet in snow. She laid the fork on the table.

"I'm really not hungry."

"The beef isn't good cold," he said, as if he'd failed her.

"Henry, it isn't the food or the wine."

His eyebrows lifted, curious. He seemed edgy, fearful of what she might say.

"This was such an amazing evening. I really mean that. I think tonight's footage will turn out beautifully."

"Did you miss Scott not being here?"

The question surprised her.

"Scott and I are friends. We used to work together at UNC-TV. I'm working on my Master's in English now at Chapel Hill."

"I like him, Scott," said Henry. "He's a bright young man, but I never knew just what he really wanted, what he might ask me. Tonight went better because it was just you and the kid." He raised his glass in a toast and smiled. "To television. And the resurrection of dead careers." For once, there was an absence of bitterness. He seemed lighter, pleased. He set down his glass and smiled. "You liked the poetry? Tonight?"

"I loved it. Everything. Dante, Baudelaire, even if I don't know Italian and my French is rusty. But I particularly liked the Holocaust poems."

He pursed his lips as if contemplating her response.

"Henry, I know why you don't want to talk about them. Scott told me about the controversy. But what does authorship really matter? Why should it keep you from owning them? Or from celebrating them for what they are?"

"I've never doubted what they are."

"Did you write them?"

"Does it matter?"

"Not really. You brought them to life, saw them published. That's what matters."

His thick eyebrows gathered in a frown. But the gate was still open. She took the risk.

"What was all that about anyway? The questions about who wrote them? Why, Henry?"

He hesitated, bent his head to stare at the floor where his yellow cat slept by his feet.

"The issue was never authorship, Rachel. The issue isn't authorship at all." He turned and stared at her, his eyes bloodshot from the wine. "What it's about is murder. And not just by the Nazis. I too was complicit."

NINE

He'd had too much to drink. Though it wasn't just the wine. The party itself was its own intoxicant: old friends at his house, well, not exactly friends, but former colleagues, and then the music, the poetry. And Rachel, her lovely face illumined in firelight, eyes lit and dancing from him to the recorder and back to him as he recited the poetry he had long loved—and then the other poems. In the kitchen afterwards, he'd almost blown it with his stupid words about murder and complicity. She wasn't ready for that. He saw it in the flicker of her eyelids, the tensed shoulders, ever so slightly tensed, as if she worried she'd stumbled into the lair of Hannibal Lecter. But Rachel was no fluttery female. Rachel had character and poise. He'd known that from the first. Whatever she might have thought at that moment, she had taken a sip from her wine glass, set it down slowly and looked directly at him. "Are you going to tell me about it?"

He'd nodded and begun with a sketch of his childhood and the years at Duke, launching then into the real story, what he had told to another only once before, beginning where it first began—the journey by ship to England, the few days in London, the ferry across the channel, how he had arrived in Paris in May of 1956. And those early weeks—when he wandered the streets stupefied, like a boy lost in an enchanted forest. The weather was cold, rainy, yet despite the rain, the City of Light dazzled him, and had he been a different sort of young man, he might have burst into song, done a two-step along the quay or let fly a raucous rebel yell. But he did none of those things. He merely walked. Walked everywhere. Passersby taking note of the young American would have seen a tall young man, heftier now, with a babyish face marked by mournful eyes and a slightly puzzled frown. The one perceivable oddity about him was that he neither carried an umbrella nor seemed in the slightest hurry to get out of the rain. He barely slept, spent every waking moment exploring the city. He wound his way up Montmartre, was propositioned by whores in Place Pigalle, took mass at Notre Dame though he was raised a Baptist, and tracked along the Left Bank and down its narrow streets near the river to St. Germain. A full two weeks were given over to the Louvre. He took it room by room, studying each masterwork carefully, as if to leave one unnoticed might offend the artist.

He ate while he walked, grabbing bites of food from street vendors or in the small groceries and *charcuteries*, staggering exhausted to his room late each night. He climbed the Eiffel Tower by foot, not once but whenever the mood struck him, usually after dark following a few drinks at a café. On one of those nights, half drunk, he ran the steel steps, gasping for breath and to his surprise shouted Baudelaire to the filmy sky and the delight of lovers snuggled in the tower's recesses. During these first weeks, he met no one, associated with no one, knew only his landlord, although he developed nodding acquaintance with a few neighborhood merchants, particularly the Tabac owner down the block who called him Yank. Henry reveled in this anonymity. The great city embraced him, protected him. It didn't matter that he was indolent, that he rose at noon and stayed late drinking in cafés. It didn't matter that he gave no thought to poetry and study and wrote only in a journal. Most days, he forgot even that. For the first time in his life, the furies were quiet.

He lived in the Marais, in a room rented from M. Forain, a bent man in his 60s. A retired furrier, Forain solaced himself after the death of his wife by renting out his extra bedroom to students. Henry learned of the arrangement from a professor at Duke, and although the room was comfortable and well lit, he wasn't happy there. M. Forain was a pleasant, doting man, but much too chatty for Henry's monkish sensibility. And the flat was on the fifth floor of a stone building off Rue Turenne, a rather dismal block of eighteenth century buildings, their facades coated with centuries of chimney smoke and, in this particular century, black auto exhaust. Once residential, most nearby buildings now housed factories. Formerly quaint courtyards were crisscrossed by steel rails where machinery and large bales of wire were rolled onto heavy cars. Twenty-four hours a day, the street thrummed with noise. When Henry opened the window in his small room, he looked down on an alleyway and across it to boarded-up windows of a chair factory.

The break with M. Forain came his second month in Paris. Things went quickly sour when Henry bought a guitar and spent the early evening hours in his room learning to play. He had, of course, asked M. Forain's permission and was assured there were no objections. But soon afterwards, the landlord, usually so agreeably talkative, began complaining, about petty things mostly: Henry's habit of sleeping until noon, his failure to hang his bath towel on the proper peg on the back of the door, the magazines and papers left scattered across his bed. Henry wondered whether M. Forain went through his things when he was out. He hid his journal, though he doubted the man read English. Even though he preferred the sullen (and quiet) M. Forain to the garrulous one, he set about to find another place to live. Within days, he located a room in an old Left Bank hotel on Rue Sommerard, a few blocks from the Seine. The room wasn't as pleasant as M. Forain's, but the neighborhood more than compensated. Now, he was close to the Sorbonne and the quays along the Seine and in walking distance of St. Germain where he imagined everyone he passed was a student or an artist. There were probably more tourists than genuine *artistes* here, but he felt at home on the Left Bank, his spirit set free in the heady air of these ancient streets and busy cafés.

The move to the Left Bank brought another change in his life. He began to meet people. The hotel, unlike M. Forain's pristine flat, had its own community. Most, like Henry, were renters rather than transients and tourists. The hotel was small, shabby and cheap, without baths or toilets in the rooms. The toilet for his floor was at the end of the hall. The shower, one flight up, was shared by two floors, so that showering became a communal event. While he waited for a free stall, Henry met other residents. One of the first was Bert Yeager.

"Duke?"

"What?"

"Duke? You go to Duke?"

"How did you know?"

"Shirt on. The other day. Saw you coming through the lobby."

"Oh that."

"Bert Yeager."

The young man extended his hand, not bothering to remove the towel, which slipped down over both his and Henry's wrists. Henry took the proffered hand and mumbled his name. Yeager, also an American, was short and wiry, his sandy blond hair slicked back with oil.

"Michigan State. You Greek?"

"What?"

"Greek. Fraternity."

"No."

"What you doing here?"

"Here?"

"In Paris. What brings you to Paris?"

"Oh. A fellowship. To study the French Symbolists."

"Hey, a bona fide intellectual. Me, I'm a reporter. String for the

AP. Been in Paris about a year now. Got sick of college. Well, maybe college got sick of me. But here, gaîté Parée, I'm having a blast. Pleased to meet you, Henry Beam. I've got friends, Americans, if you're looking for company. Good fellows."

He wasn't looking for company, but he didn't say that to Yeager, and soon found himself invited to join Yeager and friends for dinner. The invitation initiated a new phase in Henry's life. Yeager was 27. As a stringer, he pretty much worked on his own time, probably why he never seemed too busy. Henry suspected he was handicapped by his French, which was passable but unexceptional. Henry's fluency in the language immediately interested Yeager. He quickly latched on to Henry and sought his help translating French periodicals and an occasional letter. In return, Yeager introduced Henry to the good fellows he'd mentioned. Yeager's friends prided themselves on knowing the right cafés and provided Henry an endless stream of trivia.

"There's Lenin's table, where he came in the 20s."

"Sartre holds court here."

"Camus lives on this street."

"In that building they published the *Midnight Press*, the resistance, you know."

Henry had little use for this information. He considered Yeager's friends bourgeois expatriates, resident tourists, gawkers and hangers-on. Their conversation was studded with sightings: Sartre at Le Dôme today, Blum at Le Méphisto talking with a Communist. These minor incidents seemed to fuel their resolve to remain in Paris, as if to *see* meant to *become* and by proximity one found significance for one's own life. But if they appeared at times frivolous and at loose ends, these young Americans weren't without interest for Henry.

Doug Spaulding was also a Southerner, from Mississippi. He lived on an inheritance and did not appear to do anything that might be termed work. Jake MacNally had been a Classics major at Chicago before he chucked it all to bum around the world. He survived in Paris with a job as a runner for a wealthy American financier who made regular trips to France to purchase artworks. Another of Yeager's friends, William Rice, had been a Catholic seminarian but quit after a few weeks. "Nest of queers," he told Henry. Rice was now making up for his celibate adolescence and young manhood—what he called his lost years—by screwing every woman he quite literally got his hands on. Rice had also renounced religion and become a Communist. Henry found him more bitter than ideological and greatly preferred the company of MacNally and Spaulding. He began spending evenings with Yeager and these friends and discovered he could even enjoy some of their conversations. In Paris, no one knew him, no one was privy to the grim truth of his childhood. And there was one fact about Henry that made them equals. Henry was published.

He and Yeager made an incongruous pair, yoked more by the chance proximity of their rented rooms than by a genuinely personable bond. The short, thin Yeager, who'd been a college sprinter, was a restless, fidgety man. His work for the AP was spotty and paid very little. His mother sent him money every month, enough to allow him to scrape by with what he earned writing. One reason for his interest in Henry seemed obvious. Yeager fancied himself a literary man, his idol another Henry, Henry Miller.

"I've got at least one novel in me," Yeager liked to say, referring often to this one novel, although Henry never knew whether he'd committed a word of it to paper. But it took only a few drinks to set Yeager off. He would wave his hand or raise a clenched fist and begin a high-voiced staccato description of scenes and characters and which publishers he felt were right for it and the advance he expected, as if the book was already at the printer's. He never showed a word of it to

Henry, or to any of the others as far as he knew.

Early on in their friendship, Henry gave Yeager a copy of *Nightshade,* his published poems. Yeager had seemed pleased, but never afterwards mentioned the book or if he'd even read it. Several times Henry started to ask but didn't, fearing Yeager's response, that he hadn't found them worth commenting on. Henry brooded about this and felt Yeager's silence as a rift in their friendship, though he never voiced this resentment. If he didn't always enjoy Yeager's company, he enjoyed the idea of his friendship, saw it as something fine and worthwhile, something that until now had been another of the absences from his life.

In October that year, world events altered the genial banter among Yeager's friends. News out of Hungary sobered Paris: bold young Hungarians challenging Russian tanks with bottles of gasoline and raw courage. In France, where the Communist Party was a power to be reckoned with, the events sent shocks through the country. Henry had never concerned himself with politics. The artist, he believed, observes history, comments on it, perhaps reveals history. Yet the photographs and newsreels from Hungary deeply affected him. Young men, his age, battling columns of tanks. He pondered the choices surely pondered before him by artists like Camus and Malreaux when faced with Nazi horrors. When does an act of rebellion, he wondered, like one man alone against the tyranny of a tank, become an artistic act, a transcendent moment of TRUTH?

One evening Henry asked this question out loud. He, Yeager, MacNally, and Rice were engaged in a spirited discussion at a café along Boulevard St. Germain, a discussion that like more recent conversations had grown heated. Rice, the Communist, defended his loyalties, though he too, like other French Communists, was dismayed by

Soviet tanks in Budapest. Yeager and MacNally weren't in the least dismayed. They were outraged and let Rice know it. Henry, who hated bullies, agreed with them, but argument made him uncomfortable, so as usual, he ate and drank his wine and listened.

"It's a matter of ends," argued Rice, after a rant from MacNally about communists.

"Yeah, the end of Hungary, the end of dissent, the end of all those boys out there," snapped Yeager. "Did you see the photographs in *Match*? Some of those street fighters are kids, twelve- and thirteen-year-old kids, against fucking tanks!"

"I pose a question," said Henry suddenly, and since he had never posed anything before, they turned his way, surprised.

"Okay, Beam, pose away," said MacNally, squelching an amused smile.

"The role of the artist in revolution. I mean, is it the artist's role to use art as a tool of rebellion, or to actually participate, to join the street fighters? Isn't the pen a more powerful tool than a Molotov cocktail?"

"The guy who shot the photos of the Hungarian fighters," Yeager said, "now he's the artist, right? If he'd been holding a gun, we'd never see them. We'd never know what the bastards were doing in Budapest."

"But he's a photographer, that's one thing," MacNally chimed in, "but nobody's going to sit down in the middle of a revolution and write a novel or a collection of poetry, for Chrissake. It's not art, per se. It's art if it works to further the revolution. Journalism, news photography, the newsreel guys, things like that."

MacNally was warming up, but Yeager looked bored. He hopped up to get cigarettes and when he came back coaxed them on to the next café. At Deux Magots, a man came through passing out flyers. Yeager grabbed one, glanced at it and dropped it on the ground.

"There's your artist as revolutionary," said a laughing Yeager.

Henry picked up the flyer. RENARD MARCOTTE screamed in large black letters at the top. Underneath in slightly smaller letters were the words MOUVEMENT LIBERTÉ FRANÇAISE. Smaller type announced that Renard Marcotte would address an M.L.F. rally that evening to condemn the events in Hungary. "Who's Renard Marcotte?" asked Henry.

"A Pierre Poujade impersonator," said Yeager, "thinks he can replicate the Poujadists' success. Good luck to him. Marcotte is strictly small time. But an artiste nonetheless. He puts on quite a show."

Henry knew of Pierre Poujade, the stationer from the provinces who'd rattled French politics with his shopkeepers' anti-tax revolt. Poujade's political party had just won 53 seats in the National Assembly.

"Marcotte's a joke," Yeager continued, "a neo-fascist in the guise of man of the people."

"A fascist?" asked Henry, startled. "This soon after the war?"

"Marcotte doesn't claim that, of course, but I've a few sources who think that's what's behind his incendiary rhetoric. He's certainly no friend of the Communists and socialists. Or parliament or the republic, for that matter." Yeager scrubbed his face with his hands. "Who gives a shit, anyway?" Yeager sounded tipsy.

"I give a shit." MacNally stood up. "For all you know, Marcotte may be a hero of the new France, another DeGaulle."

"Here's to fascists." Rice hoisted his glass.

"I'll take a good fascist any day to a commie," said MacNally, baiting Rice.

Yeager came up from his chair. "Well then, why don't we hear what the man has to say? Maybe we'll be witnesses to history."

Yeager's challenge elicited nods and thumbs up. They'd had

too much alcohol or were simply bored, likely the latter. Even Rice seemed up for a lark. "Okay, let's go watch the little Hitler crawl all over the Fourth Republic."

Yeager laughed. "Hell, I might even get a story."

Rice paid the bill, and the four friends left the café. Before they reached the Metro, Rice begged off. The others hopped a train that took them under the Seine to the Right Bank. They walked four blocks to an old building, like those in the Marais where Henry first stayed, an apartment building converted into a warehouse for a restaurant supply distributor. People milled outside. A few picketers, communists, marched in front. Some of Marcotte's crowd shook fists at the picketers and shouted "massacrers" and "assassins." The mood was ugly. Henry was having second thoughts. But he didn't want the others thinking him cowardly, so he followed them through the picketers into the warehouse and climbed stairs to a storeroom on the third floor. It wasn't a large space, so the eighty or so people seated on benches and old wooden chairs seemed a full crowd for the rally already underway. The room's high windows had been boarded over outside and were blocked inside by shelves loaded with neatly stacked oven units. Enough shelves had been moved aside for seats and a small podium at the front. Henry wondered why the need for a microphone, particularly with the intermittent feedback that screamed in his ears. The man speaking into it, who Yeager whispered was not Marcotte, ignored the feedback, his speech more ranted than spoken and little more than repeated platitudes about freedom and tyranny and the restoration of France. Smoke from cigarettes floated in thin layers above the audience's heads. Although large electric fans stood in the corners of the room, the space felt close and airless.

A second speaker who was also not Marcotte followed the first. Henry grew restless and ready to leave. He started to say so when the speaker suddenly stopped and people began to shout Marcotte's name.

"That's him," Yeager whispered.

Renard Marcotte strode quickly to the podium and cut off the microphone. He slid an empty chair to the podium's front edge and stood on it, looking out at his cheering followers like a Roman emperor at the Forum. A muscular man of medium height, he looked to be in his forties. Even before he'd said a word, his face shone with sweat. Strands of grayish hair, greasy in the garish light, stuck damply against his forehead. As Marcotte began speaking, the three friends edged to the far back of the room and tried not to look out of place among the true believers. Yeager nodded toward four clean-cut beefy young men standing near the doorway. They wore similar dark blue shirts under their jackets and blue bands around their upper arms, printed in black with the initials M.L.F.

"Marcotte's thugs," Yeager hissed in Henry's ear as Renard Marcotte's voice rose in both pitch and decibels.

The tension in the room grew palpable, enough so that Henry, like Marcotte, had begun to sweat. The hair on his arms tingled. Marcotte stepped suddenly from the chair to the floor with loud thumps, wiped a handkerchief across his face, which he quickly stuffed back in his pocket, and pumped his fist. His voice, masculine and deep, resonated through the room. There was little logic to his speech and fewer facts—the stock accusations of the right: Communists in the government, burdens of taxation, evils of socialism. He even threw in a jab at unidentified Christ haters. The longer he spoke, the more his voice gathered fire. He closed his eyes and jerked his arms high in the air—staged, clumsy gestures, yet Henry experienced the man's power as he lunged from the podium and bent toward the first row of listeners, his face in their faces.

When he was a boy, Henry's mother had taken him to Baptist

revivals, mother and son seated on plank benches under canvas tents in grassy fields. The aisles were layered with sawdust, down which the faithful and faithless were exhorted to come to salvation. Marcotte was like that. Henry remembered the one time in his childhood he'd considered the call and might even have made the trek to the flimsy wooden altar had the preacher not been so poorly educated, the fire and passion of his sermon tempered in the boy's mind by the man's poor grammar. "A man mus' get hisself right with Jesus, or the devil'l be on his coattails." But Renard Marcotte wasn't some ignorant preacher and Henry was surprised to find himself stirred. Perhaps it was the heat in the room or the resonance of the man's voice, or that he'd had too much to drink, but as Marcotte warmed to his audience, Henry's face warmed with it. When the sentences flowed faster from Marcotte's tongue, Henry's heart accelerated, until an odd sensation flooded his chest: a sensation of oneness—with Marcotte and the others in the room. They believed in something. He loved them for believing in something. He too wanted to believe in something.

Marcotte appeared to be reaching a climax in his speech when Yeager moved away from Henry, worming his way through the crowd to approach a young woman near the door. She had not been there when they first entered the room, for Henry would certainly have noticed her. She stood out among these shopkeepers and clerks and their frumpy wives—a lovely girl, barely twenty, he guessed, a blossom among the sweaty stalks of Parisian petite bourgeoisie. Her wavy auburn hair shone in the smoky light, her face round and rosy, an image from Renoir. Henry, aroused by Marcotte and in love with the crowd and his tingling body, let his passion extend to the girl. Yeager leaned toward her to whisper in her ear. Henry watched. They whispered and smiled until one of Marcotte's arm-banded young men glared them into silence. Though Yeager shut up, he moved closer to the girl, his shoulder against hers. Henry hated Yeager for this intimacy, yet loved him too. Marcotte's fervor had mellowed him. He wanted to embrace them, Yeager, the girl, Marcotte, the others in the room. His head hurt, his throat burned from smoke and heat, but he hardly noticed. Marcotte stopped speaking. The audience screamed for more and he launched into another heated attack on the Communists. Henry edged toward Yeager and the girl. By the time Marcotte finished, he was beside them. People began to leave. MacNally joined Yeager and Henry.

"Hello, Eugénie," MacNally greeted the girl.

Henry waited to be introduced. When he wasn't, he took the introduction on himself.

"*Bon soir, Mademoiselle.*"

The girl glanced his way and Yeager seemed finally to notice him. "*C'est* Henry." He jerked his thumb in Henry's direction.

She acknowledged Henry with a slight smile and turned back to Yeager.

"Can we go now?" Yeager asked in French.

"Yes, *oui*," she answered. "Now."

Yeager winked at Henry. "You boys want to meet the guy?"

"Who?"

"Renard Marcotte, who else?"

"Sure," MacNally answered.

Henry wasn't sure. Marcotte's speech had disoriented him. He didn't want to talk with anyone about it, much less with Marcotte. Reality was an intrusion. Reality could scatter the exhilaration he'd felt into a thousand sterile bits. He wanted to hoard the experience. The real Renard Marcotte was something else again. He doubted he'd like him. But Yeager and MacNally didn't wait for his answer. They followed Eugénie through the dispersing listeners and out the back way.

"Glad we came," Yeager mumbled to whoever was near enough to hear him. "I think I can get a story out of this. Some show wasn't it? The guy's a real case."

These last words were mumbled to Henry, who didn't respond. He was too embarrassed. He didn't want Yeager to know how Marcotte had affected him. Yeager would laugh and rightly so. He should be laughing too.

Eugénie led them down a flight of stairs to a long hallway with doors along either side. A single electric bulb dangled from a cord midway down. From the corridor's far end, there came sudden trampling footsteps and loud voices. Young men in blue armbands swept into view. Henry looked for Marcotte among them but didn't see him. The young men disappeared through one of the doors, the same door to which Eugénie now led them. It was open and Henry could see into a suite of rooms. In the outer room, Marcotte's young men bantered and popped corks from bottles of wine and began to wolf down bread and pastries. Yeager stepped past Eugénie and in among them.

"Press, United States," he said in French. He flipped open his wallet to flash an AP card.

Marcotte was nowhere in sight.

One of the young men pointed at Yeager's wallet. "Dollars?"

"Press, newspapers," Yeager repeated, though with less confidence.

Another young man snatched Yeager's wallet from his hand. Yeager lurched for it, tripped and would have fallen had not one of them grabbed him, jerking him roughly upright. The young men laughed and taunted Yeager. Henry edged farther back into the hallway as the men passed around the wallet, each one making a show of examining it. Yeager, furious, leaped on a burly fellow with dark hair and grappled with him for the wallet. There were joyous shouts as the others joined the fray. Henry looked for MacNally. He was gone. Eugénie screamed for Yeager to go too, to get out of there and quickly. Henry felt the heat in him ignite. These men were bullies, hooligans, like the farm boys back home. He hated them. He stepped into the room, decked one with his fist and grabbed another off Yeager to pull his friend free. Two of the young men jumped him. He slung them away, flailed and slammed them with his fists. Blows hit him in the side, on the back of his head, but he kept hitting back until the room suddenly stilled. Whoever had hold of Henry released him. Renard Marcotte stood in the doorway. His deep voice rumbled in the silence. He spoke in French, to the effect that a man can't even take a crap without things getting out of control. His young men backed off Yeager and Henry. Yeager was on his knees. He got up slowly and rubbed a hand across his face. Blood dripped from his nose onto his coat collar. One of the men handed him his wallet.

"You want to see me?" Marcotte asked in English.

The question was ludicrous. Yeager's face contorted, like that of an injured child trying not to cry. He slipped the wallet into his back pocket and turned toward the door. Marcotte waited, a question in his face. When he spied Eugénie across the room, he brightened.

"Ah, lovely girl," he said with a laugh, his attention diverted from the two Americans. But only for a moment. He remained in the doorway, through which Yeager would certainly have fled had Marcotte not been standing there.

Henry felt he'd wandered into the midst of a bizarre play. The young men had returned to their wine and food. The two Americans waited awkwardly near the door, anxious to bolt, the door blocked by an animated Marcotte chatting happily with Eugénie. Yeager looked frightened. Henry was exultant. He had never spent a more stimulating evening. His fists throbbed where he had smacked several of the young men. His back and side and neck ached from their hard punches. But he didn't care. He realized he was smiling.

Marcotte and Eugénie talked a few moments before Marcotte nodded toward Yeager and Henry. They were to follow him. Yeager grumped at the invitation, but Marcotte insisted. "Please, *merci*," he cooed sweetly, his face sorrowful, like a repentant boy that his thugs had behaved so badly. "I make amends to you. My young fellows think to protect me. I have enemies, Messieurs."

Marcotte, his arm through Eugénie's, led them to a back office with a large desk and swivel chairs. A cot was set up in one corner. A table against the wall held a bowl of fruit and several bottles of wine. There was a small room off the side with a toilet and sink. Marcotte motioned for Yeager to use the bathroom to wash his face. Yeager slunk away and shut the door with a thud. Marcotte took a bottle of wine from the table and opened it. He waited for Yeager's return before he offered a brief toast to a new France, this time in French.

"Please. Forgive me that I have no fine crystal goblets to serve you with. We're poor men. Poor men who speak for poor men." He smiled and turned to Yeager. "You, Monsieur?"

"Bert Yeager. Associated Press, out of New York City. I'm an American journalist."

Yeager's French was awkward but he made himself understood.

"And you, Monsieur?"

Henry was startled by the question directed to him. Until that moment, he had thought of himself as an observer, a tourist in alien country. But Marcotte was waiting for an answer.

"Henry Beam. I'm a writer." He wondered why he'd put it that way, *writer*. He had never before referred to himself as a writer. He still thought of himself as a student, even if he had yet to attend any classes at the Sorbonne. Student was closer to the truth. Or poet. But in the charged masculine atmosphere among Marcotte's coterie, the word poet seemed effeminate. So he said writer, and saw he had given the right answer. Marcotte seemed pleased.

For the next half hour, Yeager asked Marcotte questions, grudgingly so, Henry thought. He'd pulled a small notebook from his jacket pocket in which to scribble Marcotte's responses, but Henry could see from over Yeager's shoulder that he wrote little of substance, the interview a charade, an attempt to mollify Marcotte so they could make their escape. But Marcotte was enjoying himself, his answers windy and prolix. In the flesh and close up, the man wasn't in the least impressive. Handsome, yes, with a broad face and muscular, athletic body, but also brusque, crude, and, Henry believed, ill educated. His clothes were rumpled, his shirt collar dirty, the blondish gray hair oily and matted against his head. What Henry had felt during the man's speech ebbed away. He grew conscious of the smells in the room, the odor of perspiration, mold from layers of grime on the walls of the cramped space. From the next room came the raucous chatter of Marcotte's bullies. Henry now agreed with Yeager: he was ready for Marcotte to shut up so they could leave. Only the girl Eugénie held his attention. She sat quietly in a chair near the wall while Marcotte talked, paging through a magazine. She was lovely with wide eyes and soft curls about her face and obviously as bored with this interview as Yeager and Henry. Perhaps afterwards, they could find a café somewhere and he could learn more about her.

Yeager brought the interview to a close with a ruse. "Got a deadline," he complained. "Got to get this stuff in."

Yeager never had deadlines. He worked for himself.

Marcotte nodded. Henry and Yeager started for the door. Eugénie remained behind.

"Monsieur Beam. One moment."

Surprised, Henry turned back. Marcotte held up a finger and waggled it, like a conspirator with a secret.

"Monsieur Beam, please." He bent over the table and wrote something on a scrap of paper and held it out to him. Henry hesitated before taking it. When he looked at it, he saw an address.

"I like you, Monsieur," Marcotte said. "You have *élan*, spirit."

Henry felt dumb. What had he said?

"Tomorrow, if you will come to this place, in the afternoon. I need a man of your talents and sensibilities. Tomorrow. You must promise me."

The whole scene seemed so absurd that Henry mumbled "yes" for fear if he said *no* he might be detained forever in the small office. Marcotte smiled. Henry swiveled to the door and hurried after Yeager, eager to be gone, to leave the entire bizarre evening behind.

"But I assume you didn't leave it behind," said Rachel. She propped her elbows on the table and held her face in her hands.

Henry was grateful she had stayed awake, had listened. He glanced at the clock. It was past two in the morning. He saw how tired the young woman was. "No I didn't leave it behind," he said, with a sigh. "It was as if that night I'd been reborn, become a man I had never been, who could fight and defend himself, whose heart could be stirred by fiery words and, yes, a woman's beauty." For a moment, he experienced an old and nearly forgotten despair. "Some might call it a come-to-Jesus moment. But there was no salvation in it, Rachel, no salvation at all."

TEN

René's mother was startled to find him standing at the door when she opened it to go out. He had not knocked but waited like a beggar for someone to come. She called his father at the warehouse. His response was unambiguous. He was furious. What had happened? Why had this gifted son again failed?

René remained with his parents a year, sometimes working with his father at the warehouse or running errands or shopping for his mother, although his parents could not hide their disappointment. What made it worse, his younger brother had surpassed René in the esteem of the *lycée* teachers. Michel Étienne was a sunny child, as bright and cheerful as René had been gloomy. His classmates and teachers doted on him, considered him a budding star in mathematics. M. Durand hinted to René's parents that Michel should attend a university. The small attic room that had been René's was now Michel's place of study, though he spent little time there, too gregarious a youth to be cooped up with books. René could not sleep in the room with his sisters, so he was allotted a small cot, which he set up each night in the parlor.

He accepted the arrangement without complaint, keeping his clothes in the worn leather suitcase brought back from the seminary and stowing it in the pantry. His only other possessions were books, which he stacked on a shelf in the cellar. In the dampness, their covers filmed with mold. After eight months, the stack had spilled onto the floor and been replicated into a dozen stacks, each more than a half meter high. In these months at home, the black angel was René's constant companion, but now he welcomed its brooding presence, like a familiar friend. For he had discovered a cure. When his despair grew too great, he escaped to his books, spending hours in the damp cellar reading. But this brought on frequent colds and a bout of flu that forced his parents to summon a doctor.

René's parents quarreled frequently—about not enough butter, his father's long hours at work, his sister Magdelena's flirtations with the butcher's son. René wasn't fooled. He knew these quarrels concerned him. The longer he remained at home, the more distracted his mother became, the angrier his father. One day his mother screamed at him, scolding him for the time spent reading in the cellar that made him sick and cost the family money for medicine. She locked the cellar door and hid the key.

René left Orleans. In a gesture of good will, his father wrote a letter to the foreman of a shipping company in Roanne. The man gave René a job and he stayed eight months before dissension among the other workers caused his dismissal. He moved to Besançon. There he worked as a clerk for a wine distributor, at the rail depot unloading cars, as a runner for a watchmaker. He was a competent worker, but he made people uncomfortable. Most said it was the eyes like polished slate, the cold tone of his voice. People did not trust him. The eight years after he left Orleans were stuporous, lost years. He slept, woke to go to work, ate and slept. If he felt the hovering wings of the *ange noir*, he buried himself in books. His landlords complained about the clutter of books in his room, the cheap editions he bought with the little he had left after paying his rent and providing enough food to keep him alive. He had long given up on biology, and after leaving the seminary, abandoned theology as well. But there were subjects he had never explored. He went on binges, like a drunkard, greedily imbibing the German philosophers, Nietzsche, Kant, Schopenhauer,

A Stone for Bread

Marx, Spengler. He ravaged literature, the French poets Baudelaire, Rimbaud, Verlaine, the English poets in translation. When he could not find books of literature or philosophy, he read what was available— shipping instructions and watchmakers' manuals. He found little pleasure in this reading. Books were medicine, swallowed in regular doses to keep him well. Once into a book, he disappeared where the black angel could not reach him.

He had few contacts with his family, although he wrote faithfully once a month and visited at Christmas. During these visits, he was warmly greeted and fretted over, but he sensed how relieved they were when time came for him to leave. He returned home for his younger sister's wedding, a rather drab affair. The groom, a pudgy middle-aged man, had a pronounced lisp. A good match, René's father confided to him. The groom's family owned a tract of valuable land near Amboise. René did not like the man and was sorry for his sister toward whom he had always felt affection. He returned to Besançon after the ceremonies. His mother wrote when Michel finished the *lycée*. He had not passed the *baccalauréat* and had gone to work at their father's warehouse.

René's most fortuitous opportunity came when he found employment at a small hotel in Besançon. The hotel's owner, Mme Gourou, a widow in her fifties, had inherited the place from her late husband, and for the childless woman, the hotel seemed husband, child and lover. It wasn't a large hotel, eight upstairs rooms over a café, Mme Gourou living in a cramped attic apartment. A large, robust woman, she possessed a cheery nature which proved an asset for her business. She was also a shrewd judge of people. She hired René without references, despite the fact that several weeks before he had lost his job with the watchmaker. Though she, like others, found his austere nature unsettling, she refused to be put off by it. Did he not tell her he had lost his job at the watchmaker's? Did he not do everything as precisely and carefully as he was told? And the young man was excellent at the most basic repairs and maintenance. René understood electric circuitry and plumbing: he had read manuals about these things. Whatever he might not know, he quickly learned. Even more important for Mme Gourou, he never complained. If she desired something done, it was done fast and competently. He installed two new bathrooms, unclogged toilets in the middle of the night, cleaned the chimneys and oven flues. And what was most exemplary about him, he was quiet. Mme Gourou's last employee had been much too garrulous, spending more time chattering with the guests than doing what she needed.

She gave René a small room off the café with instructions that no disagreeable sounds or odors must ever emanate from there. René's meals were provided in the café. He helped with the cooking and kept the oven and kitchen utensils spotless. That sometimes the guests found him unnerving did not seem to concern Mme Gourou. René was a marvel—and cheap. She paid him low wages, explaining that the room and food provided the difference. René was satisfied. Though a hard and stubborn businesswoman who demanded much from René, Mme Gourou was also kind to him. He never minded the long hours that saved her the necessity of hiring other staff. Before a year was out, René and Mme Gourou were running the hotel virtually alone, with only part-time help and, in the busy summer season, one or two extra employees.

In matters other than business, Mme Gourou was cheerfully gusty and irreverent. She refused to allow René's gloominess to shadow her hotel. When he grew silent, she prattled at him; when he moped, she teased. René warmed, only slightly perhaps, but yes, definitely, he warmed to her spirit. He looked forward to the late evenings when the guests were in bed, the café empty, when he and Mme Gourou rummaged in the kitchen for leftover bread and pâté or prepared an omelet. They would sit in the dark with only a single light or sometimes a candle—Mme Gourou ever conscious of the cost of electricity—talking softly, though usually it was Mme Gourou who talked. She chatted about the day and the peculiarities of their guests. On less chatty evenings, they smoked and listened to the radio, its music entering the room like a friendly acquaintance.

Only once did the relationship pass the bounds of propriety. On the day of the Armistice, when France capitulated to the armies of the Third Reich, Mme Gourou led René into an empty room on the second floor of the hotel. Surrounding him with her fleshy arms she took him into bed, undressing as she talked aimlessly about trifles, an elderly guest, the beef that needed ordering from the butcher. She gripped his hands and showed him where to caress her naked body, and when he had done everything she asked, she put her head against his chest. René found the smell of Mme Gourou disagreeable, but the heat of her skin surprised him. He wanted to press tightly against her to absorb this heat, allow it to burn him. An image of Georges flashed in his mind, swelling his penis. Mme Gourou did the rest. René was awkward and finished quickly, but she kissed him gently on the lips and released him, putting on her clothes and wiping a stream of tears from her cheeks. "You are a good boy," she said.

Mme Gourou did not speak of the incident afterwards. Nor was it ever repeated. In the weeks that followed, the hotel was transformed. The Germans now occupied Besançon. Mme Gourou—who had been quite outspoken in her feelings about *Les Boches* and their ridiculous Charlie-Chaplin Führer (she had described Hitler to René as a rooster strutting on a manure pile)—reconciled herself to the new state of affairs, capitalizing on France's adversity. She no longer denounced

Germans to René after the guests had gone to bed, but told him that they must be accepted, though she sighed when she said it. One day, René watched from the sidewalk along the Grand-Rue as a line of German troops marched by, followed by tanks and a convoy of trucks. A dim memory stirred in his mind. His cheek and left eye twitched. All week he grew increasingly apprehensive. He was not a reflective man, but for once he wondered if it wasn't wise to consider what might soon occur. He had not taken sides in the war. He was French, yes, but governments and politics meant little to him. He had read the German philosophers, knew the great strengths of the German people. But now, this entry of soldiers into Besançon ignited new and unrelieved fears. Surely, something of grave import was about to occur. He felt it in his body, the involuntary tics of muscle that caused him to rub his hands so hard together that his palms sometimes bled.

Mme Gourou's hotel remained open. Only the clientele changed. Now, it was mostly German, officers of the Occupation. Despite this, Mme Gourou remained warmly solicitous of her guests. If she harbored anti-German sentiments, they were kept to herself. She fawned over the majors and colonels of the Third Reich, pampered the civilians who came to Besançon to administer the occupied city. The hotel, more hospitable than many in Besançon, became a popular spot for these Germans. Buoyed by her success, Mme Gourou expanded the café into a restaurant and hired a full-time chef and two waiters. René fretted over these changes. Mme Gourou focused her attention on the new employees and was soon ignoring him. The new employees also ignored him, speaking to him only when necessary and avoiding friendly chatter. René's duties changed. He no longer worked side by side with Mme Gourou but was relegated to the hotel desk and running errands.

He continued to oversee the maintenance, kept the heat functioning in winter, the toilets unstopped, the electrical wiring repaired, but he was no longer Mme Gourou's confidante and companion. The evenings spent smoking and talking after the guests had gone to bed ended. Mme Gourou preferred the companionship of her new chef, a large, red-faced man named Jean who seemed more intent on huddled conversations with the proprietor than supervising the kitchen staff. René tortured himself with fantasies of Jean and Mme Gourou in an empty hotel room, Mme Gourou revealing her naked bosoms to Jean and showing him how to caress them, where else to touch on her body. He saw no signs of this, though it was quite clear that Jean had displaced René from his employer's affections. Now when the guests were in bed and the restaurant closed, it was the kitchen staff to whom Mme Gourou turned for conversation. René was fed before the supper hour and put to work in the evening cleaning and sometimes repainting empty rooms. He was not invited to the late night suppers. René experienced the despair he'd known years before in Orleans, when he came home from the seminary to find Michel in his old room in the attic. In this first year of the Occupation, the black angel returned, but his books no longer protected him.

Mme Gourou at least kept René busy. She sent him off on all kinds of small errands, many previously assigned to a schoolboy in the afternoons. René spent more of his time on the street than at the hotel, off to the butcher for meat, to the bakery for bread, to the *fromagerie* for the fine cheeses she served her guests. The black angel that hovered over René swooped nearer, and although he did not know what it wanted of him, he feared that Mme Gourou, like all the others in his life, would soon send him away. The black angel would not rest until she did.

One day on his way to the market, he watched a column of German soldiers march through the streets. A chill passed through his body. Their cadence, the stiff uniformed soldiers awakened in him a haunting dread. The next morning he did what he had not done in years. He slipped from the hotel and its incessant errands and attended Mass. The Latin words were a surprise, as if he had never before heard them. He had abandoned religion since the seminary. It wasn't that he had stopped professing it. It just made no difference to him. God did not choose to hear his prayers. The vision of Christ reaching down to him from the brass crucifix had long ago been attributed to a hallucination. Perhaps he had seen it, yes, or perhaps he had only imagined it, his sensibilities heightened by the dark angel. In the years since, René had read the works of many philosophers, but had not reflected on what he read. Some things, he believed, defied reflection.

There were only a few people in the church, straggled about St. Pierre's rectangular nave. René tuned out the droning priest and let himself be lulled by the Latin rhythms, the smell of incense, the chill of the stone walls. How tired he was. If only he might flee into the cold stone or be consumed in the flame of the altar candles. If only he might rest. These thoughts brought him no peace, no peace at all, merely heightened his dread. Dark wings hovered over him, carrion, their beaks aimed for his chest. He felt his heart shrivel, imagined blood spilling from it, spilling onto the stone floor and flowing about the pews. He did not partake of the Eucharist, but crossed himself and bowed to the altar, uttering a whimpered vow that came from a dark crevice of his mind, a vow that until he spoke it was unknown to him. I am willing to pay, he whispered toward the priest and the altar before ducking hurriedly from the church.

He did not attend Mass again. Whatever words he had whispered in the solitude of St. Pierre were quickly forgotten. Mme Gourou seemed to sense René's unhappiness and took an awakened interest in him. She added new duties to his work. With the success of her restaurant and hotel under the Occupation, she bought an automobile. René was amazed. It was almost impossible to buy automobiles in these war years. Everything was rationed. But Mme Gourou had ties with her German guests. The car was old, used, a clattery wreck of a Renault. But a car nonetheless. Mme Gourou made René learn to drive it, which only heightened his anxiety. He could not make the car stand still, but sent it bumping and spurting along the road. He seemed unable to coordinate his foot on the clutch with the one on the gas. Mme Gourou persisted, and when he was more confident, she set him to ferrying hotel guests from the train station or taking them about the city to sightsee or shop. Most of the guests were Germans, although a few French travelers and an occasional Swiss stayed at the hotel.

As the months passed, René forgot the war, forgot his fears about German soldiers, even as war gossip swirled about Besançon. At the hotel, the gossip decidedly favored the Führer. To hear the majors and colonels talk, the war would soon be over: Hitler was winning in every part of Europe. Occasionally, René heard a tidbit that countered this optimism, usually in the whispered conversations of the new employees or even from Mme Gourou herself, but he did not concern himself with gossip. War or peace, what difference did it make?

The Occupation was in its third year, when one day René was stopped by two policemen as he walked from the butcher's to the hotel. They demanded his papers and asked where he was going. One grabbed his shoulder. René shrieked. The policeman slammed him against the wall of a building. René dropped the packages of meat that had been under his arm. As he bent to retrieve them, a policeman kicked him, sent him sprawling on his back. He struggled to find his papers, but he lay on the pocket that held them. He stared up at the policemen. What had he done? The man roughly rolled him over, searched him to find the documents René could not reach. René struggled to his knees as the other policeman tore the paper off the chops and legs of lamb from the butcher. The man crowed and let out a loud laugh. René did not understand. He saw things spill from the packages of chops, pieces of paper and photographs. He could not imagine why they were there. He started to say this, when more policemen came. They jerked René to his feet and dragged him to a car. René tried to explain his confusion but no one listened. He was shoved onto the floor of the car, face down, a foot on his neck. He could hardly breathe. They drove him to the police station, made him sit on a stool before a corpulent man in a gray suit. The man was smoking. He blew smoke in René's face and smiled. Name. Age. How long have you worked at the hotel on rue des Granges? Who else works at the hotel? Who is staying at the hotel? René was cooperative. He was certain Mme Gourou would want him to be. She needed him at the hotel. She would not be pleased the police had taken away the meat for her restaurant.

He was surprised when later he discovered Mme Gourou also at the police station. He passed her in a corridor of cells. She sat on the floor of a large cell, among twenty or thirty others. Her face was bruised. The police must have pushed her down too. He tried to motion to her, but she seemed not to see him. He was placed in a cell with ten other men. A few were Jews. The others, like René, were not. They talked very little with each other. Several had been injured—beaten by the police. Only one was someone René knew, a local grocer from whom he had bought provisions for the hotel. The grocer ignored René, his attention fixed on a small Bible. The only time he spoke to him was the next morning when a guard led René from the cell. The grocer tapped his foot against René's. René looked down. "Betray her and I'll kill you myself," the man said through clenched teeth.

René did not understand what this meant, but the interrogator explained. He showed René papers and photographs found among the lamb chops. He showed him documents taken from Mme Gourou and the chef, Jean. Spies and resisters, the man said, filthy scum. All of you. You think we are stupid. René was astonished, though the interrogator did not believe he was astonished. He slapped René's face, twisted the little finger of his right hand until the bone snapped. René screamed. What did he know of Mme Gourou's treasonous activities? He knew nothing. A hand slammed his ear. The ringing drowned out the interrogator's voice. Nothing. I know nothing. René was returned to the cell, warned he would be called again. Think it over, they told him. He huddled in the corner, shivering. Pain burned through his body. The grocer was not there when he was returned to the cell. But there was no comfort in this. The interrogators would hurt him again. He did not know the correct answers.

He was kept in the cell six weeks. Many others shared his misery, some for a short time, others for weeks. Many taken away by guards never returned. Two died in the cell. René shared his evening meal— liquid from a bowl of watery soup—with one of them before he died. He held another man's head in his lap. The man cried and clawed the floor. René grew used to the sound of men sobbing. He learned to endure the cramped cell, the stench of urine and feces and vomit, the discomfort of relieving himself in such an exposed situation. He lost weight on the paltry rations. His eyes bugged from his head. They no longer chilled so much as startled, like glittering lights. His hair began to fall out in hunks. His broken finger twisted oddly. He was surprised he was not questioned again. Perhaps Mme Gourou told them the truth about him. But he was not released.

Some who shared the cell in later weeks were more talkative. They spoke about summary executions, the camps in Germany and Poland where resisters were taken to be slaves for the Germans. René tried not to listen. He preferred quiet prisoners. As weeks went by and he was ignored, his terror eased. He became a spectator to his fears, like the spiders that climbed the walls of the cell, looking down. René looked down and saw a calm take hold of him. Perhaps the dark angel had refused to enter such a wretched place. He found himself thinking about his family, his sister's marriage, his two nieces and the new nephew about whom his mother had written him. Was his father still the strongest man at the warehouse, able to lift heavy cartons without strain? Had his mother ceased worrying about him? He dreamed about his old village, the frail bent body of his grandfather. Once he even dreamed of his nearly forgotten brother. Étienne was standing in the garden behind the house, his arms held out to René as if to embrace him.

In this time of calm, René comforted new prisoners. He spoke gentle words to a boy of sixteen to help prepare him for what was certain to be a sentence of death. He shared his food and didn't worry he might grow weaker. He began to pray. Not formal prayers, but babbled half sentences, not to ask anything of God but only to explain.

One day, René was taken from the cell and marched with others outside to a truck. The sun burned his eyes. He could barely walk. They were driven to a railroad siding miles from Besançon. More trucks arrived at the same site. Hundreds of prisoners, René among them, were herded up ramps into wooden boxcars. His car was so tightly packed, he was shoved to the back and forced to squat. As others crushed in against him, he believed he would suffocate, until he discovered a knothole close to his head. Through it he could see the gray countryside. It was winter, the railroad siding surrounded by woods and large sheds like warehouses. Cold air came through the knothole. René breathed in the air and was grateful. As the car groaned forward, accompanied by cries and moans of the people crowded in like hogs, he felt his body warm with relief. At last. He had waited a long time.

ELEVEN
Eleven

Henry had offered her a bed in an unused room upstairs but she'd refused. "I have to go to Charlotte tomorrow. I promised my mother I'd be there for New Year's." This was more explanation than she needed to give, as if she were seeking excuses. But she didn't want to stay, her mind an eddy of questions and doubt. She sensed he knew this, for he responded with his own excuses, warnings rather—the lateness of the hour, the lonely roads to the Interstate, the dangers of driving when sleepy. He sounded like her mother.

She laughed. "I'm a big girl, Henry. If you'll heat me some water for coffee and let me borrow a mug, I'll be on my way."

She slept late the next morning, toasted an English muffin for breakfast, packed and drove to Charlotte. She stayed until the start of classes the second week of January, her physical self with her mother, her thoughts tugged back to Henry and what he had told her. He'd startled her with the comment about murder and his complicity. He had always seemed so benign, a sad and somewhat lonely man. So she had shrugged off his confession as a writer's hyperbole. "A terrific lead," Netta Holmes, her undergrad freshman comp instructor, might have said. But the more he talked, the more she'd begun to wonder about him. What burden of guilt had Henry carried into his decades-long exile? She thought of his sudden outbursts of anger when the *Stone for Bread* poems were mentioned, how furious he'd been with Scott when he asked about René. Yet he had recited several of these same poems to his party guests. As she pondered the hours she'd spent with Henry, another thought came to her, this one more unsettling. What if he'd just invented the stories about Paris, the same way many thought he had invented the mysterious René as back story for poems he had written himself? How did one ever truly know another human being? Ted Bundy had also seemed benign.

While she was home, she stopped by the Charlotte Main library and searched the card catalog for Renard Marcotte. She didn't find him. She checked indexes of a half dozen histories of post-WWII France. Again nothing. On a whim, she had the reference librarian help her find a list of current journalists and ran down the names of anyone named Yeager for whom Bert might be a nickname. She found two dozen or so Yeagers with first names Albert, Bertram, Elbert, Gilbert, Hubert, Herbert and Robert, and one Bert. She dutifully listed all of them and their employers in a small notebook, purchased that morning for this purpose. The sole Bert Yeager was identified as a reporter with the *Des Moines Register*, a newspaper the library didn't carry. She would try to find it at Chapel Hill. She scanned back copies of the *Philadelphia Inquirer* and *Los Angeles Times* for the reporters named Yeager she'd copied to her list but came up with nothing.

On her way to her mother's house, she stopped by the offices of Southern Bell. They directed her to a telephone book for Des Moines, Iowa. She jotted down the number and address of the one Bert Yeager and wondered why she bothered. This was needle in a haystack stuff. She didn't have time to waste on it. She had planned to use the holidays to narrow several ideas into a proposal for her Master's thesis but had hardly given it a thought. Until now. It was Scott who'd first planted the idea in her mind. But would they let her write about Henry Beam? She would have to ask Henry, of course. Make it his decision. How could it not be? If he disapproved, he'd tell her nothing. And she would never know the rest of his story. Probably the English Department wouldn't let her do it anyway. Henry wasn't important enough. But what about the concentration camp poems?

After her first classes in the new semester, she poked her head into Dr. Terry Schwartz's office. Schwartz's specialty was Southern poetry. It was even possible he might direct her thesis if they allowed her to write about Henry. She wouldn't ask that now; instead, she told him about the documentary and asked him if he'd heard of *A Stone for Bread*. Dr. Schwartz rotated in his chair, stretched out his long legs and adjusted his rimless glasses. "You're asking about Henry Beam?"

She nodded.

"I haven't heard that name in a long time." Schwartz smiled as if bemused. "There was quite a stir about him some thirty or so years ago, Rachel. Before my time, however. But I guess you already know about that."

She nodded. "Have you read *A Stone for Bread*?"

"Actually I have. When I was a grad student. I just kind of stumbled on it looking up North Carolina poets."

"He lives near Durham," she said.

"I'm assuming then you've already met him and will possibly meet him again."

"Yes."

He touched his fingers together in an arch against his chin. "Then you might ask him the sixty-four-thousand-dollar question. Did he or didn't he write those poems?"

She heard Henry's voice in her head and repeated the answer he'd given her, "Does it matter?"

"Not really. It would just be an interesting footnote to the controversy. Lay it to rest, so to speak."

"But you don't think they're good poems?"

"It's been a few years now since I read them. I looked up Henry Beam one other time after that and discovered that the poems were a bestseller, exceedingly rare for serious poetry. But then controversy generates interest. But I'd probably say the poems' artistic value lies in the truth of them, that they exist as witness. Once that gets debunked and they're read only as works of a poet's imagination, it's hard to know what to make of them. Like a violin that turns out not to be a Strad, despite its fine workmanship." He squinted over his glasses at her, as if trying to come up with a more precise explanation. "I think I really liked them when I read them. But probably if I went back to them I'd find them passé. You know, some things affect you at one time in your life, like your first love, and then you look back and think, God, how could I have been so taken with her."

She nodded, then thanked him and turned to leave.

"You might talk to Jim Green," he called after her. "He may have known the man, may even keep up with him for all I know. Good luck with the documentary."

She stopped by Professor Green's office later that afternoon. The older man, gray haired and bearded, echoed Schwartz. "I audited one of his seminars years ago at Duke. He was dull as hell but good on Baudelaire's Theory of Correspondences."

He knew Beam had returned several years ago to North Carolina and launched into the tale Scott had already told her about Henry's brandishing a shotgun at several students who'd gone out to interview him. "He scared the hell out of them." Green rubbed his fingers through his beard and smiled. "Unless, of course, the students made up the story to excuse themselves from completing the assignment."

Davis Library was her next stop. She checked out a book of critical essays on Adrienne Rich. A real poet, and acclaimed as such, someone to consider for her first paper for the seminar on women poets. She didn't have time to look up newspapers for Bert Yeager. But that evening, when she tried reading through the essays, her mind wandered to Henry. Frustrated, she shut the book and stared mindlessly at a Georgia O'Keeffe poster she'd bought on Franklin Street when she moved into her apartment. "Winter Cottonwoods," O'Keeffe had titled it, the bare twisty limbs against an orange sky, wisps of gray fog caught among the branches. She felt suddenly sad, felt the loneliness of her own life. Her five-year marriage had been unhappy, almost from the beginning. For a moment she believed she understood Henry, his sense of failure, or whatever haunted him, his own loneliness. Her search at the Charlotte library shamed her, that she'd been spying on him as if to prove the duplicity of his stories and poems. She went to her satchel and removed the notebook with its list of Yeagers. She was going to toss it down the garbage chute in the hall but instead stuffed it at the bottom of a drawer under tees and sweatshirts she wore on her morning runs.

The next evening, she called Henry. It took several tries before she reached him. He didn't own an answering machine. When he finally answered, he sounded contrite, apologetic, as if somehow he had disappointed her. She was about to invite him to her apartment for dinner when he preempted this with an invitation of his own. "Saturday evening? A light supper, maybe around six. I promise I won't keep you up late."

"Yes," she said. "I'll bring a salad and wine."

TWELVE

e had wanted to call her a week ago but didn't. He must tread cautiously with Rachel. Certainly, he was attracted to her, the tilt of her head so like Eugénie's, chin slightly angled left, the way light burnished her auburn hair, the *okay, prove it* smile. He doubted she realized the effect she had on him. To a woman Rachel's age, he was like a grandfather. If she did notice, the attraction was certainly not reciprocated, and would never be. Friendship, yes, but otherwise, he imagined a *don't touch* sign dangling from her neck. And he wouldn't touch her, not as a lover. That notion was as ridiculous and inappropriate as Rachel would consider it. He wasn't a sexless old man, far from it, and had not led a sexless life, not since Paris. He'd been married, twice, with several long relationships along the way. Most had foundered on a woman's need for an intimacy deeper than sex, an intimacy of soul, which he had not been able to offer. Other times, it was a desire for marriage and the supposed financial security that would follow.

This last they were wrong about. He wasn't a wealthy man, as the success of *A Stone for Bread* would have him. Early on, he had donated most of the royalties earned to The Simon Wiesenthal Center, which tracked down former Nazis. Soon after the poetry's publication, he'd moved north, in search of anonymity and solace of mind, finding it eventually in Cincinnati. No one knew him there. If they'd heard of the controversy, they never linked him to it. He had spent twenty-nine years with an insurance agency, starting as a temp in the records section. Though he lacked ambition for the work, in time he'd risen to become an Assistant Vice President. This did not make him all that much money, but eight years ago, having accumulated sufficient savings, he retired, left Cincinnati and bought the old house near Durham. Like coming home. And maybe so, for only then had he begun to write again.

Now as he chopped onions and celery for rice pilaf that late Saturday afternoon, he fretted about what he had told Rachel about Paris. He had stopped his story at the wrong place, with the Marcotte rally and his youthful exuberance afterwards. That wasn't what he wanted to convey. His enthusiasm for Renard Marcotte barely lasted the evening. He wanted Rachel to know that, know that he wasn't a naïve country hick when he arrived in Paris. The truth was, that by the time Henry reached his hotel, any lingering fascination with Marcotte had vanished. He understood Yeager's scorn of the man as a buffoon of the petite bourgeoisie. If somewhat attractive in his clumsy way, he was bombastic and stagey. The time spent with him following the rally had cheapened him in Henry's eyes, reduced him to life-size. But the girl—before that night, he'd had no experience with women. In the rowdy male culture of rural Cleveland County, he was a freak of nature, that rarest of young men during his adolescent and college years—a virgin. Before he reached Paris, he had loved only one woman, Anna Fincastle, his fourth grade teacher. The day she caught him slipping a book from the school library into his gunny was the most fortuitous day of his young life. Miss Fincastle reprimanded him and made him stay after school. Books weren't allowed to be removed from the library.

"You know the rules, Orville Henry," she scolded him.

"Yes ma'am."

"So what were you doing with that book?"

When he answered he'd wanted only to read it, and to her amazement listed the other books he had already taken from the library and smuggled back the next morning, a conspiracy was born. All Henry had to do was mention an interest in a particular subject or suggest a book, and by that afternoon, the book would be in a tin breadbox on Anna Fincastle's back porch. The young teacher lived with her parents a half mile from the school and Henry passed the house every day. If he had time enough in the late afternoon, he would sneak from his chores to the Fincastle back porch, take the book from the box and read sprawled on the rough slats of the porch until dark. Miss Fincastle never acknowledged his presence or came to the door, but sometimes he detected a sound or movement at the window. Winter afternoons, he shivered while he read, but the thought that just maybe she watched him through the curtained window warmed him enough to keep him reading. She was his first love, his only real love before Paris, an ideal, yes, he knew that, Aphrodite, Helen of Troy, Beatrice.

Miss Fincastle was the daughter of a white-bread family. Her father owned a hardware store in Shelby. She had gone to Queen's College in Charlotte, returning to Cleveland County to civilize and redeem the county's ruffian children. That she got very far with most of them was debatable. But she had redeemed him.

"You are my light," she'd told him, when she came to his graduation from Duke.

And he had tried always to be a light for her, to achieve everything she desired for him. When his book was published, he sent her a copy, the dedication penned on the title page, "For Miss Anna," and signed just below it, "Your light, Henry." A note came back from Miss Fincastle's niece that the teacher had died of cancer a few weeks before. One year later in Paris, the night he met Eugénie, Henry had stood at the window of his hotel room, his face wet with tears, and understood the truth of 23-year-old Henry Beam. He was no one's light.

By the time he had the pilaf made and the table set, Rachel was at his door, plastic bowl in one hand, bottle of wine in the other. He was suddenly shy. How to greet her? What to say? And why had he involved this young woman in his past? He hardly knew her.

"I brought a tossed salad," she said, quickly, as if she sensed his uneasiness.

"Good, yes, excellent, I have a rice dish."

"The wine, well, I'm not a connoisseur," she apologized. "You don't have to drink it to be polite."

"Wine is about the company it's shared with," he said, then added, "But perhaps in this case since I'm the company, it won't help."

"Of course it helps, Henry," she said, sweetly, which ended the stalemate of nerves.

Over dinner, they chatted easily with each other, except each seemed to need to apologize: he'd cooked the rice too long, her salad greens had wilted on the drive over. "I don't have a cooler," she lamented. "But then my former husband used to say what I really didn't have was a talent for the kitchen. I guess he was right."

"You were married?" A stupid question, since she'd just said so.

"Un-huh, for five years. What about you?"

"Twice. What I didn't have was a talent for marriage." He offered her an uneasy smile, as if needing to apologize for that as well.

"Do you have children?" she asked.

"A son. He grew up without me. You?"

"Fortunately no. I doubt I have much talent for motherhood either."

She laughed and a relaxed geniality ensued as they recounted tales of their former spouses.

"Randy was a control freak. Maybe all men are, you know, possessive." She smiled ruefully. "The man of my dreams, damnably handsome, smart, a most likely to succeed kind of guy. Until we were married. Who knew that under all that charm and good stuff lurked Svengali. He had serious anger issues. I guess I was naïve. I'm amazed we made it five years."

"Is Singer your husband's name?"

She gave him a curious look. "I took back my maiden name after the divorce. Why?"

"Rachel Singer sounds Jewish. I was just wondering."

"My family's been Presbyterian probably since John Calvin."

There was awkward silence. She was the first to speak. "Well, are you going to tell me what happened next? In Paris?"

He nodded. "If you're interested."

"Of course, I'm interested."

He began where he'd left off, the night of the rally. "Marcotte had intrigued me at first, but the events after the rally disabused me of any admiration for the man. Still, when I thought about him, I felt I knew him—a provincial man, maybe even peasant stock, yet a man who'd risen to want more from life. Like me. Of course, I was from another culture, but I asked myself that night if he and I were really so different."

By the next morning, however, he'd put Marcotte out of mind, until he remembered the scrap of paper in his coat pocket, the address Marcotte had given him. Come to see me here, he'd said. How ludicrous, the American student agog in Paris venturing into the lair of a French demagogue: *Come into my parlor said the spider* … He dug the address from the pocket and tossed it in the wastebasket. Despite last night's euphoria from the rally and brawl afterwards, in daylight, he was quite clear-headed. He wanted no part of Renard Marcotte. But Eugénie—the girl glowed in his mind through the morning. Over coffee with MacNally, he inquired about her.

"Careful," MacNally tweaked him. "Everybody wants a romp with Eugénie. A pretty thing, but she's no easy lay."

The coarse remark offended him. He wanted Eugénie pure. He dropped the subject. MacNally asked about the fight with Marcotte's men.

"Thanks a lot for running out on us," was Henry's response.

"Bare knuckle stuff's not my style. Give me a gun and I'm your man. Besides I don't plan to get my nose busted so Yeager can get a goddamn story. Serves him right." The broad-faced American laughed heartily.

Henry told him about the conversation with Marcotte, his interest when Henry had said he was a writer.

"Writer, huh? Good response, boy," the *boy* meant as banter. Mac-Nally was probably all of twenty-six years old. "You know, you *ought* to write about the guy. I mean he's interesting. I give him that. The elitist s-o-b's of the world could use a little shaking up every now and then."

The exchange cheered Henry. He reconstructed the events of the night before as a grand adventure: the rally, the brawl afterward, the girl and the flamboyant rightwing politician. Maybe he *should* write about Marcotte. He could do that. Not poetry, but a book, a journalist's account, better yet, a novel. He had not written a single line of poetry since his arrival in Paris, having convinced himself he was due a break. Well, he'd had his break. He returned to his room and retrieved the address from the trash and an hour later showed up at a gray building off Sébastopol on the right bank. The directions indicated the place was on the fourth floor. He took the elevator and ended in front of a door, glassed from halfway up with a smoked semi-transparent pane. There was no sign, no identification, only a number painted in black on the glass. Henry knocked. No one answered. From inside came the clank of machinery. He turned the knob and opened the door into a small outer office.

Marcotte wasn't there. No one else was either. Though Marcotte had said nothing about meeting him here, only that he come, Henry experienced a vague disappointment. The room was furnished with a well-used wooden chair and desk, the desk stacked with flyers and posters. The walls, cracked and peeling paint, were decorated with M.L.F. posters—Marcotte's face in close-up, mouth open in a Marcotte harangue, Marcotte with a defiantly raised fist, Marcotte's Gallic profile superimposed on France's tricolor flag, the M.L.F. slogan in French, which in English meant "Break the Elitist Chains," in black letters across the top. Henry saw a door off the office and that it was open. Through it, he peered into a large room. A thin, gray-haired man was bent over a table, collating pages and stapling them. A small printing press burped out the ubiquitous posters. Henry rapped on the door-frame, hard enough to be heard above the press. The man looked up. He was the only person in the room.

"What do you want?" he shouted in French.

Henry responded in French. "I was sent here. Marcotte sent me."

The man scowled. His face was gaunt and chinless. A brush of moustache covered his upper lip. "Marcotte?"

"Yes. He told me to come here."

It was a silly, shouted exchange. Henry felt like an idiot. He told the man his name and handed him the address.

"Henry Beam?" The question didn't seem to be about his name, but why he was even here, why Marcotte would send him such a worthless fellow.

"*Anglais?*"

"American."

The man's scowl deepened. He turned away as if to dismiss him. Henry felt a sense of relief. He was eager to leave. Coming had been a mistake. But the man wasn't dismissing him. He had only turned to point toward a corner of the room, offering Henry a single word of direction in English, "There."

Henry looked to see what *there* was. This was a print shop, a rather rudimentary one at that, with two mimeograph machines and a small offset press printing the M.L.F. posters. On the floor and on long tables were rolls and stacks of paper. Cardboard boxes rose halfway up one wall. The room smelled of ink and a piquant odor like rubbing alcohol.

"There," the man repeated, as the press stopped. Henry, grateful for the silence, moved in the direction he indicated, stopping before a small table. Sitting on it was a yellow plastic radio. On the floor beside the table were stacks of newspapers and magazines: English-language periodicals, mostly British newspapers, *The Times*, *The Daily Mirror*, with one stack of *Herald Tribunes*.

"I'm authorized to pay you," the man said in French, his tone matter-of-fact as if this wasn't in the least unusual.

"To do what?" asked Henry in French.

"Cull through the newspapers for articles about the Mollet government. Articles critical of Mollet or favorable to Marcotte, corruption, favoritism, anything useful. Clip and make a brief translation for us to understand what the article says. Simple, hey?"

Henry nodded. The image of Henry Beam, novelist, evaporated in the banality of the cluttered room. Had the man not offered money, he would have walked away. It was a small sum, francs equal to a few dollars for three mornings a week. But he needed money. The food and wine in cafés were draining his meager budget. So he agreed to the job, his fantasies surrendered to practicality.

The man who hired him was Dreux. Bony and slightly stooped, he was a sour man who complained about everything: the quality of paper stock and ink, the clutter in the room (although it was *his* clutter), the bad manners of Marcotte's young men who made unannounced forays to cart in supplies or haul off bundles of leaflets and posters. The only thing he didn't complain about was Henry. Dreux seemed to quickly recognize the trait of diligence that had served Henry well through his school years. After the first week, he added to Henry's hours, had him also monitor BBC radio broadcasts. If Henry had sought adventure in this place, he was quickly dissuaded from any such hope. Dreux tinkered with his press and mimeograph machines; Henry read newspapers and listened to the radio.

He reported in around nine o'clock, three mornings a week, although he was free to set his own hours, so long as he put in at least four hours each day (Dreux paid him a flat daily sum). Sometimes Henry chose to stay late and into the afternoon. The small table faced a window that overlooked an alley and apartments across it. When he grew bored with newspapers, he entertained himself with the vignettes of daily life from the building's balconies and windows—the elderly woman in her apartment who would lift a canary cage from its stand, kiss the wood slats, the bird presumably inside, as she waltzed about with the cage. On one balcony, a young man sometimes stepped into the cold air to smoke, often clutching his head in his hands as if to shut out some turbulence in the apartment behind him. Sometimes a little boy appeared on the same balcony. Spotting Henry at his desk across the way, he would chuck cookies at the window, or when he missed, which was most of the time, stick out his tongue and make grotesque faces. Henry usually laughed.

The print room was cold. He learned to wear his heavy coat and sat bundled at the table with his hands in the pockets. He did whatever Dreux asked, which was easy enough, this sifting through back issues of the *London Times* and other British papers for articles about France and the Mollet government, monitoring BBC news. He dutifully translated anything of interest onto sheets of cheap newsprint, noted the date and newspaper or broadcast. He found occasional mentions of Marcotte, although it was soon obvious the English press had no interest in the man. One columnist called him a rabble-rouser who was "more rabble than rouser." Most articles dismissed him as a fluke, expecting him to sink quickly into political oblivion. He didn't translate these articles for Dreux. And when Dreux wasn't hanging over his shoulder or was off on other errands, Henry forgot politics and read through the *Times'* art and literature sections or scanned the papers for news of home. Except for Dreux and the unpleasant room with its acrid smells and cold draft, the constantly clanking press and mimeograph machines, the job was a painless means to a few extra francs.

When he wasn't at the print shop, he stayed in his room or wandered the city alone. He saw less of Yeager's friends. Sometimes he worried he had slipped into his monkish habits and might again become a recluse. There was little conversation between him and Dreux. The others who came and went from the print room were couriers with messages for Dreux or supplies and Marcotte's muscular young men, minus the blue M.L.F. brassards. Mostly they ignored him. Henry never saw Marcotte. Or anyone from the night of the rally. He never saw the one person he most wanted to see.

He had not forgotten Eugénie. He'd made discreet inquiries among Yeager's friends, but not with Yeager. He recalled their air of intimacy at the rally, Yeager and Eugénie whispering shoulder to shoulder.

He feared Yeager would tell him things he didn't want to hear about the girl. He didn't want to know why Yeager and his friends all knew Eugénie. MacNally said she worked in a *pâtisserie*, somewhere not far away, maybe in Montparnasse. On the days when he wasn't at the print shop with Dreux, Henry canvassed Montparnasse, ducking into every *pâtisserie* he passed. When he didn't find her, he tried the *boulangeries*, then the *charcuteries*. Frustrated and miserable, he resolved finally to face the situation head on and speak to Yeager. But fate, or possibly providence intervened. Years later, Henry decided the encounter smacked more of whimsical chance.

Their paths crossed one frigid afternoon on Rue St. Michel as he was returning from Montparnasse. It was late afternoon, the light fading. She was accompanied by a short, slender young man with black hair and eyes, a gypsy of a youth, neatly dressed in dark trousers and a heavy jacket. Eugénie was bundled in a long overcoat, a green felt hat perched on her head. He might not have recognized her except that as they passed, she looked his way, startling him by the sudden familiarity of her face and eyes, although he saw no trace of recognition in them. In fact, he realized, she hadn't actually looked at him so much as away from the young man, with whom she was quarreling. Henry's heart stirred. He waited a moment then followed after them. They were headed toward Pont St. Michel, the bridge that crossed the Seine to the Île de la Cité. Henry remained a discreet distance behind. Eugénie and her companion's quarrel grew heated. By the time they reached the bridge center, the young man was shouting. Eugénie abruptly stopped and turned toward the stone balustrade. Henry gaped. Was she going to jump? He hurried toward them. The youth grabbed her shoulders, but she jerked away. When she did, the felt hat came loose from her head and was swept by a gust of wind beyond the balustrade. She shrieked and turned to retrieve it, but it was gone, spiraling downward to the Seine.

Henry saw the hat drift like a feather on the wind that lifted and floated it softly toward the water. He raced to the end of the bridge and the stone steps to the river, until at the bottom he jerked off his coat and dropped it behind him. From the quay, he spied the hat bobbing on the water, moving slowly away. Off came his shoes and socks. He stuffed watch, wallet and keys in a shoe and dove from the quay. The icy water hit him like an electric shock. He came up sputtering water that tasted of gasoline. He tread water until he spotted the hat some eight or ten yards away, then swam with strong strokes toward it. When he had it clutched in his left hand and held above the water, he awkwardly propelled himself to the bank with two legs and one arm. From the bridge, the girl called encouragement. Two boys fishing from the quay jeered and called him an ass.

He realized he had not the slightest idea how to get back onto the quay. His teeth clacked in his head. He began to worry about hypothermia and that he might actually drown. But the few spectators who had gathered to watch were now shouting at him. One gestured toward a wall cut, where steps led up to the quay. Smiling and snapping his picture, an Englishwoman helped him from the water. Eugénie and her young man waited on the bridge. The girl laughed and waved. Henry, quaking with cold, waved back. Relieved to see his watch and wallet still there, he grabbed up his coat and shoes and ran the steps to the bridge.

"Mademoiselle," he stuttered, presenting her the hat.

"*Oui, très belle,*" she cried, with not the slightest sign she had seen him before.

Her companion stood back, his lips in a pout.

"*Le chapeau, c'est très belle,*" said Henry stupidly, repeating her French and trying not to sound like a tourist.

"She means you, imbecile," the young man said in accented English. "A pretty deed."

Henry flushed. The girl seemed not to notice. She rattled on in French about his valor and kindness, how distressed she was to see him so wet. *C'est dommage.* "Come. To dry off. At my shop."

"*Merci, non,*" he said, feeling foolish now. "I live close by."

He slipped on his jacket and turned away from her. His face burned. He'd been an idiot. He started across the bridge. The girl followed, caught up and laid her hand on his arm and walked beside him. Her scowling companion trailed behind like a rejected puppy. He spoke sharply to the girl in French, which Henry understood perfectly: how anyone that leaps into the Seine after a cheap hat is a lunatic. The girl retorted hotly and called him a bastard.

"Mademoiselle," said Henry in French through chattering teeth, "we have met before." As he said it, he looked at the girl to be certain. He had seen her only the one night. But yes, he was positive this was Eugénie.

She squinted up at him, confused. She had totally forgotten him.

"With my friend Bert Yeager. At the M.L.F. rally."

Her eyes widened. "*Ah, oui,* I remember. You were crazy then too. Crazy American."

He laughed and wondered what his college classmates would think of her description. They walked to the end of the bridge, where she informed him she must leave with the young man who'd remained a few paces behind. Henry was still dripping water. He shivered in the cold air.

"I would like to see you again, Mademoiselle."

She smiled, but it wasn't an acceptance, only an uncertain toss of her head, as if to question why he was worth her time. She did not look toward her companion.

"I would give you a thousand roses," Henry blurted, without thinking. Idiotic gibberish. Certainly, the foolish pledge would do nothing to dissuade the girl from the ridiculous image she must already have of him, the crazy American, face flushed, wet hair matted wildly, as he stood there trembling with cold, river water puddling at his feet.

Eugénie seemed perplexed. "Perhaps."

"When?"

She shrugged. "Some day. I work there." She pointed to Rue Huchette.

"I'll find you." Henry grinned and waved his hand in that direction before he hurried away. Behind, he heard her laughing and the sound warmed him. He amused her. If that's what it took to get her attention, so be it.

Rachel was also laughing. "You actually leaped into the Seine, Henry? My image of you just underwent a radical transformation. Yet somehow that seems so French, although I've never been to France. Maybe that's just from movies. *C'est la vie.*"

"I was young, Rachel."

She picked up her plate. "I want to hear the rest of the Eugénie story. You can tell me while we wash the dishes."

"There's more to it than just Eugénie."

"Whatever," she said, heading into the kitchen.

That same evening, he met Yeager outside the shower stall. Though he knew better, he couldn't stop himself from mentioning the encounter.

"Eugénie? You saw her today?"

"On the Pont St. Michel. She didn't remember me from the other night."

"Figures. You had your clothes on."

"What?"

"Kidding you, Beam. Just kidding."

"Tell me about her."

"About her what? Pretty girl. Sort of, in a French kind of way. I like mine a little thinner myself. Shop girl. Which is what most of them are. The pretty ones. Except for an aristocrat or two, who won't, believe me, WON'T give you the time of day. Their papas would shoot them. Oh, don't shake your head, Beam, happens all the time. Pretty girl gets her throat slit. Usually her lover, though sometimes it's her own father." He shrugged. So what's the rag? With Eugénie? Wanna lay her?"

"N-n-no. I mean I just ran into her today. Spoke to her. There was someone with her. A guy."

"Always a guy with them. That's how it is, Beam, you got to stand in line."

"You know her well?"

"Sure." Yeager let a grin slide across his face.

Henry hated him.

"Want an introduction?"

"We've been introduced."

"I mean a real introduction. Like an arrangement or something."

"No."

Henry lied. Of course, he wanted a real introduction. But Yeager was dangling the girl like a worm on a fishing line. And he didn't believe him. He was bragging. So he changed the subject, asked Yeager what he was working on for the AP and ignored his response.

What kind of man was he, Henry later wondered, this crazy fellow who leaped into the Seine after a girl's hat? A man who'd never slept with a woman. Did Yeager suspect that? Among Yeager's friends in the libertine air of Paris, one was supposed to have sampled all the vices. They were so available. Women were easy. So was hashish and heroin. If it was a prostitute Henry wanted, that was simply negotiated. But Henry Beam, Duke poet, backwoods valedictorian, was as innocent as grass among these worldly Americans. He didn't want a good lay. He wanted romance. Despite what Yeager said, he saw Eugénie as a goddess of romance—her rosy face, bright eyes, rounded figure. Eugénie was beauty and truth and sweetness. Henry was old-fashioned. He wanted love.

He found her shop easily and began his campaign. If he wasn't handsome like other young men or gifted with wit and charm, he possessed tenacity and soon discovered he could delight this girl by surprising her. He learned what time Eugénie arrived at work each morning and got up early, stopped by a florist at Maubert to buy a single rose then hurried to the *pâtisserie* to be there before she arrived. He left the rose on the counter for her with a number on it to remind her of his promise. The shopkeeper, Mme Péguy, a fat, gray woman, seemed pleased by Henry's little game and became a willing conspirator. "Tsk, tsk, so much money for love," she would giggle when he came in. She allowed him to place the flower in a different place each morning but always where Eugénie would see it. After two weeks of this, he showed up one afternoon with a bouquet of roses as she was leaving the shop. She smiled and took them and let him walk her to the Metro where she caught her train. She lived, she told him, near the Gare d'Austerlitz.

"May I come tomorrow?" Henry asked, as they waited for the train.

"Who knows tomorrow?" She laughed and gave him a quick kiss on the cheek, then stepped aboard her car. Henry was euphoric. His face burned where her lips had touched him. He knew it was an innocent kiss, a typical French gesture, but he took it as a sign of favor. He ran the steps of the Metro and felt the cold wind of the November street like a caress. Yeager was wrong about Eugénie. Yeager was an ass. That night in his hotel room, Henry wrote a few lines of poetry, the first since he'd arrived in Paris.

> Alchemy is the art of changes,
> dull things, materia prima,
> sparked to life in
> a marriage of elements.
> Flash of feminine mercury,
> explosion of sulfur,
> two essences fused
> by fire.
>
> Dante, pious muse,
> to the eighth
> dark circle of hell
> you banished Hermes'
> magic stone.
> Did you forget
> how earth is formed
> of dross,
> that love
> feeds not on air
> or dust,
> and drowns
> in fathoms
> of inconsequence.

Only

in fire's consummation,

comes the flash

and burning

of souls,

base metal reborn

as bright and transient gold.

He titled the poem "Ancient Arts" and worked another hour to translate it into French. Folding it into an envelope, he wrote Eugénie's name on the front. It was well past midnight when he left the hotel and walked to the *pâtisserie* to slide his gift under the door. When he returned, he found he wasn't sleepy and went out again to the quay, admiring the ghostly towers of Notre Dame in the fog.

He met her after work the next day with more roses. This courtship was costly. He had asked Dreux for a raise or more hours but was refused. He would soon run short of money. He'd been forced to hassle Yeager's friend Doug Spaulding for the francs loaned him during the summer. But Eugénie's pleasure at the sight of the roses was worth the cost. She smiled warmly as Henry entered the shop. He did not ask her about the poem, waiting for her to mention it, which she did as soon as they started toward the Metro station.

"Mme Péguy says there is a letter for me. And I tell her she is lying. No one writes me letters. And she says no, it was under her door this morning, like a messenger put it there. At first, Henri, I'm so frightened. Maybe it is a threat. Because I am political. Or something bad has happened. But no, it is a poem. A poem from Henri! My crazy American!"

"You liked it?"

She frowned. "So many words. What do they mean?"

He flushed.

She put her hand on his arm. "But yes, I like it. Even if I don't understand it. Because I know it is a beautiful poem, like Baudelaire. Do you know that no one has ever given me a poem? And in a letter under the door of a *pâtisserie*! So all day I find myself thinking about how in movies young men are romantic. They say pretty words and write pretty letters like Cyrano. But no French boy does that for me. So I like it, Henri."

He grinned and put his hand over hers. As they walked, he explained the poem, who the alchemists were, how they tried to make gold from ordinary dull metal. Whether Eugénie understood, he didn't know. But she listened.

At the train platform, she fixed him with a puzzled look. "What do you do, Henri? What work?"

The question startled him. He took it as an interrogation.

"I, uh, I write. I'm a writer, some poetry but other things too."

"Like Bert Yeager?"

He wondered why she asked that. Was she testing him? He didn't know the right answers. He thought of her statement that she was political.

"I work for Renard Marcotte."

"You? No!"

"Yes, really I do."

"Henri, you are too crazy and too American to work for Marcotte."

Was she laughing at him?

"But I do. Three mornings a week, I report to an office off Sébastopol, to M. Dreux."

"Do you write poetry for Marcotte?"

She *was* laughing at him. His face warmed.

"I write important things," he snapped, "press releases and news articles. For the British newspapers."

That wasn't true, of course.

Eugénie frowned, as if trying to decide something. Then she smiled. "Don't be serious, Henri. I don't like you serious."

"But I *am* serious about Marcotte." She was slipping away. He hadn't said what she wanted to hear. He felt his heart sinking. She wanted him to be her goofy, rich American, who brought her roses and poetry. A journalist was a hack, even a journalist who worked for Marcotte. He thought desperately for something to salvage the conversation. Perhaps she sensed his panic for her demeanor changed, and she spoke in a somber tone he had never heard before.

"Marcotte is a great man, don't forget that, Henri."

"Of course not," he answered in irritation. He didn't need to be lectured.

She responded heatedly. "You Americans are rich. So that you come to Paris and pretend to work while you drink and sit around all day in cafés while we serve you. That's why we believe in Marcotte. He is for ordinary people, while our politicians care only for the rich. For that I love Marcotte."

Henry was thrown off balance, his strategy to win this girl shredded by talk about Marcotte. What had happened? He struggled for words with which to extract himself. But it was too late. Eugénie's train slowed beside them. He waited, frozen with fear, for some final word from her, dismissal. But she kissed his cheek as usual, smiled, and called back "tomorrow," as the car doors closed.

That should have heartened him, but nothing could hearten him. He walked to his hotel in despair. He had said all the wrong things, destroyed his chance with Eugénie. She would never take him seriously. The more he thought about this turn in their conversation, the angrier he became, foisting his fear on her, that she was an ignorant shop girl. Yet even in his anger, tears ran from his eyes. He would not abandon Eugénie. Never. And because Henry was a creature of habit, his tenacity quickly reasserted itself. The next morning, he rose early and made his way to the flower shop, where he purchased with his last few francs a single rose and left it at the *pâtisserie*.

He walked to the M.L.F. print shop, too broke to take the Metro, walked home again that afternoon, his mind continuing to reconstruct the conversation from the day before. Did she prefer him rich or poor? She seemed delighted with his flowers, his poetry, his impulsive acts. But the persona that delighted her was little more than a diversion for the girl, a clown, whose antics kept her mind from serious matters. That she cared about serious matters was obvious from her passionate words about Marcotte. Henry remembered her eyes when she spoke of the man, the conviction in them. He remembered too how she had scorned rich Americans. If he remained her clown, she would tire of him. But there was one serious thing they had in common. Renard Marcotte.

When he met her after work and walked her to the Metro, he brought up the subject of Marcotte. She shook her head. "Serious things do not become you, Henri."

He persisted. "You think I don't care about Marcotte. That because I'm an American I can't understand. But I do care. I'm not rich, Eugénie. The family I grew up in was poor."

"Poor, yes, only three automobiles."

"They didn't own an automobile."

She tossed her head in such a way as if to say prove it.

"In America there's opportunity for people like me. I was born to a poor family, farmers, but I had the opportunity to be educated with the children of wealthy families, because I worked hard. In America, we believe everyone is equal. Doesn't Marcotte believe that, that ordinary people have the right to the same opportunities?"

"Yes, of course." Her skepticism softened. "But Americans are so arrogant. They think because they won the war, we owe them great homage. They think with their money, they can buy the French. Well, I don't like Americans. But I like you, Henri. You aren't like them. So maybe I believe you were poor, but now you are here in Paris, so now you must be rich."

He didn't correct her, the part about being rich. Maybe he could have it both ways.

"You really work for Marcotte?" she asked, puzzled.

"Yes."

"You are a strange American, Henri."

They entered the Metro tunnel. Eugénie took his hand and gently squeezed it. This time on the platform, she kissed him, still on the cheek, but with ardor. "You must also believe in him," she said suddenly, before she disappeared into the subway car.

Long after the train had pulled away, Henry still fretted. He hated the intrusion of politics into their relationship. He wanted Eugénie as she first seemed to him, naïve and pretty, a girl who should be worrying about clothes and perfumes, not cluttering her head with a man like Marcotte. He didn't remind himself, of course, that he had first seen her at Marcotte's rally. His imagination had taken him far from there. He wanted her to be a lovely rose of a girl, but politics wilted this image. Eugénie said he must believe in Marcotte, yet if he let himself think about the man at all, he found him nothing more than a petty demagogue. Taking money from him, for whatever innocuous purpose, seemed suddenly shameful. He vowed to quit the work with Dreux.

The next evening, MacNally talked Henry into accompanying

him to the Arc de Triomphe for a rally in support of the Hungarians. Henry had seen the posters plastered on the Left Bank, photographs of tanks in the streets of Budapest, boys hurling Molotov cocktails. The brave young Hungarians awakened his conscience. Many were his age, some still teenagers. Young men dying for freedom. Maybe Eugénie was right. Wasn't he just another American wasting his time in cafés? The night sky was clear as he and MacNally walked across the Île to the Right Bank and along the Avenue des Champs-Élysées. A large crowd had gathered at the Tomb of the Unknown Soldier. Music blared through loud speakers, "La Marseillaise" and the Hungarian national anthem. Demonstrators wore black armbands in support of the doomed Hungarians. Henry felt his heart once more stirred. The long walk, the cool air were tonics to his spirit. The music roused him. He cheered and sang "La Marseillaise" as lustily as the Parisians crowded about him. They were brothers. They were all brothers, in pursuit of truth and freedom. The crowd roared with outrage as a speaker blasted the Soviet Union, the Soviet tanks, the death of the valiant Hungarians. When it was over, people lingered, unwilling to leave. Henry and MacNally headed back to the Left Bank. MacNally met a friend near the Louvre and went off with him to a café. Henry walked on alone, the music and crowd reverberating in his heart.

On the sidewalk outside the hotel the next afternoon, Yeager greeted him with a copy of *Paris-Soir*.

"Boy, look what happened." He stuck the paper under Henry's nose. "Heard you and Mac went to the rally."

"Un huh."

Henry read the headline and scanned the article below it. There had been a riot, beginning at the Arc de Triomphe. Hundreds had marched off to the Communist Party headquarters and destroyed the place, tossing file cabinets and furniture into the street and lighting a bonfire.

"You didn't get in on that part of the rally, I guess?" asked Yeager, grinning.

"No," said Henry, annoyed by Yeager's sarcasm, even as it shamed him. He had done nothing except feel sorry for the Hungarians.

"Well, your buddy Marcotte isn't about to be upstaged. He's having his rally tonight."

"Marcotte?"

"Yeah, the goddamned thug." Yeager's indignity at his treatment by Marcotte's bullies had lingered, especially when the AP didn't buy his story. "But I have better things to do," he said. "Party at a friend of Mac's. You wanna go, meet me downstairs at eight. Should be a doozy."

Henry waved him off. "Got other things."

He ignored Yeager's quizzical look and headed to his room. A few minutes later, he went upstairs to shower and shave, came back to his room and dressed. He put on a tie and slipped on his one sport coat. He grabbed something to eat at a corner grocery and walked around Place Maubert trying to spot an M.L.F. poster advertising the rally. But there were only anti-colonial posters and the usual Communist flyers (painted over now with contemptuous anti-Communist slurs) tacked on the kiosks and buildings. The Left Bank wasn't usually M.L.F. territory. So he started walking, across the Île to the Right Bank, to the print shop off Sébastopol. The front office was dark through the glass, but Henry heard the churning mimeograph machine. The door was locked. He knocked and was admitted by a man who wasn't Dreux, but a young man, blonde and muscular, who eyed Henry suspiciously.

"I work for Dreux. In there."

"The American?"

"Yes, Henry Beam."

The man shrugged but did not step aside. It was obvious he considered Henry's arrival irregular. Henry asked about the rally, which seemed to mollify the young man.

"We're leaving shortly," he said.

Henry didn't know what that meant, but the man gestured toward the back room. Henry followed him into the print shop where there were other young men. They wore the blue shirts and armbands of the M.L.F. Henry wandered over to the corner of the room, *his* corner, to the table stacked with British newspapers. A lump of anxiety settled in his stomach. He heard the others murmuring, about him he thought, although they spoke too softly for him to know. But he knew they didn't trust him. What if they thought him a spy or snitch? He had encountered Marcotte's young toughs before. Perhaps some of these men had been among them, although he couldn't recall their faces. But he too worked for the M.L.F. now. He had a legitimate right to be here. But did they know that?

Henry sat on the edge of his familiar table. The others talked among themselves with an occasional glance his way, seeming as edgy as he was. They waited for twenty minutes more until sounds from the outer office roused them.

"Here. Go. Come on," a voice shouted in French.

A head came through the door. The face was familiar. But whose? Henry searched his memory. The day on the bridge. The young man with Eugénie. Following the others to the open door, Henry tried to duck past Eugénie's companion, but the young man stopped him.

"Hey you. What are you doing here?"

"I, uh, work here, sometimes, during the day, for the M.L.F."

The young man sneered. "Who is he?" he called after the others.

None of them knew, but at least he hadn't recognized Henry from the bridge.

"You're lying," the young man said.

There was something ugly in his voice. Henry's skin tingled. When would the young man realize who he was?

"I work for Dreux."

The name had its effect.

"Doing what?"

Henry stiffened. This young punk had nothing to do with him.

"I don't have to tell you."

"Bastard. What do you mean you don't have to tell me? American bastard. Bastard."

He kept repeating the word *bastard* as if it were the only weapon he had. Henry guessed Dreux's name carried weight.

He felt more confident. "Renard Marcotte asked me to work for Dreux."

The young man started to say something else, thought better of it, and stalked from the room. Henry, like the others, picked up a stack of posters and followed to the street. A truck was parked at the curb, an old army transport, with canvas top and benches along the side. Henry, heart thumping, climbed aboard. Eugénie's young man, whom the others called Claude, hopped in the driver's seat and gunned the gas pedal. The tires screamed; the truck lurched ahead. It shimmied and swerved through Paris. Henry was jostled into the man next to him every time the truck turned a corner. At each turn, the man shoved a hard object into Henry's ribs. He glanced down and saw a key gripped between his fingers. Henry clenched his teeth and refused to acknowledge the pain or the young man gouging him. He stared straight ahead. What was he doing? What mindless impulse had urged him into this truck? He was wading into deep water. This time he might actually drown.

The truck stopped several times to load more of the young men. Henry slid down the bench and let a new arrival get between him and the man with the key. The truck was soon crowded and began to reek of body odor, tobacco and hair oil. It was dark in the truck, illuminated only by matches and cigarettes and the flash of streetlights and yellow automobile headlights through the open back. The men around Henry were strangers and paid him no mind. They cursed and laughed and handed about blue armbands to those who had none. Someone passed one to Henry. He clasped it in his hand, let it dangle between his knees as the truck bounced through the city. It was one thing to come along, another to wear the M.L.F. brassard. He thought about Eugénie. She had said he must believe in Marcotte. Was this what she wanted? What would she think if she saw him? He fingered the soft cotton of the armband. Such an innocuous piece of cloth. What did it matter? This wasn't real. The truck, the noisy young men, the blue brassard in his hand. Tomorrow he would wake and realize he had dreamed it, or perhaps written it, a novel of post-war Paris. He was an actor and this was a film. Why should he take any of this seriously? He had come to Paris on a fellowship to learn. Certainly he was learning. He should have brought along a notebook.

A young man next to him offered a cigarette, and though he had never smoked, he took it, let it droop unlit from his mouth. He slipped the armband over his jacket sleeve and asked the fellow who'd given him the cigarette to tighten it in place. He then asked for a light. A match flared. He leaned against the ribs of the truck, smoking and trying not to cough. He watched the smoke curl away from him, mix with smoke of other cigarettes. He had no idea where they were headed. But in that moment, it satisfied him to be going.

The truck stopped again and Claude's face appeared at the back. "Out. We're here."

Henry stumbled from the truck with the others. They had come to an open city square he didn't recognize. Only a few people milled about, mostly M.L.F. operatives stringing lights from poles and setting up a platform with chairs and a long table. A sound system was already in place. A microphone stood near the platform. Martial music blared through loud speakers. Henry followed the young men and tried to make himself inconspicuous. Whatever they did, he did. Occasionally someone asked his name, if he were a new fellow, but it was obvious a new fellow here or there was not unusual. That he was American was. They unloaded folding chairs from a truck and set them in rows, strung more lights and rolled large metal drums onto the pavement and lit fires in them so those standing around could warm their hands. By the time they finished these jobs, people had gathered, perhaps seventy or eighty, Henry thought.

The young men in armbands took up positions around the chairs like sentries. Henry found a spot toward the back. He looked for Eugénie and wondered if she came to all Marcotte rallies, but obviously not this one. Claude positioned himself near the podium. He was a handsome young man, probably a year or two younger than Henry. His face was sharp, but pretty, shadowed by dark hair that curled over his forehead. His full upper lip seemed frozen in a pout. He reminded Henry of students he had met at Duke. A young man who knew who he was, whose bearing projected confidence and presence. Henry envied him. And was furiously jealous. They weren't equals and never would be.

There was one preliminary speaker before a cheer went up and Marcotte mounted the platform. This time he used the microphone so that his voice boomed through the open square, echoing off the buildings around it. It was the same speech from the earlier rally. Henry hardly listened. Marcotte was just getting warmed up when Henry spotted a familiar face at the edge of the crowd. Yeager's friend Rice. He tried to edge away, but Rice had seen him.

"Well, what brings you to the party?" asked Rice.

"Curiosity."

"Wearing that?" He tapped a finger on the blue armband.

Henry was too embarrassed to answer.

"Yeah, well, let me give you a tip, friend. You'd better get yourself out of here or else get rid of that." He tapped the armband again. Henry flinched at the disgust in Rice's voice.

"Why?"

"This party's going to get busted up." Rice spoke normally, as if he assumed no one around them understood English.

"What do you mean?"

"A little retribution. For last night."

Henry tried to remember last night. What was Rice talking about? Rice grinned. Henry moved away, farther back from the listeners. As Marcotte's voice got louder, a quiver passed through the square. Something screamed overhead. Exploded. Shadowy figures, armed with bats and cudgels, lunged in among the chairs. Those seated in them leaped up and ran panicking about. Some fell to the ground and were trampled. For what seemed an endless moment, Henry froze. Then his instincts took hold and he ran—past the struggling spectators and across the street, away from the square. He stopped, his breath coming in gasps, and looked back. Near the podium a wild melee was in progress, rioters with cudgels against Marcotte's blue-banded toughs. Henry didn't see Marcotte. Someone threw a smoke bomb, and the brawlers scattered as people fled the square. Several rioters headed across the street toward Henry, pursued by Marcotte's young men. Henry ducked into an alley and let the dark enclose him. He stumbled against a pile of bricks and rubble. Sounds of running came nearer. He grabbed a brick, gripping it as the rioters swept past his hiding place. He grabbed up more bricks, stuffed two in his pockets, clutched another in his free hand and darted from the alley. A group of M.L.F. bluebands caught up and surrounded Henry. Like a charging herd, they pursued the rioters along the sidewalk.

The bricks weighed heavily in his pockets and he slowed. A young man ran beside him, the fellow who had gouged him in the truck. He yanked a brick from Henry's left hand and hurled it, not at the rioters but into a shop window. Glass sprayed the sidewalk. The young man hooted and raised his fist, groped with his other hand toward Henry and received the gift of a second brick. More glass. Henry's heart beat wildly. His side ached and he gasped for air. His feet pounded the concrete. The pavement jarred his legs as if to shove him along faster. He slid a brick from his pocket and hoisted it, sent it in the direction of the fleeing rioters. His last brick he kept tight in his right hand until rounding a corner he let it fly—toward a wide glass front of a butcher shop. He raced to catch up with the others, the shattering glass in his ears like bells. He threw back his head to gulp in the cold air and laughed. He had never been so happy.

THIRTEEN

Thirteen

The train gained speed. More than a hundred people had been crammed into the small space. René found himself squeezed in a corner, a large woman in front of him, her broad back a wall. His legs tingled and grew numb. He wiggled his toes, forced his hands up and down his shins to stimulate the blood. An old man was propped against his shoulder. The man's mouth was in his face and he exhaled a sour odor. René bent close to the knothole. Air, mixed with grit from the smoky engine, blew against his cheek. This chill of air was all he had to soothe him and give him hope. If he twisted at a downward angle, though to do so was torture, he could place his left eye to the hole and see outside the car, observe the whir of trees and grass until this dizzied him and his body cramped. The knothole was his secret. He hid it from the others with his body, afraid it would be discovered and taken away.

As the car rattled along, prisoners began to speak, some begging for more space or water. Voices grew louder until people were shouting. A young man at the other end of the car forced himself into an upright position and demanded their attention. Listen, he called, we are going to have rules. It is the only way.

A baby screamed, but otherwise the car quieted.

Break the damn door out, someone cried.

A panicky voice rose from deep among them. No, no, they will shoot us.

More shouts and angry voices.

Quiet! the young man shouted. Listen to me!

Resistance, someone near René whispered.

The young man eventually prevailed, assigning tasks to a chosen few. A quick inventory was taken: what was in the car, the location of the doors. Were there loose boards in the floor or along the sides? Did anyone have among their possessions anything that might be of value? Many like René, taken directly from jail, had no possessions. Others had small satchels, as if only to stay overnight. René did as the young man instructed, feeling along the boards where he was pressed against the wall. He did not tell the young man about the hole. It was only a knothole, hardly larger than a coin, and offered no escape. But it was his escape. In the corner of the car opposite René sat a metal pail provided by the soldiers, he assumed, for a toilet. There were jeers when the young man reported this. Several women wailed, but René felt relief. His bladder was about to burst.

How many women and children? the young man asked.

Reports were shouted across the car. There were six children. These were easy to locate, since most were crying. One man, pinned upright into a standing position, held a baby as if to keep it above floodwater. They worked out a system with the metal pail. When anyone needed to use it, the pail was passed through the car. They soon found this unworkable, particularly when the pail grew heavy and its contents sloshed over the side. The car stank of urine and feces. They began a system of shifts when some would stand and others sit to rest. Every hour or so, they would all stand, allowing passage to the pail. René was afraid to leave his place, afraid the tiny hole would be discovered by someone else and he would lose it. But his bladder forced him to move. He struggled through the swaying bodies. The train was rounding a bend. He wasn't afraid he would fall; there were too many people in the car. He reached the pail, let his penis loose from his pants and gagged. The pail was close to overflowing. It would soon be full. Then what? He peed into the disgusting pail. Bits of fecal matter floated in it. The odor was horrible. Someone beside him shouted for him to hurry. He buttoned his pants and felt no relief as he squeezed across the car to his spot. His knothole was still there! Everyone was standing and no one had found it. When the order came from the young man to sit down, René sank in relief. He pressed his face against the tiny space, felt the cold air like a cooling breeze. His neck and back ached from the contorted posture and he feared he might vomit. But the air consoled him. Near him, a baby screamed. People mumbled under their breaths. Somewhere in the car, a man spouted obscenities.

René withdrew into himself, his face against the hole. His legs became numb, his back screamed with pain, his stomach cramped. He was thirsty. He licked his arms, searching with his tongue for beads of sweat. It was winter outside and he found no moisture on his skin, only the bitter taste of dirt and body oils. Unable finally to ease the pain in his back and neck, he sidled upright and pressed himself against the car wall. He closed his eyes. The old man next to him gasped for air. Bereft of his air hole, René panicked, terrified these strangers crowded around him might shift their weight and crush him. He listened to the old man gasp and found himself gasping in tandem. Yet despite his panic, René experienced a tremor of anticipation. Where was he going? Unlike these others, he did not ask himself the more nagging question: why? He knew why.

Three days passed in the crowded boxcar. The stench became unbearable. There were several stops when the soldiers opened the doors and allowed the slop pail to be emptied beside the track. But this was never a sufficient remedy. The pail filled and overflowed several times. People got sick and vomited into it. The young man who had organized them tried to keep order among the increasingly panicked

A Stone for Bread

prisoners. He forced several men to give up their jackets to be used as mops to soak up the refuse and prevent its spread through the car. People grumbled but did what the young man said. His name was Joseph and he recruited allies among the others, so that soon a gestapo existed within the car equal to the one outside.

The grumbling increased, but Joseph kept order. He grouped the prisoners into teams, one team to keep the area clean around the slop pail, another to help anyone who was sick. Another team of three young men, strong men, likely resistance fighters like Joseph, gathered in one corner of the car. René was invited to join them. René was young, muscular from his years of hard work. They could use him. But René refused. He knew what they were doing. They would devise a means of escape, though they told none of the others. René did not want to escape. He had been chosen for this dark journey. He would see it through.

The fourth night, the old man next to him died, his eyes open and fixed on René. Spooked by the man's lifeless stare, René averted his gaze. Yet still he saw him, the pasty face, stiff oval of mouth like the brass crucifix in the church at Orleans. The man's right hand clutched René's knee, and he felt the warmth drain from the dead fingers. Finally, René forced himself to look, surprised he wasn't afraid. He touched the old man's face, leaned close and let his forehead touch his cheek. For a moment, they were brothers. René then did something he had seldom done since leaving the seminary. He prayed for the man, the prayers for the dead. The next morning, the old man's body was taken off the car at a stop along the rail line and tossed into the snow with the slops from the pail.

That same morning, the train stopped again. The prisoners fidgeted. Their talk grew louder. Every stop agitated them. From his knothole, René saw German soldiers walking beside the train. The door to the car opened. A soldier ordered them outside. Where were they? René expected to see a station or compound, one of the camps about which the prisoners had jabbered so frantically since they were first herded into the boxcar. But there was nothing outside except snow-covered trees and fields. René stumbled awkwardly into the cold air. His legs hurt and his knees buckled. He fell against another man, who cursed and shoved him. Something struck him in the back. He couldn't breathe and felt himself falling toward the snow. The shock of snow on his face stunned him. He tried to get to his feet and was struck again.

"*Aufstehen!*" A soldier was behind him, a foot on his back.

René was confused. How could he get up? The man's foot prevented it.

"*Aufstehen!*"

René struggled to do just that, but the man pinned him. It was likely he would have died in that moment from a bullet to the head had shouting not diverted the soldier's attention. He left René and ran toward a clump of trees. There were shots, the stutter of a machine gun. René got up quickly. He looked around. Prisoners from his car were wandering dazed beside the train, afraid to venture off. René gulped down a handful of snow then peed on the ground. His mind was weary. He wanted to weep or laugh, bemused by the yellow stain in the snow, the steam that rose in the air from his hot urine. Why had they stopped the train? Offered this sniff of freedom? Did they mean to taunt them with the world beyond the stinking railcar? René breathed in the icy air, felt his chest swell with gratitude.

Several soldiers remained in the field, their machine guns aimed at them. The other soldiers came back from the woods, dragging two bodies. They flopped the bodies on their backs beside the tracks. René gasped to see Joseph, his face and chest torn by bullets. Alien tears stung his eyes. A good boy, he heard himself say aloud. A sudden burst of machine gun fire startled him. Several prisoners loitering beside the boxcar crumpled to the ground. One was a child. Bright red stains spread through the snow. Had René not been so stunned, he might have found the crimson blood against the white snow oddly beautiful. But all he could do was tremble in terror at this inexplicable act. The soldiers herded them back onto the cars. The shock of the killings and the fall into the snow had awakened René's senses. His face burned from the wet snow. His aching arms and legs and neck no longer bothered him. There were worse things to consider. And the stop had cost him his precious knothole. He was now in the middle of the car, wedged between a father and mother and their two teenage children.

A gloom settled over the prisoners. One man, obviously a Jew, keened in Hebrew under his breath. The death of Joseph and the random shooting outside the train had cast a pall on them, silencing them, until their baser instincts, held in check by Joseph and his allies, loosened. People snarled at each other and shoved for space. A fight began in one corner and ended with a prisoner beaten to death as the train rattled on its incessant way. René pulled his knees to his chest and closed his eyes. He had grown used to the smells. But not so the sounds—the crying children, muttered curses of old men, the sobs of women.

They traveled another day before the train stopped again. They were ordered off the car and, this time found themselves in a depot. A perceptible shudder moved through the prisoners. There were more soldiers here, units of them outside the train. Some had dogs, sturdy Shepherds restrained on leather straps. The soldiers lined up the prisoners in rows of five beside the train. René could hardly walk. Pain shot through his legs. Somehow he summoned the resolve to move into place. Those who did not move quickly or stand straight enough to suit the guards were slammed with cudgels—heavy sticks and rubber hoses weighted with sand. It was late in the afternoon and they were in a village. Schoolchildren sent on their way home stopped to watch. A young woman carrying packages hurried past. She shot a glance toward René and the prisoners in his line that he could not understand. Was that pity in her face? Or hatred? The children shouted taunts. One boy chucked stones at them. The soldiers with their guns and cudgels strutted down the rows, checking lists.

René did not understand what was happening. They seemed to be waiting. The prisoners remained in their neat lines for an hour, then another. The children had gone home. It grew dark. Lights came on in the village. Some prisoners tried to sit down but drew shouts and blows from the guards. Several fainted. They were beaten and taken away. One, a young man about the age of Joseph, was shot in the head when he refused to stand. René wondered if he had grown accustomed to such horror. It no longer shocked him.

He kept himself alert by unobtrusively shifting his weight from foot to foot. When the man beside him sagged, he reached a hand behind him in a way the guards wouldn't see to give the man support. But there came a time when he doubted even he could continue standing. He was weak from hunger. They had eaten nothing the last five days but bread tossed into the cars when the train stopped to empty the slop pails. Before Joseph died, the bread was rationed and divided. Afterwards, it went to whoever was strongest or lucky. One loaf had landed in René's lap, but he had given most of it away to the family who shared his tiny space in the middle of the car. They had taken it greedily, stuffing it down before he changed his mind.

The prisoners continued to wait. A convoy of trucks roared up. Women and children were culled from the neat formation and loaded onto the trucks. Crescendoing wails and weeping rose from

A Stone for Bread

the separated families. When the last of the trucks had rumbled off, a soldier, who seemed the one in charge, signaled for the prisoners to move. They were marched through the village, where they could see into windows of houses, families at their evening meals. René thought of his own family and experienced a burning in his chest. It amazed him that he could walk another step. Or breathe. But he did what the soldiers ordered.

They were marched beyond the village to a road that wound up a mountain. The road grew steep. The cold wind stung their faces and chilled their bodies. René did not have a coat—his coat had been taken from him at the prison. He shivered in great jerks. His legs trembled. The rows of five loosened into straggling clumps of men. Guards marched on either side of the road, raining blows on anyone who did not keep up. Some guards ran beside the prisoners with the dogs. René was glad he was in the middle of the lines, protected from the dogs' teeth. Many older prisoners lagged behind or fell. It was quickly apparent that it was in a man's best interest to keep going, no matter the aches of the body or the throbbing of his feet. The laggards were dealt with swiftly. Occasionally, a soldier running alongside would cut in among them and jerk someone out. No one knew why. The hapless victim was shoved into the ditch by the road and dispatched with a shot to the head. René wondered how such a person was chosen. What did the soldiers see to make them target someone for death? Perhaps they would target him. He expected it. Perhaps he would welcome it. Yet something in the senselessness of such deaths, the utter caprice of them, repelled him. That was not how he wanted to die and was careful to do as the soldiers commanded. When they ordered the prisoners to move faster, he stepped up his pace.

René was a strong young man. During the years at Mme Gourou's hotel, he had undertaken any task she asked of him, painting rooms, repairing the roof and furnace, tearing out the pavement in the hotel courtyard. He had hauled in barrels and boxes of food and supplies. Even as his mind had filled with knowledge from the books he lapped up greedily, his muscles had hardened. And there was a further skill he had developed at Mme Gourou's. He learned languages. His German, at least his understanding of German, was excellent. He seldom spoke it, but Mme Gourou had used these skills with her German guests. When they needed anything, she referred them to René, who would listen solemnly then attend to their requests. He had learned the language as he had learned everything else, from the books that sat in piles in his room. During the time of the *ange noir*, he had poured over books of German grammar, moving on to Goethe and Heine, even a little Freud. So now René understood the soldiers as they shouted and joked with each other while they chased the prisoners along the road. Some were taking bets, picking out prisoners: him with the brown jacket, that one there, the curly haired one, betting who would collapse first. René did not slow but moved along quickly. They had not yet wagered on him.

They rounded a bend in the dark road. The prisoners gawked. Some cried out. Above them, the road curved toward a high fortress. It sat on its mountain crest illumined by floodlights, its massive stone walls topped with barbed wire. From the walls' corners rose towers where guards watched from behind mounted machine guns. René stopped walking. The scene before him was magnificent. Terrifying. Beautiful.

Someone shouted at René and shoved him. He moved on. They passed stone outbuildings until they stopped before the high wooden gates of the fortress. René's feet burned. His head throbbed. He shook from cold. The soldiers kept them standing in front of the gates for another hour, until finally the gates opened and they were marched through, into an area between buildings of the prison. Once again they waited for hours, left in this area through the night. At least, the guards allowed them to sit down. The temperature dropped to freezing. The prisoners huddled in groups to keep warm. On the wall above, guards trained machine guns on them. The bright lights made the night into day.

At the first pink streaks of dawn, René noticed figures moving among them like ghosts, men dressed in blue-striped pants and shirts. They wore funny caps, some with slashes of red paint on them. The men set up tables and the prisoners were formed into lines. When René reached one of the tables, he was told to hand over his valuables. None, he declared, I have none. The man in the striped uniform did not believe him. René explained he had been in prison but he did not finish speaking before a guard hit him on the shoulder with a rubber hose. He reeled, caught himself, and forced himself to stand upright, despite the terrible pain in his shoulder. He emptied his pockets. The man at the table scowled, pushed a piece of paper in front of him to sign. René did not read what was on it but wrote his name where the man pointed. He moved forward to the next prisoner group.

They were lined up in twos, paraded by soldiers on either side of the lines. The soldiers nodded and gestured as the prisoners passed. Sometimes they ordered the line stopped and had someone taken from it. Usually it was an older man or a prisoner who'd been lagging. A young man with a heavy limp was pulled aside. René held himself erect as he marched through the gauntlet. He waited for the hand on his shoulder, the growled *you!* but nothing happened. He marched on and did not look back. The next order was to undress. René stripped off his clothes—pants, shirt, shoes. The air was icy. He could see the breath of the others like puffs of mist. His teeth clattered in his head. The prisoners—in his group possibly 200—stood naked in the courtyard in the early morning light. From elsewhere in the camp, orders blared over loudspeakers. There were sounds of men moving about, ordered to line up. But the men with René waited naked an agonizingly long time, until they heard the other prisoners in the camp being marched away. Only then was René's group prodded into an open area between buildings and driven by shouting guards into the basement of a stone building and told they were to shower. René heard groans around him. There had been talk about showers on the train, rumors repeated about camps where instead of water, gas streamed onto unsuspecting prisoners. But now there were few unsuspecting prisoners. René wondered if he was going to die. But to the prisoners' relief, water came from the nozzles. Hot water. It scalded their skins. René didn't know whether to be glad to no longer be cold or to scream from the pain of the blistering spray.

They were herded from the shower into a room where a barber shaved the hair from their bodies—scalp, beards, underarms, legs, crotch. The barber used the same razor over and over until it dulled. Blood streamed into René's face from cuts in his scalp. He stared at his fellow prisoners, their shorn heads and unrecognizable features. Who were these men? He wondered if he too looked so insignificant and foolish. They spent the morning shuffled from one place in the prison to another. They were given clothes—a bundle of the striped suits handed to each man but were not measured for size. René was lucky. His trousers were too large, but that could be remedied. Some had clothes too small for them, that pinched and chafed their skin still raw from the hot shower. They received shoes, though not really shoes, but odd, rough-crafted affairs of canvas strips nailed to wooden soles. They chafed René's feet and hurt when he walked. There seemed to be few other prisoners within the fortress walls, only those handing out shoes and clothing. These were ghostly men, scalps partially shaved, faces gaunt, eyes furtive and fishlike. From elsewhere in the compound came the clank of shovels or picks.

When they had dressed, the prisoners with René were marched to a different building and ordered to halt outside. Soldiers in the black uniforms of the SS pointed machine guns at them and made them crouch into knee bends, their hands at the back of their heads. They were left this way more than an hour before finally being allowed to stand, but only at attention. After awhile, the guards again ordered them into the crouched position. This went on for hours. The pain in René's legs grew intense. When the guards weren't watching, he lowered one knee to the ground, but was quick to raise it should a guard turn his way. A man several yards in front of him fainted. The guards were on him like dogs, beating him until blood ran from his nose and mouth. They carried him away. René searched inwardly for a means to divert his mind from his tender knees and aching back and discovered an astonishing skill. He recalled the book he'd read just before his arrest, Maurois' *History of England*, and realized that not only could he remember it clearly, he could see the pages in his mind, could read them without the book in front of him. He had never known he possessed such a faculty. Why had he not known this before now? He pictured other books he had read, Verlaine, Goethe, a technical manual on watches and discovered the same was true with each of them. He could visualize the pages and read them from memory. He forgot his throbbing legs in the glow of this feat. The library which he had spent years pursuing was here in this bleak prison, intact in his mind. He had only to summon it. He explored the trick, how far back it was possible to recall a book, until shouts interrupted him.

Aufstehen! Aufstehen!

He stood. He was at the door of the building. Though annoyed to be roused from his discovery, a prod from a gun barrel moved him in the door. He followed the line of men to a desk. Behind it sat a prisoner in striped clothing, a stack of small white cards in front of him on which he wrote information. He asked René questions. Nationality. Name. Birth date. Place of birth. Family. None he replied. The man asked his profession. Profession? Mechanic. For some reason, the little lie amused him. He felt better. It was only on the last question that he balked. Reason for imprisonment? A mistake, he answered. A nearby guard shouted at him. The question came again: reason for imprisonment? Mistaken identity, René repeated, and was slammed in the back. He was at a loss. What was he expected to say? The question was asked a third time. Before answering, René turned to the guard and stared directly at him, confused. A mistake, he repeated. The guard's eyelids flickered. He signaled the prisoner behind the desk and René was passed through. He felt grateful to the guard. He had believed him. He tried to thank him as he was ordered into another line. The man grunted and stared at the ground.

The prisoners were given patches to sew on their uniforms. The patches identified each of them by number, nationality and prisoner category. Criminals received green triangles. Homosexuals pink. Jews yellow. René's triangle was red, which meant he was a political prisoner—resistance. The letter F for France was stitched across the triangle. Underneath was his six-digit number. The whole day blurred into one terrible ordeal. It wasn't enough to stand in so many lines and be pushed and jabbed at each step, but the guards constantly taunted them, hitting them or spitting on them, occasionally pulling one from the line and beating him for no apparent reason. At sunset, René was assigned a barracks. This was temporary, he learned. They would be held in a quarantine block for three weeks. To separate the dead from the living, a guard said and laughed, his mouth gaping wide at his joke.

But it was not a joke. The quarantine barracks was an empty room, neither lit nor heated. Temperatures at night dipped below freezing. There were no beds. To keep warm, the men piled on top of one another. One man was suffocated. The guards here were themselves prisoners—called kapos. Most wore green triangles, which marked them as criminals. Many of the greens were German, which seemed to grant them special status. They maintained order by viciously bullying the other prisoners. The kapos who ran the quarantine block kept the floor of the barracks wet, hosing it down, sometimes several times a day, for proper hygiene, they explained. The men stayed chilled and wet. Food arrived haphazardly, and when it did there was little of it. The men subsisted on bowls of weak soup, an occasional piece of sausage and chunks of stale bread. Many in René's barracks became sick. René observed this ordeal with curious detachment. He wondered why some men sickened and others did not. Why more men did not become sick. What could a man endure and still live?

He remained surprisingly healthy and did not catch even a cold. How was that possible? He searched his memory for books he had read on medicine and the intricacies of the human immunological system. But nothing he'd read explained this miracle of physical resistance. Not all men, of course, possessed such resistance. Twenty prisoners of the more than one hundred in his barracks died the first week. Most, René believed, died of chronic ailments worsened by prison—heart disease, diabetes, weak lungs. Many were afflicted with varying degrees of dysentery. The slop bucket steamed with their liquid bowel excretions. Some of them died of dysentery. Toward the end of the quarantine, others showed signs of onset diseases, like tuberculosis and pneumonia. René could hear incipient TB in a man's seemingly mild cough. He could read the first stages of other diseases in the coloration of a man's eyes, or the paling of his skin. The one disease that seemed to alarm their masters most was typhus, why the block was continually hosed and disinfected.

When the three weeks of quarantine ended, the survivors were sent back to the barber. Their heads were again shaved, but this time only down the middle, leaving the sides to grow back. Now René looked like a veteran, marked by what prisoners called the Hitler Street on their scalps. After the haircut, they were subjected to *lausjadg*, lice inspection, stripped naked and doused with a burning liquid. When they were again allowed to dress, they were assigned a permanent barracks. René's was Block 13. He felt a delirious happiness. The barracks was heated and, though crowded, had bunks, three tiers of bunks, furnished with straw pallets. René shared his bunk, four feet in width, with two other prisoners. Space was so cramped that he experienced every breath and movement of the others. Even so, the first night he slept peacefully and without dreams. But the respite was short. The prisoners were awakened roughly at dawn with shouts of *Heraus! Heraus!* Come out! Come out! from the kapos in charge of his barracks, ordering them immediately from their bunks.

Outside the barracks, music blared. There was a quick breakfast of watery broth. René found a tiny shred of cabbage floating in his bowl and sucked it up greedily. They were given a half cup of something the guards called coffee. It was bitter and tasted like tree bark. The kapos ordered them outside for roll call. They lined up six deep with the other inmates of the prison in an immense open space in front of the first row of barracks. Prisoners began to fill the area. René was stunned. The prisoners kept coming. There were thousands of them crowded into this open space. He never dreamed the prison held so many. A city of lost men emerged before his eyes. Stick men, in bizarre striped suits. What crimes had they committed? He again heard music and saw a straggly band of prisoner musicians across the yard, emaciated, ghostly figures with shaved heads, playing jaunty tunes on mismatched instruments—an accordion, several guitars, possibly a dozen woodwinds and a single trumpet. The music floated across the yard and over the heads of the prisoners like a summons to step forward into a macabre parade. René was dizzy. He felt he might swoon. Someone next to him put out a hand.

Straighten up, a voice whispered in Spanish. As if it were an order from a guard, René did as he was told. He focused on a spot of color on a stone building across the yard. The dot was a tatter of cloth stuck to the stone. He grew fascinated by it. What was it? From whose clothing did it come? None of this, of course, mattered, but it helped him survive his first roll call. He was so tired. He wanted to lie on the ground and sleep. Every prisoner's number was called by their barracks' *blockschreiber*, the elite prisoner second in command of the barracks. The numbers were called again. And again. René glanced right and left. How many thousands of men must be lined up and down the prison yard? How many times would their numbers be called? Finally came a shout: *Mützen ab*! The prisoners jerked their caps from their heads. The lines broke up. Most marched off with work groups. Some were forced to sing as they hoisted tools or pushed wheelbarrows and carts in front of them.

René's group, the new prisoners, were left standing. Mid-morning, when they were led to the latrine to relieve their bursting bladders, an old prisoner shoveling wastes from the open ditch confronted him. The man was testy with René for taking too long to pee. Learn to do things smart, man, he snarled, or they'll shovel you out like this shit.

The words echoed in René's mind. *Do things smart*. He knew that meant more than being wary. Do things quickly. Do them correctly. Find ways to survive. Yes, these were skills he possessed. Had he not done things smartly at the hotel? Mme Gourou was proud of his clever hands, his talent with machinery and equipment. Mechanic, he told the man writing on the white card. Perhaps it had not been a lie. He knew machines. Had read about them. And now he could summon diagrams in his mind from manuals read years ago, diagrams of machinery parts for furnaces, radios and watches. His reverie was broken by a shove. Move along! a guard shouted. René shuffled quickly after the others toward the high front gate. Kapos with their green triangles and slashes of paint on their caps wandered in among them, like slave traders at auction.

Skilled workers, stand front, a guard barked.

René stepped forward with most of the others. A soldier went down the row. What do you do? What skills, horseface? You, hah, what do you do? When René was asked the question, he repeated what he'd said before. Mechanic.

Liar, the guard grunted.

René was grouped with forty men and marched away. It was obvious he would not be employed as a mechanic. Instead, he spent the day in a stone quarry just outside the camp. They were marched along the winding road to a place where stone steps descended the face of the mountain, a steep 300 feet. What looked to be a thousand prisoners moved about the quarry floor like maggots. Going down, they passed prisoners coming up, carrying blocks of stone in hods attached to their bodies by webbed harnesses. René's job was to load stone onto open cars, which were then pushed along narrow gauge tracks to the foot of the steps. Everything was done by hand. Even the heavily loaded cars were moved about by prisoners—two dozen men to push one car along the tracks. The work was brutal. Dynamite blasts hurt René's ears. Grit from explosions rained down on them, stinging their noses and throats. René's eyes burned. He comforted himself that he was not made to carry stones up the steps, that task a perverse torture reserved for prisoners with yellow triangles on their uniforms—Jews.

René could see from the corner of his eye as he worked how many stumbled under these heavy loads. Some fell or were kicked down the steps of the quarry. Such scenes no longer startled him. The rules of ordinary society meant nothing here. He meant nothing. There was an odd comfort in that thought. It was what he expected, had anticipated. It was what he deserved.

There was a short break for lunch. Other prisoners served the workers a hunk of bread and a cup of bitter liquid. René gulped down the sparse rations. There was no water. They were given time to use the latrine—slop buckets carried from the quarry and emptied by Jews. After the break, they worked through the afternoon. René felt he would fall or faint, but each time his body threatened revolt, he fought back with the remarkable mind trick. He went to his books, conjured up pages read years before and forced himself to see the print, read the words in his head. Safe among these mental images, he ceased to feel the agony of his muscles or the trembling of his back and legs. He no longer noticed the guards and kapos not ten yards away, clutching their rubber hoses. Nothing mattered, not life, not death. He disappeared into his mind, like a mouse into its dark hole.

The work ended at dusk. Every man stopped at the foot of the steps and took a stone to carry to the top. They were then marched to the prison. Some did not march but were carried in carts or by other prisoners. These were the men who had collapsed that day. Many were dead, moved aside like the blocks of granite. René's group was marched into the huge open space, the *Appellplatz*, for evening roll call, which lasted several hours, every prisoner counted by number not once but three times. René burrowed into his mental images, until they were released to the barracks for another cup of liquid and piece of hard bread. He was exhausted, his body a torment of pain. That night he hardly slept. Every sound woke him, every twitch of the men beside him on the bunk. The barracks was alive with noise and movement and stench. When he did sleep, he dreamed of dismembered torsos and pools of blood in the snow. By morning, he understood that soon, very soon, his own body would join them.

FOURTEEN
Fourteen

"Forgive me, if I shocked you."

They were seated at Henry's kitchen table. Rachel's coffee cup, its contents ice cold, had sat untouched for the last hour. From the living room, the clock chimed ten p.m. Henry's face shone from the overhead kitchen light. But it wasn't the light alone illumining his cheeks. The glow seemed to come as much from the re-lived memory—the brick, the shattering glass. That's what shocked her, not his youthful foolishness, but that forty years after that night, Henry still gloried in it.

"Understand, Rachel, I don't condone what I did. But there was something so alive in the experience that's hard to explain, like a rite of passage." He shifted toward her. "I'm ashamed, of course."

She didn't see a trace of shame in his face. "I suppose it's good I don't shock easily," she said casually, too casually, for she saw this was not the response he wanted. In a blink, no longer than it takes to shift in a chair, the glow drained from his face as if she'd switched off the overhead light. He was again dull and bookish Henry Beam, jowls saggy, face stoic.

"I'm sorry, Henry, it just seemed so unlike you, at least not like you as you seem now."

"I'm not certain that's a compliment."

She saw she'd hurt him and offered a hasty, "I certainly understand we all do crazy things when we're young, things we would never do later."

"It isn't just that, Rachel, as you may one day learn." His smile was forced. "The truth is we never know who anyone is, like you said about your former husband. We don't even know ourselves, until circumstances force from us the truth of who we are."

She thought about that later and felt a twinge of guilt. She had tried to slough off her dismay at Henry's story, the enthusiasm with which he told it. But he'd sensed how she really felt. And now, several days afterwards, she found herself pondering just who Henry Beam really was, that he could have once, even though a young man, allied himself with someone like Renard Marcotte and violently so. What else might he have done from youthful ardor? Sometimes she found herself again thinking that perhaps none of this was true, that Henry had invented it, everything, the poems from the concentration camp, René, Renard Marcotte, Eugénie. He was a writer after all. Could she trust anything he told her?

But then, she too had not been completely forthright with Henry. He had asked if her name was Jewish. Her answer had been truthful. Her parents *were* Presbyterian, her mother's family for years. She had been baptized and confirmed at the age of twelve at one of the oldest Presbyterian churches in North Carolina. But that wasn't exactly Henry's question, which was about her name, if it was Jewish. Because it was. She wondered why she hadn't told him. Was she ashamed? Or was it that she wasn't supposed to know this and therefore could not be certain. She had been a high school senior when she spent a Saturday morning rummaging in the attic in search of letters from a Vietnamese friend she'd met at last summer's Governor's School, seeking a quote for a college application essay.

She never found them but found something else, when she spied a shoebox taped shut, tightly shut, with the words "letters" inked neatly on the lid. Her mother was a tidy freak. Had she boxed up Rachel's letters among others of her own? She had pulled off the tape, but what the box contained, she saw immediately, did not belong to her. The dozen or so letters tied into a packet with string bore an APO address in the upper left hand corner of the top envelope. Surely these were her father's letters. He had been an Army sergeant when her mother met him but left the military when his tour was up. A year after the death of their son, he'd reenlisted, perhaps his way of coping with the tragedy. Carefully, almost reverently, Rachel had lifted the letters from the box and put them to her nose to smell them, as if she might sniff some trace of the father she had barely known. He had died when she was three. She didn't look at the letters. She would not invade her parents' privacy.

But she did look at the only other item in the box—a black and white snapshot. It had seen its share of wear—stains and torn edges, the surface cracked as if the photo had been folded or even wadded into a small space. It was a photograph of a family standing in front of a house on a street of houses: a beautiful young woman in a belted print dress, hair lush and dark, in her arms an infant, the man beside her slightly stiff in his dark suit, the brim of his felt fedora angled so that it partially shadowed his face. They might have been going to church. On the back, barely legible words identified the family as *Rachel, Jakob, Daniel, Stuttgart 1938.* Her father's name was Daniel. But there had been no parents or aunts and uncles, no Jakob or Rachel that she had ever heard of in her family. Danny Singer had grown up in an orphanage in Elmira, New York, supposedly given up by his parents at an early age. Who were these people in the photograph? Who was Rachel?

She never told her mother about the photo, returning it along with her father's letters to the box. That same afternoon, she resealed the box with tape to make it appear it had not been opened. Yet even then she knew, though no one told her, she knew that these people had been family, her father's family and hers, before they vanished from her father's life and history. Rachel, Jakob, Daniel. Jews surely. Jews in Stuttgart, Germany. In 1938.

FIFTEEN

Fifteen

He waited two weeks before he called. In fact, he considered not calling at all, not ever. What had he expected? What had he always expected from the women in his life? That they would understand? Forgive him? Love him no matter what? Our most paradoxical human desire, he thought, more basic than sex: know me fully, know every weakness and awful thing I have ever done, then love me without condition. Of course, he would eventually call her, he knew that. He couldn't stop himself. He was too far into his confession—Father, I have sinned, or mother, friend, whatever. He would not back away now, damn the consequences. But would he find a shred of relief in the telling? A cleansing? He doubted it. So far he'd experienced only sleepless nights and a growing agitation of mind. But when he finally gave in and reached her, he came away pleased to find himself invited to her apartment for dinner Friday evening. Perhaps it was her way of apology and to let him know she had not given up on him, though all she'd said was, "I'm not that great a cook, Henry. But it's my turn."

He appeared at her door precisely at seven, dressed in his one sport coat and a tie. He brought wine and flowers, not the roses he'd first considered, ill considered, he realized, but a bouquet of gold and yellow mums. He saw she was uncomfortable with him at first, and the reservations she'd mentioned about her culinary skills were not unfounded: she wasn't a great cook. No, that wasn't the problem—she was too nervous a cook. She fretted and fidgeted over the chicken casserole in the oven, apologized for the beans. When he asked about the band-aid on her left index finger, she admitted she'd nicked herself slicing cucumbers for the salad. But the meal was passable. And since he'd brought the wine, that was excellent. After the second glass, they both seemed to relax. She chatted amiably about her second semester classes, describing the odd facial tics of one of her professors. He told her more about where he'd been most of his adult life, the insurance agency, Cincinnati. But it was only when they turned to books that the conversation soared. She seemed to delight in his take on *To the Lighthouse*, delight in his delight over the novel itself—one of her favorites, she said. His favorite was Fitzgerald's *Gatsby*, which she also admired. He didn't tell her that sometimes he thought he had lived Jay Gatsby's life. In his own way, of course. Neither said anything about Paris. He had promised himself he would not bring it up, that she would have to ask. It was only when they'd finished dessert, the best part of the meal, an excellent homemade chess pie, that she finally did ask. They moved to her living room with a second cup of coffee and settled in. He sat on her small sofa, Rachel across from him in a frayed upholstered chair, and began the story where he'd left it.

Running.

Along narrow Paris streets. When he finally stopped for breath, he was alone. Marcotte's young men had scattered. The rioters, if any remained about, were blocks away. He heard distant shouts, but the street on which he found himself was deserted except for a few stragglers likely headed home. He cut through an alley to a quiet boulevard where he found a Metro station. Once underground, he checked his surroundings. If anyone had pursued him, he'd lost them. He waited on the platform for a train. Other young men, students, laughed and talked loudly nearby. One pointed at him. Henry's face warmed. Was something wrong? His neck and cheeks were sweaty, probably dirty. He glanced down at his clothes and noticed the blue M.L.F. armband. Pivoting away from the students, he slipped it from his arm to his pocket.

It was after eleven o'clock when he exited the Metro stop at Pont St. Michel. Though the subway ride had calmed him, he remained fidgety and awake. He found a café on Rue Huchette and sat alone drinking coffee for an hour. The caffeine jangled his nerves, and he watched his hand shake on the cup. Like a scientist studying the body's reflexes, he mentally traced the tremor, the network of nerves and ganglia that led from his fingertips to his brain. But the trembling came not from his fingers, he knew, but from a quiver deep in his belly. What had he done? What craziness had taken hold of him? He quit drinking coffee and began on wine, but was soon down to his last francs, so he left the café and walked along the Seine, as far as Pont Royal and back again. With nowhere else to go, he returned to the hotel and sprawled on the bed fully clothed. The last time he checked the clock before falling asleep was at four a.m.

He woke in a panic. Someone was pounding on his door. No, it wasn't his door, but down the hall. But what if it was police? Searching the hotel? He dragged from bed and stood mid-center of the room shaking away his grogginess. The pounding stopped. He went to the window. Outside was gray. He glanced at the clock. Eleven a.m. He had overslept. Where was he supposed to be? At Dreux's? No, not this morning. There was nowhere he had to be. He could sleep all day. Guilt caused him to grab a towel and head for the upstairs shower. He met Yeager on the stairs.

"Damn, what happened to you?"

"What do you mean?"

"I mean you're a wreck."

"I was out late, slept in my clothes."

"Yeah, well nothing that a good pressing room can't fix. Out late, huh? With whom?" He gave Henry one of those I-know-what-you've-been-up-to looks.

Henry ignored it.

"Well, glad I ran into you," Yeager said. "I need to borrow some cash. I'm strapped."

"I don't have much."

"A few dollars worth of francs, that's all. Got to ship a package to the States and I'm flat busted."

"Me too."

Yeager shrugged.

"Wait a minute." Henry turned toward the stairs and Yeager followed. In his room, Henry dug under the mattress and came up with two franc notes, added another from the pocket of the coat he'd tossed on the bed rail. As he withdrew the note, the blue armband fell out with it.

"Thanks." Yeager took the money and shoved it in his wallet. "What's that?" He pointed to the M.L.F. band.

Henry stared, perplexed, his mind still befuddled by sleep. Yeager plucked the brassard from the floor.

"That?"

"Of course, that? What the hell you been doing anyway?" Yeager's look was both curious and amazed.

"Found it."

"Okay, sure."

"I'm working on a book."

"About Marcotte?"

"Yeah."

"Great." He leaned toward Henry with a friendly smile. "Look, if you come on any tidbits, you know, a good story, clue me in, will you? I'm running dry."

"Sure. But it's a novel, what I'm working on. I'm not a journalist."

"You go to the rally last night?"

"What rally?"

"Marcotte's toughs got in a brawl with a bunch of commies in St. Denis. A few explosions, literally."

"What did you hear?"

"Didn't hear anything. Read it. Two-inch blurb in *Paris-Soir*. Riot of sorts. A few smoke bombs thrown, windows broken, nothing too serious."

"*Paris-Soir*?"

"Yeah, but you'll have to really look to find it. Buried deep in the first section. You know, I finally sold that story, the interview with Marcotte. Changed the angle. Talked about anti-communism in France. If I play it with the France-in-political-chaos angle, they seem to like it. I mean Americans don't even know who Marcotte is. But they care about Communists."

Yeager left and Henry went upstairs to shower. The lukewarm water woke him. He tried to reconstruct the previous evening. Sleep had robbed him of his exhilaration. He had awakened sober. And panicked. Would he be arrested? But who knew who he was? Marcotte's young toughs didn't know his name. And who even knew where he lived? He wondered why he had gone to the rally. A lark, done on a whim. But then the violence. The bricks. Yet Marcotte's people hadn't started the brawl. They'd been attacked. Why was it wrong to fight back? Whatever the truth of the last night, Henry decided he'd been little more than an observer. What American had such an opportunity? When he returned to the States, there might well be a book in this. Why not write a novel? He smiled at the thought, hastily dressed and left the hotel to find lunch.

He returned to the print shop the next morning. Dreux greeted him as usual and set him to work at the table in the corner. But Henry felt a changed atmosphere. Whenever any of the young toughs happened by, they stopped and spoke to him. A few patted him on the back or commented about the rally. A few days later, a man Henry had never seen showed up at the print shop. He spoke quietly with Dreux, while Dreux ran the offset. Several times, the strange man glanced Henry's way. Henry kept his head down, afraid he might be a policeman. When he finished with Dreux, he approached the table where Henry worked.

"*Monsieur Américain.*"

"What?"

"I saw you the other night," he said in English.

Henry looked confused.

"You know the brick?"

"Brick?" He wasn't a good liar. He stared down at the table.

"Don't dissemble, Monsieur. You were magnificent. Magnificent. I'll buy you a beer, yes. An American beer." He patted Henry's shoulder.

Henry wondered if this was a trap.

"Who are you?"

"Brisson," he said, as if his surname was all that was required.

"You're M.L.F.?"

"Of course, aren't you?"

"Yes," Henry mumbled.

"Come, the beer." Brisson motioned toward the door.

This seemed more a requirement than an invitation, so he accompanied Brisson to a bistro a few blocks away. Henry ordered a demi of beer and an omelet.

"I have been with Marcotte since the beginning," Brisson began, with no prompting from Henry. "A great man, Marcotte, you know. Like your Lincoln, he wants to free people, as Lincoln freed your slaves."

"Some think he's a fascist."

Something about Brisson, his sophistication possibly, made Henry wary. He was older than most of the M.L.F., probably close to forty, and spoke fluent English.

"Fascist, no! Who says that?"

"I mean I read that in the newspapers."

"Stupid labels from stupid people. Renard Marcotte is for freedom."

"Yes, of course, I know."

"But you cannot have freedom where there's chaos, Henry. In chaos, evil rules. You know that. And France, since the war, has experienced nothing but chaos. This president, that president, a new government every few months, the socialists in power, the conservatives, ridiculous. Nothing but chaos, chaos. And the people are the ones who suffer, those who work, own businesses, this chaos is destroying them. But Marcotte offers them order, from which will rise a new prosperity for France. It must be so. We must make it happen."

"And how will Marcotte do this?"

Brisson seemed unruffled by Henry's questions, as if he regarded this chat over beer an opportunity to convince Henry of the cause.

"One must win the hearts of France. This is not done with violence like the Communists do it, although we're sometimes forced to fight back. As you understand. But Marcotte will win this battle by winning the hearts of France. That's it, you see. The hearts of France."

Henry finished his beer. Brisson ordered two more demis.

"Even though you are an American, I think you sympathize with us, yes?"

"Yes." A feeble yes.

Brisson took the answer as a ringing endorsement.

"Marcotte needs a man like you."

"Why me?"

"You're not like the others, aimless boys who show off their muscles. You're educated, a sophisticate. You speak French well. If you work with us, you'll be rewarded."

Henry shrugged.

"You are a writer?" asked Brisson.

"Yes."

"And you write in French as well as English?"

"Not too well in French."

"You write well in English?"

"Yes."

"Then you see, you can be of use to Marcotte."

"I don't know."

"If it's money, there will be money. Marcotte does not expect us to be slaves. Like Lincoln, you see. He will reward you."

Brisson was handsome, despite his rough complexion. His hair was brown and his blue eyes friendly. He smiled easily, revealing a broken upper front tooth. The beer relaxed Henry, and he began to enjoy the man's company. Brisson appealed to him more than Yeager and his sour friends. He treated him like he was important. Brisson paid for the beers and walked him back to the print shop, shook Henry's hand and left. A week later, Henry received a note from him, an invitation to his flat for a political discussion. That same evening, Henry met Yeager and Rice for dinner. After listening to their arguments about the French in Algeria, he decided he was tired of Yeager's friends, annoyed by their cynicism. He thought of Brisson, the man's open face, his words about freedom and a new France. Brisson believed in Marcotte. He thought of the freedom fighters in Hungary. They had failed against the Soviets, but what magnificent failures. Prometheus stealing fire. And so unlike the boozy chatter of these expatriate Americans. Henry excused himself after dinner and went to the hotel. He wrote a note to Eugénie, whom he had not seen that week, went out and slid it under the door of the *pâtisserie*.

The next evening he showed up at Brisson's flat, a small, cluttered apartment near Montparnasse, unpretentious but comfortable. A dozen or so others were there, mostly people Henry didn't know and had not seen before. He had expected M.L.F. loyalists, the young men who came through the print shop or had been at rallies, but this was a different crowd, older, urbane, educated. They sat around Brisson's living room speaking casually about Marcotte, France's political problems, the Mollet government. Most were in their thirties or older. One man, gray-haired, might have been fifty; the woman next to him was a striking woman of similar age. Henry imagined her quite beautiful when she was younger. The only guest close to Henry's age was the one person he knew besides Brisson. Claude. The boy on the bridge with Eugénie, who had driven the truck to St. Denis. He now sat on a sofa beside an antique Edison phonograph. When Henry first entered the flat, waiting awkwardly just inside the door, Claude had looked up and seen him. "*Américain*," he said, his face somber.

Henry nodded just as Brisson greeted him warmly, took his arm and introduced him to the others. He never once called Henry by name. He was always *Américain*. Henry acknowledged those he met with a stiff *bon soir* and felt stupid. Brisson offered Henry a drink and motioned him to the sofa next to Claude. He sipped the drink nervously and wondered what he should do or say. But Claude took the initiative, turned and spoke directly to him in French, while the others continued their conversations.

"So, everyone is talking about you."

"Me?"

"They say the American is a beast who when aroused becomes dangerous. Is this so?"

Henry felt his hands sweat. He took another sip of what was a fine and probably expensive cognac.

"Of course not."

Claude's beady eyes and pretty face rankled him.

"Do not take offense, Henri. I mean no offense."

Henry was surprised Claude used his name.

"I mean no offense," he repeated. "I mean to congratulate you. I heard about you. It was a consecration, don't you think, the other night. The American consecrated a true partisan. A patriot for France. I will shake your hand." He reached toward him.

Henry was confused. He expected Claude's enmity. The praise baffled him. He gripped the outstretched hand. It was strong and hard. He felt a pang of admiration for Claude. He knew why Eugénie would be attracted to him.

Brisson began speaking to his guests. There was nothing inflammatory in what he said. These people weren't the ones who sat rapt at Marcotte's every utterance. They were sober and reflective, men and women of intelligence, sophistication, their conversation centered on the election of deputies to the French Chamber, the country's parliament. They seemed little different from Democrats back home in Cleveland County discussing campaign strategy. Henry was disappointed. He had expected more. Yet he was also relieved. The M.L.F. was nothing more than a political party, vote counters, campaigners. Marcotte wasn't a sinister neo-fascist, merely a brash conservative politician.

Brisson finished speaking and others spoke up, mostly to echo his ideas. When the meeting ended, some hung around to drink and talk. Claude left. So did the older couple. Henry was ready to leave as well, but Brisson cornered him.

"Well, *Américain*, what did you think?"

"Think?"

"Our discussion."

"Oh, fine, good," he stuttered.

"I thought you would like us. You're not like them, Henry. The boys who wear the armbands. You're one of us."

"Who are us?"

"Marcotte's brains."

Henry was puzzled.

"You think we are all shopkeepers and farmers?" Brisson smiled. "Dr. Reynaud is a chemist. Helene lectures in serology, and Charles, the one who was seated on the floor, is an attorney. With all respect to our brothers in the cause, shopkeepers do not elect deputies to Parliament. Marcotte's vision is more ambitious than that. This is an excellent time to be in France, Henry, believe me. We have survived shameful events in this century and allowed our cowardice to defeat us. But France still has greatness in her. You will see. Even if you are an American."

"Yes," Henry said, dumbly, as Brisson wandered away. How had he gotten himself into this conversation? Why had he even come? The attention flattered him, certainly. He was warmed by it—and by Brisson's cognac. These people weren't like Yeager's friends. They *believed* in something. They wanted to change France. But what place did he have in this? He was ready to make a polite exit when Eugénie arrived. She smiled and greeted the others as if perfectly at home here, chatting a long while with Brisson before she made her way toward

Henry.

"You like my friends?" she asked with what sounded like a giggle.

"Your friends?"

"Yes, Brisson and the others."

"Did you tell Brisson about me?"

"Of course. Everyone wants to know about you." She leaned in close and whispered in his ear. "They call you Wild Yankee."

Henry flushed.

"It is a great compliment. They do not usually like Americans. Like your Yeager friend."

He started to follow with a question, that he thought Yeager was her friend too. Instead, he let Eugénie rattle on. He loved her praise, and he'd had enough cognac to forget his shyness. If he was Wild Yankee, so be it. He put his hand on Eugénie's arm. "I was just leaving. Come with me."

"But why?"

"Because I want …" He stopped.

"You want what?"

"Because there are roses I haven't yet given you, and a hundred poems." Henry reached his arm lightly across her shoulders. Eugénie frowned as if she thought him a bit too wild, then laughed.

"You're so silly, Henri."

"Of course. I'm American."

"Yes, so American. Okay, we go."

Brisson did not seem to mind their leaving, although Eugénie had just arrived. The elevator was stuck between floors, so they walked down the stairs. He took Eugénie's hand and tugged her along. On the street, he stopped, put his arms around her and kissed her. He was surprised by the warmth of her lips. A charge zinged through his body.

"Henri, Henri," she whispered, "silly American."

"Come on."

She pulled back.

"Where?"

"My hotel."

She stopped. "No, Henri, not tonight."

He was hurt and knew she saw that in his face. "But why not?"

"It is not yet time. That will come or will not come. It depends."

"Depends on what?"

"When it is right."

"What isn't right about now?" he fumed.

She took his hand. "You go to movies, Henri?"

"Yes, sure, I go to movies."

"Then you know in American movies that a woman and man, well, things must make their way in a right manner."

He felt confused, wounded. What movies did she mean?

"Your movie stars, Doris Day, do not just fall into amour. No, they must dance slowly toward it. It is a fine tango, Henri. That is how I describe it."

He was completely lost in this conversation. He'd never seen a Doris Day movie, knew nothing about tangos. He sputtered a grumpy "Who cares?"

"But it's true. You must believe me, Henri."

He did not want to argue. He nodded in resignation and changed the subject. For a moment, he felt his hunger for Eugénie fade. Movie stars. Tangos. What happened to revolutionary fervor? Under the streetlight, she appeared plainer than he'd imagined her, her face plump and a trifle ruddy. A Paris shop girl. Doris Day! But then she grasped his arm and her magic rushed through him. He burned with desire and was mortified by his swelling penis.

"Then you'll go with me to a café?"

"Yes," she said, and happily smiled.

They soon came to a place, went in and ordered wine. He watched her across the table, bewildered. What had happened? He had felt her lips, her body against his. Was she playing with him? Because of Claude?

"Tell me about Claude," he asked.

She shook her head to shake off his question.

"No, I want to know."

"That isn't fair, Henri."

"What isn't?"

"I am here with you. Why should I talk about Claude? I want to have fun with you, laugh with my crazy American. What if you don't like what I tell you about Claude?"

"I don't care what you tell me," he lied, fearing his face betrayed him.

"Oh no? You're American tough guy, right."

"Not very tough."

"Pah. I hear from everyone, how tough you were at St. Denis. You would fight anybody."

"I probably got a little carried away." Did everyone in Paris know about that night?

"Yes, you are that way. You can fly away from yourself. Go wild. Wild Yankee."

He felt the blood flow into his face. "I'm not a wild man, Eugénie."

"What do I know?"

"Tell me about Claude." He'd had enough alcohol to insist.

"Claude is very great. He will be a great man. Like Marcotte."

Her answer unsettled him. He wanted Claude to be only a handsome punk. "Why is he great?"

"Because he is serious."

"What's that supposed to mean?"

"You don't know, Henri, because you are not serious. You are an American who is on holiday in France. Marcotte is fun for you. A grand adventure. But Claude is serious. He wants France to be great and will die for that."

Henry was sorry he'd asked. He hated this slight gypsy youth, Eugénie's praise of him. Yet he could not deny her accusations. It *was* a grand adventure. That's all. Her accusations shamed him.

"Then you love Claude?" Why did he ask that? Why did he have to ask that?

"*Oui* ... and *non*. Sometimes I hate him, he is so mean and bossy. Claude wants to rule everything. Me too. I don't like him for that. But yes I love him, of course."

"He's your lover?"

Her eyes flared angrily. "See, you are all alike. You want to own us. And I despise that. From Claude or from you, Henri."

"I'm sorry." His face burned with shame even as he hated Claude. "And what about me?" he asked, furious that he had left himself open to her answer.

"You are my good angel."

"I'm what?"

"Do you believe in fortune tellers?"

"Huh?"

The turn of conversation dismayed him. Eugénie flitted from subject to subject. This was ridiculous.

"You know, palm readers, mystics."

He wanted to pounce on this, declare heatedly that he didn't believe any such rubbish, but he shrugged instead, offering a lame, "I don't know."

"My friend at the *pâtisserie* is a fortune teller, she says so, a gypsy.

She told me I would meet a stranger who would be my angel, my guardian angel, to watch over me. She told me this only last year. Is that amazing? I think that is you, Henri. Yes, I do believe that. You are like Maurice, my brother."

"Your brother?" Eugénie had never talked about her family.

"When I was a child, my mother took us to the sea, to Nice. One day, I swam far out, but Maurice, who is younger than me, swam after me and pulled me back in. He would not let me float away. You are like that, Henri. I believe you will not let me drown, like you would not let my silly hat float away on the Seine."

"I don't know if I want to be someone's angel."

"But of course you do. You are a crazy American, Henri, but you are good. You are not serious like Claude. Claude will kill a man or be killed himself for France. He will even allow me to be killed. You would not do that."

"But that's terrible. It's evil!"

She shook her head. "No, it is heroic. And I love Claude for that, and even though I want to be, I am not heroic. I believe in Marcotte, but I do not believe I would die for him."

"Would Claude kill me?"

"Only if you are an enemy of Marcotte. If Marcotte needs you, then Claude will need you too."

Henry's confidence wavered. Did he care anything about Marcotte, the M.L.F.? Wasn't it only as Eugénie said, a grand adventure? What would happen if Claude discovered Henry Beam wasn't serious about Marcotte?

"Tell me more about Maurice," said Henry, to change the subject. He was sick of Claude.

"He is tall, taller than you. And proud. He is a student at the *lycée* with plans to go to the university. We are a poor family, but Maurice has rich men's dreams."

"Why not? I came from a poor family too."

She wrinkled her nose as if she doubted him. "Pah, you came from a poor *American* family. That is not like here."

"No, really."

"I don't believe you, Henri."

Her stubborn insistence worried him. Did she think him wealthy? All Americans as wealthy? Was that her interest in him? How would she feel if she knew that after he paid for their wine, he would be nearly broke?

Eugénie allowed him to accompany her on the Metro to her flat. She lived in an old building on a run-down street near the Gare d'Austerlitz. He left her at the outside door, but not before she let him kiss her again.

"I want to see you tomorrow." This wasn't a question but a declaration.

"Yes," she said, and sighed.

Henry wondered about the sigh.

He met her after work. This time, he brought flowers, bought with the few francs retrieved from Yeager. He walked her to the Metro. They didn't talk about politics or Marcotte or Claude. In fact, he didn't talk at all, only listened as Eugénie rattled on about a dispute with a customer in the shop. The next morning, he asked Dreux if he could work more hours for more money. Dreux shrugged, but did not say no. He seemed willing to let Henry spend as many hours as he wished culling through newspapers. Henry asked about Brisson.

"He comes around now and then," said Dreux.

As if summoned, he came later that afternoon.

"Ah, Henry, you were, what is it you say in America, you were a big hit last night."

He laughed and patted Henry's shoulder. "You wanted to see me?"

"You mentioned work for Marcotte?"

"I don't know. It will involve many hours."

Was he reneging? "I have time."

"It involves commitment."

"What kind of commitment?"

"To Renard Marcotte and the M.L.F. We do not need half-hearted soldiers."

"I've been working for Marcotte for weeks now." He heard his voice and thought it sounded weak. Time he could give. But commitment? "I write French, not perfectly, but I can."

Brisson seemed lost in thought.

"Perhaps. Perhaps we can use your talents." He wrote something on a slip of paper and handed it to Henry. "Come by here, Wednesday, after the noon hour."

"Will I get paid?"

Brisson raised his eyebrows in a silent question.

"I mean, I'm running out of money because I already give too much of my time to Marcotte." He was fumbling badly. "I have to live. I have no time to write."

"Ah." Brisson brightened. "I will talk with the others. Perhaps something can be worked out."

Henry was relieved. Brisson believed him.

"And here, an advance from me." Brisson pulled a handful of thousand franc notes from his pocket.

When he was gone, Henry counted the money. Ten thousand francs, more than twenty dollars in American money. He felt rich. When he met Eugénie after work, he invited her to dinner. She said her mother expected her home. He invited her to spend Sunday with him.

"What on Sunday?"

"I don't know. What would you like?" He felt awkward, indecisive. Why didn't he know how these things were done? He should present her with an exciting plan for the day, one so wonderful she would not turn him down.

"Movies?" he said stupidly. "Doris Day?"

"I love American movies."

"Then we'll go to the movies."

She gave him her best smile. On his way back to the hotel, Henry berated himself for how inept he was. Eugénie expected to be wooed. That's what she'd meant. A relationship must unfold. One didn't just fall into bed, the way Yeager and his friends described it. He had written poetry for her, brought flowers. But he hadn't had the money to take her places. Now he did. She deserved to go places, to be treated to wine and entertainment. Back at his hotel, he spent the evening thinking about the girl, imagining her white flesh under the billowing skirt, how her breasts must feel, how he would feel when he entered her for the first time.

They spent Sunday in theaters. If it was movies Eugénie liked, then movies it would be. They went from the matinee to an early evening show, then to a nine o'clock and finished with a midnight run. It was all American. Jane Russell in a stupid film about gypsies and a Dean Martin-Jerry Lewis comedy *The Caddy*. They ended with Doris Day in a drama about twenties' singer Ruth Etting. Insipid films, but Henry didn't care. In the dark theaters, he put his arm around Eugénie, nuzzled his face against her neck. By the last film, as Eugénie stared rapt at the screen, weeping over Doris Day's torments, Henry slipped his hand between her knees, felt her hot skin. When they came from the theatre, she leaned against him, kissing him passionately once they were on the sidewalk. Henry accompanied her to the Metro— she would not let him take her home—then went back to his hotel in a fever. He could taste Eugénie, smell her, the cheap cologne filling his nostrils. His body vibrated with love. He had never known such sensation.

He met her after work on Monday. She smiled, but he felt a distance. Perhaps he had gone too far the day before. There was a rally that evening for Marcotte. He asked if she was going. She frowned, looked uncertain.

"I don't know."

"I'll be there."

"Then perhaps I'll go."

She kissed his cheek and walked laughing away from him. He started to follow but thought better of it.

Later on, he went to Dreux's offices where the bluebands gathered. As before, they piled into a truck and bounced across the city to an outlying suburb of Paris. Henry leaned against the side of the truck and felt every bump rattle his spine. The night was cold. His eyes burned from the chimney smoke that layered the city like fog. He shivered in the cold truck. He felt for the blue armband in his pocket, let it lay limp against his fingers until he slipped it over his coat sleeve. Was this a dream? What was he doing here? For a moment, he fancied himself Hemingway behind the wheel of his ambulance in the Spanish Civil War. He told himself he had found his adventure. He glanced around the truck, at the rowdy young men. Brisson said he was not like these young toughs, that he had intelligence and education. But he didn't feel so different. They reminded him of boys in Cleveland County with their dirty hands and rough faces.

"You bring your bricks, *Américain*?" one called.

"No."

"Don't let the commies get a brick after you, ok?"

"Yeah, they give you a flathead. Right, a flathead."

"A flattop!"

They laughed, like soldiers kibitzing before a battle.

"Yeah, you get a brick to the head, it will be like the Indian scalping."

"Should have brought my tomahawk."

They joked and bantered as the truck bounced across bumpy pavements. When it stopped, they piled out at an old warehouse and were directed inside by a young troop leader called Denis. Claude had not come. A small but noisy crowd was gathered inside, mostly men, in poor fitting jackets and baggy trousers. A few women, most likely their wives, sat beside them on benches. The hall was large. Lights from the high ceiling poured garish yellow light on them, throwing eerie shadows on the floor. Henry looked for Eugénie but did not see her. He stood at the back and leaned against the wall. He was tired.

Even before Marcotte began speaking, he knew he had seen this before. The rallies rarely differed, except in the place or composition of the crowd. Some of Marcotte's men would stomp about the platform and shout M.L.F. slogans: "Kill the beast of taxation," "Marcotte power for the powerless." The crowd would cheer. When Marcotte at last strode to the stage and stood there stiffly erect, hair greased across his brow, the audience greeted him with great enthusiasm. Henry had been enchanted that first evening he heard Marcotte speak. But no longer. He braced himself against the wall and let the deep rumble of the man's voice roll over him like warm air. He kept looking for Eugénie but she never came. He rode back to the print shop with the others and walked the long distance to the hotel.

Eugénie was in the lobby, curled on an old sofa, asleep. Startled, he bent down and touched her arm. She jerked awake and stared at him, confused. He was stunned by her face, the bruise on her cheek.

She'd been crying.

He knelt beside her. "Eugénie," he whispered.

She draped her arms around him and wept on his shoulder. "Henri, Henri," she sobbed.

"What's happened?"

"I can't tell you, Henri."

"But why?"

"Because it is so unhappy." She wiped her hands across her cheeks and looked at him, as if to ask for something he didn't understand. He felt helpless, stupid.

"I was at the hospital," she explained. "An old friend. Dying. It was so terrible, there at the hospital. I came to you."

"But your cheek? You've hurt yourself."

"I stumbled."

He felt a sudden pride, that she had chosen him to console her, him and not Claude.

"Come upstairs," he told her gently.

She did not protest.

Henry put a pot of water to boil on the small hotplate he'd bought a few weeks before. He fixed her a cup of tea. Eugénie sat on the unmade bed and drank the tea in silence. She smiled at Henry while he wandered about the room deciding what to do with himself.

"Henri, come here."

When he knelt beside her, she put her hands on his face and tugged him onto the bed. Her coat flapped open and Henry caressed her blouse and under it, surprised by the warmth of her skin, how soft and velvety it felt to his fingers. Whatever had happened that evening, she seemed to have lost any will to resist him. He slipped up her blouse. She was not wearing a bra and he stared at her breasts, the dark areolae, the tiny brown mole beneath her right nipple. He could hardly breathe. He was awkward and nervous and let the girl's flesh take and teach him, burying himself within the moist warmth of her crotch. She stayed with him that night, letting him love her twice more on the rumpled bed.

Henry broke off the narrative. His eyes watered. "I suppose, Rachel," he said in a raspy voice, "that week in Paris was the most complete of my life. It had everything. Manhood and love. I was a clumsy lover. What did I know about such things? But I don't remember it that way. The dirty sheets, the messy hotel room with the peeling plaster, none of these things clutter my memory of that night. I just remember how good she smelled. How so very good."

SIXTEEN

One hundred eighty-six steps. The magic number, negotiated twice a day at the quarry, each morning going down, work done, going up. The ascent was hellish, every man forced to carry a heavy stone to the top. Some men fell or were pushed by the guards. If that failed to kill them, they were beaten to death. Survival was in the feet. The body part that broke down first, beginning with sores from moisture and injury, the poorly fitted clogs. Infection followed. Your fate is in your feet, a prisoner warned. A man unable to climb the quarry steps was doomed. René judiciously washed his feet when allowed time at the water spigot, drying them thoroughly afterwards. He took special care with cuts or breaks in the skin, covering these with scrounged scraps of cloth and paper, no matter how tiny or soiled, sometimes tearing a scrap from the hem of his trousers.

92 days. An anniversary. He had surpassed the average lifespan for a quarry worker. 92 days and counting, each day like the one before it, noted by a scratch etched each morning with his spoon handle on the wall under his bed. Most of the men in his block were French, but there were also Spaniards, Poles, Scandinavians, Dutchmen, Hungarians, and one American. Few were friendly, many prisoners having retreated into themselves. Two prisoners, veterans who had survived a year, offered René counsel. The only goal left a man here, said one, is to stay alive. René took the man's advice to heart, though the prisoner who gave it died a week later. René learned to take short rests when quarry guards looked elsewhere. At the end of a day's

work, when forced with the others to haul a heavy stone up the long steps, René sought out the lightest he could find, one with a chipped corner or chunk gouged from its side.

If a man died in the barracks, other prisoners descended like vultures on his effects, fighting over anything of worth, a better fitting pair of pants, his bowl or spoon, his shoes. René would stand by until the frenzy abated, then scavenge through what was left for remnants of cloth or paper. Following one of these deaths, René found a stub of pencil, clutched in the dead man's hand. It was then he began to write things down if he found himself with an extra paper scrap. Mostly these were lists, the nationalities of men in his barracks, the meager items doled out to each prisoner, types of vermin that shared their barracks. He listed the many ways men died in this place, describing the onset and progression of diseases.

Pediculi defecate when they feed. Scratching rubs feces into puncture. Pediculi attach to clothing. Eggs attached through excretion. Nits form. At normal body temperature, eggs hatch 1 week. Cold delays process, sometimes month. Typhus rickettsiae in pediculi feces.

Eruptions 4th or 5th day. Chills, weakness, headache, pain in limbs. Eruptions on shoulders, torso, extend to extremities, backs of hands, feet. Rarely on face. First eruptions pink spots, disappear on pressure. Spots turn purple, brownish red. Fade into brown. Fever rises. Brown coat on tongue. Delirium.

Consumption. Cough is dry, becomes purulent.

Gas gangrene (clostridium welchii). Sudden pain in wound. Tachycardia, fever, edema, watery discharge. Odor slight at onset. Grows foul. Crepitation spreads from wound. Gas bubbles.

As weeks passed, René learned other things that made him wonder why he bothered with his feet or the worthless notes. Inmates told of the group of Jews months ago that had clasped hands and leaped from the mountainside into the quarry. Suicide was as prevalent in the camp as murder. Prisoners starved themselves to death or threw themselves against the electrified fence, expecting the guards would shoot them if they failed to reach the fence. Free choice, a veteran prisoner croaked with what René took for a laugh.

René believed the choice had been made for him, certainly so after the veteran prisoners' somber advice that was impossible to follow: get off the quarry detail. Few survived the Ditch past three months, they told him. But René knew what happened to him was not his choice to make. It had been chosen for him years ago. He counted the days and waited for the inevitable. Yet, he seemed unable to shed the disquiet that there was something ignoble about most deaths here, bodies hauled each day from the quarry, corpses of men who dropped where they stood, tools or stones in their hands. What meaning was there to such a death, like that of an ant crushed underfoot? He was already inured to them, stepping over corpses like debris in his path. He did not want to be one of these corpses.

Perhaps this was why René continued to survive when others did not. He survived malnutrition and the cruel nights when he woke trembling from ghastly dreams, vowing to throw himself against the electric fence in the morning and end his torment. He survived the onerous work of the quarry, the long hours and heavy stones, the days of rain when the quarry steps became treacherous. Even on dry days, the steps were a peril, slick with men's sweat and sometimes blood. Once he nearly slipped on several tiny hard pellets. When he looked closely he saw human teeth scattered on the step.

René seldom talked with other prisoners beyond what was needed for work and living together. Prison inmates were made to address each other by number. Names were used only out of a guard's hearing. One day a prisoner, an Englishman, spoke to René. A downed pilot, he was a young man in his twenties, though prison had aged him. The two men often worked beside each other in the quarry. On a piss break, when the kapo turned his back, the man asked René in broken French if he were a communist. He nodded toward the red triangle on René's uniform.

I am not, René answered in English.

His English surprised the man. You're not a communist? he asked again.

No.

Resistance?

No.

Then why are you here?

A mistake.

Hell of a bloody mistake, the prisoner rasped, coughing to cover his words.

René did not respond.

There were few Englishmen in the prison. This man's name, he later learned, was Cooke, but René never called him that. Like René, Cooke was a good worker, despite the near starvation that consumed the prisoners' muscle and strength. Cooke could still lift heavy rocks, although he avoided doing so when he could. The kapos tended to leave him alone. He had connections, René soon learned, even if these connections had not brought him a transfer from the quarry. Working on it, he told René one day at the lunch break.

The kapos left René alone too. This was not because of connections. Something about René inhibited the guards' usual cruelty. They did not slam his shoulders with heavy rubber hoses or kick and beat him.

Although they constantly barked orders at him, they seldom called him swine or bastard. Perhaps this was because of his strength and diligence. The kapo who oversaw his quarry section called René *Der Mystiker*, The Mystic. René did not understand this and thought it was meant as a joke. But if the kapo left him alone, he did not care what he was called. Cooke said René spooked the kapo, the fixed gaze with which he responded to orders or questions. Prisoners were required to keep their heads bowed when they addressed a superior. René tried to remember this but often forgot.

The kapo who called him The Mystic sometimes gave René special privileges. René was grateful for the extra chunk of bread or spoonful of soup at lunchtime, though the favors troubled him. What was the reason for them? He recalled the seminary, how they had tricked him in order to expel him. René didn't want to profit from a kapo's favor. Usually, he slipped the extra food to Cooke or another prisoner. Sometimes the kapo smuggled him a cigarette or square of chocolate. This terrified him more. Would the others think him a collabo? Prisoners were executed by their fellows in dark corners of the prison or shoved against the fence for such things. Except for the cigarettes, which he could not bear to give up, smoking them behind the latrine in the late afternoons, he turned the rest over to Cooke to use in his network.

One evening René was accosted by a prisoner at the latrine. The man grabbed René's shirt, twisted it in a garrote about his neck and pulled him away from the guards' sight. He tightened his grip. René began to choke.

Give me, the man said in French.

René did not know what was wanted. With the man's hands around his neck, he was unable to ask and instead gurgled and sputtered.

Give me, he ordered again. Cigarettes.

René nodded and tried to reach in his waistband for the cigarette handed him that day by the quarry kapo. The man slapped his hand away and found it himself. He released René with a warning. Tell and I will kill you. René stared at the man. He looked like every other prisoner. With their shaved heads and gaunt faces, one prisoner became indistinguishable from the next. But after that day, the man became quite familiar. He became René's tormentor. He would appear at the latrine or on one of the mud streets between barracks, sometimes before roll call to force cigarettes from him.

René told Cooke. The Englishman counseled patience. He knew the man, a Frenchman, though tagged by the prisoners with the nickname Krake, after the legendary Norse sea monster with its taste for human blood. Krake had allies among the SS. René was not the only prisoner the man tormented. There were others in his barracks who feared him for other reasons. But René knew no way to avoid Krake. The man had power.

Wait, Cooke told René. We will find a way.

Krake became a dark shadow on René's life. After he had endured months of hunger and the slave labor of the quarry, the leering face of Krake threatened any possibility of René's survival. The man sensed René's fear and added to the torments. One day, when he cornered René at the latrine to extort a cigarette, he ground his wooden clog into René's foot. René fought hard to squelch a scream. But the scream echoed in his brain. Not from pain but terror. What would happen if Krake broke his toes? A man who cannot walk cannot work. A sentence of death. In the barracks, René curled in a corner to massage his swollen foot with his hands. For the first time since he had been imprisoned, he brooded over what had happened to him.

He had entered this evil fortress like a paralyzed man, no more than a toy tin soldier, who could be moved about however his captors chose. If the guards berated him, he bore their words as just. If they favored him, like the quarry kapo, he bore that too. And when he was tormented, as Krake now tormented him, he did not defend himself or protest, believing the torment was deserved. Yet it angered him to have this sadistic man decide his fate. He did not want to give in to him. No matter the pain to his foot, he decided, he would have to ignore it when he made the treacherous descent to the quarry floor and when he hiked back up.

The camp had barracks for the sick and injured, an infirmary and *Das Krankenlager*, the sick camp, but René had been warned against these. Better to die in the quarry, prisoners said, than allow SS doctors to get hold of you. Prisoners told grisly stories: sick prisoners murdered with injections of magnesium chloride or benzene. Worse were the medical experiments that left men dying unanesthetized on operating tables, their vital organs exposed and sometimes cut into. Every prisoner knew about the dissection table in the basement of the bunker near the execution chambers.

As René pondered his dilemma, it came clear to him this was his fault. In the confusion of the ride on the train, the frantic first weeks of molding himself into the prison routine, he had ignored the meaning of this terrible journey. He had not been brought to this place to survive. He had come to die. Why had he forgotten that? God had been displeased with him for years. Yet René had told the man writing on the white card that this was a mistake. But there was no mistake. He had tried to pervert the justice of it and survive, taken special favors from a guard, hoarded cigarettes given to him. Had Krake been sent to remind him of this truth? But even as he understood that truth, he did not know what to do. That night in his dreams, a familiar voice called to him and he awoke rested. As he limped to the quarry, he felt almost happy. The day was warm. The spring sun shone brightly in a blue sky.

He ignored the pain in his foot and fixed his attention on descending the steps without a limp.

In the afternoon as he hoisted heavy stones, he imagined he heard singing. Was he dying? He raised his head and saw other prisoners glancing up. Through the noise of picks and the rattle of carts came a sweet, ethereal sound, the familiar words of the *Ave Maria*. René sought the source and found it: a prisoner standing on a pile of rock, his voice transporting René to the parish church at Orleans where as a boy he had believed the arms of Christ had reached out to him. He recognized the singer, everyone did, a Jewish youth, favored by both prisoners and guards, whose superb choirboy soprano often greeted them from loud speakers as they marched to and from their work details. Now he was singing for them alone, the quarry workers, as if to ease their agonies. The prisoners paused to listen.

René crossed himself and prayed under his breath, thanking God for the momentary reprieve. The youth sang on. The men returned to work, until an explosion shattered the quarry's altered atmosphere. Heads jerked up. The rocks beneath the Jewish youth had collapsed in a shower of stone and dust. The prisoners, although hardened by their captors' cruelty, appeared truly stunned by this atrocious act. A silence settled over the quarry, broken by a strange sound close to where René stood. He looked and saw a man, not twenty feet from him, bent over a dynamite plunger, his hands gripping it as if glued, his face grotesque with laughter. René stared. The man wore a curious uniform, not the striped suit of a prisoner but a parody of the SS Death's Head uniform, the jacket fastened by rough wooden buttons, shoulders adorned with striped epaulets made from prisoners' cloth. His hair, though now growing in, was ragged as if once shaved with a Hitler Street across his scalp. At the edge of his hairline glowed a rosy pigmentation in the shape of a heart. René knew that heart. A man with such a birthmark had once been in his prison block, a prisoner like himself. In the horror of that moment, the image of the man's face, the rosy birthmark, the mouth wide with laughter, burrowed into René's brain, where he knew it would reside until his final breath.

René spent the next week in a stupor. He went through the motions of work, but he no longer cared if a guard shouted at him or threatened to strike him. He did not care if he died. Perhaps it was Cooke who saw how his will had crumbled and set about with a remedy. Perhaps it was the guard who called him The Mystic who became his benefactor. He never knew. But two weeks later, he was transferred to a new work detail, to the stables where the camp *Kommandant* and SS kept their horses. Here the work, though hard, was a holiday compared to the quarry. The stables offered René life rather than the certain death of the quarry. But he did not want life. The scene from the quarry, the Jewish boy on the rocks, the man with his hand on the plunger, his laughter, tormented him. He dreamed them at night, heard the boy scream for René to save him. In daylight, he imagined how he might have run the short yards to the plunger, thrown his weight against the man to abort the terrible act. But always, even in his imagination, he never moved. Each time, the earth collapsed and the boy again vanished in a shower of stone. What had happened? He had believed God meant to free him from his torments but now God had added more. He went about the work at the stables in a daze. Here, there was no friendly guard, no one who called him The Mystic. Several times, he was badly beaten, though he barely felt the pain. It no longer mattered.

One day, when René's Block lined up for evening roll call, the guards began furiously shouting. There had been an escape. Two prisoners were missing. The other prisoners were made to stand at attention in the *Appellplatz*. The roll was called twice, four times. They were given no supper. The prisoners remained where they stood.

The camp was searched, the roll called again, and again. Even though counted by Block, the thousands of numbers took an agonizing time. No one was found. Beyond the walls, the sharp yelp of dogs echoed in the night. Hours passed. Prisoners fainted in the ranks. Those who fell were beaten and carried away. Long after midnight, the gates of the prison opened and SS guards hauled two bodies into the yard, dumping them before the prisoners, the corpses riddled with bullet holes. An SS officer, known to terrorize prisoners, strutted before the exhausted inmates. His face was red in the searchlights as he huffed and shrieked. One of our brothers was killed by these swine. Like an animal, strangled. They put their filthy hands on him. These are the murderers you protect. No, not just protect, you encourage them. You are all accomplices.

He ranted for another hour. More men fainted. Finally, his voice quieted as he walked the length of the yard, almost purring when he said, some of you need special instruction in how to conduct yourselves. He ordered a team of SS riflemen in their spotless Death's Head uniforms to line up at the far end of the yard. Then, seemingly at random, he selected a single block of prisoners, Block 13. René's block. Thirteen, a lucky number tonight, the SS officer laughed. He positioned the riflemen directly in front of the lines from René's barracks. Count off, he ordered, 1 to 10. Every tenth man forward. There was no need to explain. They knew what this meant. Every tenth man would be summarily executed. René, like every prisoner in his line, glanced left and counted. What was his number? 1, 2, and down the line. It was then René understood. Here was what he had waited for. He counted again. There was no mistake. His number would be ten. In the front row, prisoners began the oral count. Most shouted out their numbers. Except for those whose number was ten. Those men seldom uttered a sound as they staggered or were pushed forward. The count continued as time stretched on, slowly, a minute becoming forever. Or so it seemed before the count reached René's row. He checked again, quickly recounted the line. Nothing had changed. One, two, three, four— a man ten down from him stumbled forward, face contorted with terror. The count resumed. In his mind, René heard the familiar voice of his dreams, summoning him. There was love in that voice, and music. René's face shone. Six, seven, eight—he straightened. At last. Nine—

SEVENTEEN
Seventeen

$\mathcal{H}$*ow good she smelled. How so very good.* When Rachel thought about Henry's words, which she thought about often, her eyes filled. He had never mentioned any women in his life before Eugénie, high school or college girlfriends, only that he had been married twice—and then only after Paris and the publication of *A Stone for Bread.* But the innocence and wonder with which he described making love to Eugénie had left her agitated and sent her into a grouchy funk. Her own sexual initiation seemed adolescent, even tawdry—heavy petting in the back seats of cars, fingers probing moist places in movie theaters, her virginity lost in the bathroom of her best friend's house at a high school party after she'd had too much to drink. If she tried, she could remember the boy's name but not what he looked like. Even now, every guy who took her out, and more asked than she accepted, expected to crawl in bed with her by the second date. Occasionally she let one come up to her apartment after an especially pleasurable evening, when conversation and dinner, the alcohol had aroused her hunger for intimacy, for hands touching her body, each time with a vague hope that in the coupling she might again find love, as she had once loved Randy. But she seemed destined for disappointment. Maybe Eugénie hadn't been so wrong about how a relationship should evolve.

And Henry—there was something fine and tender in the way he spoke of this love affair with Eugénie. Rachel forgave him everything that had come before—the brick, Marcotte, Marcotte's thugs. As he was leaving her apartment that night, he had embraced her, not a lover's embrace but more a hug of gratitude that she had indulged his recounting of the story, that she hadn't laughed or demeaned it. For a moment, she'd lingered in his hug and felt safe.

He had ended the evening with an invitation to hike through the woods at his place the next Saturday afternoon. But on Wednesday, Scott called. "I'm editing the documentary. Should be done by Friday or Saturday. A rough cut anyway. Thought you might want to see it. It's not so bad. Particularly the party. What the hell did you slip in Henry's drink?"

"I would love to see the video."

"How about Saturday?"

"Sunday's better."

"I have to be in Raleigh Sunday and I'm hung up Friday."

"Maybe I can rearrange things. Is Henry invited?"

"Why not? Though he probably won't like it, but I'll give him a call."

"No, I'll call him."

"Okay."

Henry declined but agreed to postpone the hike until the next day. "You can tell me then if my TV debut is Emmy-worthy."

It was nice to hear him laugh.

She met Scott at the station Saturday afternoon. They sat in swivel chairs in front of several monitors in the editing suite. The video was ninety-nine percent complete, Scott said. All that was needed were the titles. She knew Scott was good at his job, but she was impressed with how he had interwoven snippets from Henry's taped interview and his recitations of poetry into an arresting narrative. Of course, the party had provided him more exciting footage. The musical underscoring worked exceedingly well too, she thought, contemporary instruments with a plaintive Celtic sound.

"You've done a wonderful job, Scott," she said after they'd watched the whole piece. "I think even Henry will like it."

"Probably not," he said. "It's not boring enough."

"You'd be surprised. Henry is far more interesting than you think."

He raised his eyebrows, curious. "Did you get the *Stone for Bread* scoop?"

"No, but I've learned a lot about him."

"Well ...?"

"I can't talk about it now. Maybe at some point I'll be able to. But I suggest you save your footage, even the outtakes."

EIGHTEEN
Eighteen

He nearly ran off the road on his way home from Chapel Hill, that night with Eugénie as alive in his mind as if they'd made love only hours ago. And Rachel—holding her, her body pressed against his, he had hardly been able to let his arms drop to his sides. When he reached the farmhouse, he did what he had not done in years; he slumped on the couch and wept into his hands like a boy. He had never before told anyone about that night. Even now, he wasn't certain why he had told Rachel. Yes, there were things about her that reminded him of Eugénie, her hair, its lustrous auburn color, some of her gestures. But Rachel was as different from Eugénie as two women could be. Rachel was educated and highly intelligent. Their conversation about books and literature had stirred another of his lost passions; he hadn't had such a conversation in years, not since graduate school, and in those days his innate shyness had held him back from gusty forays into books and literary criticism among his fellow students.

Rachel's sophistication limited itself to certain areas, the culinary arts not among them. He knew that her uncertainty about her present direction in life bothered her. She had told him she intended to teach, possibly continue in grad school for a Ph.D. But she seemed less than excited about any of this. He sensed a drift in her that worried her, recalling a tossed-off statement earlier that evening that she wasn't a twenty-something any more and needed to settle. He had sympathized or tried to. Only later did he realize his own heart was far from settled at this moment of his life, as his poem "Going Gentle" might imply. Damn settling anyway! He'd spent the last thirty years settled. He rose from the couch and opened a bottle of his best wine, drank it down, slowly, tearfully, an old man crying in his cups. Where had he been for so many years?

He declined Rachel's invitation to view the documentary. He did not want to see himself on video. These past months, his thoughts had bent themselves back to Paris. He had no interest in the old and overweight man he'd become. They had postponed the walk a day, and Rachel drove out to his place early Sunday afternoon. As they strolled along the path he had cut through the old farmstead, he resumed his story of Paris. He didn't rush into the telling. He allowed himself to enjoy the sunny afternoon, the scent of pine and the dank, dark earth, the smell of smoke curling from his chimney. And the young woman beside him, listening to him, lovely in suede jacket and tight jeans, her auburn hair blown about her face. If only he could be a young man, he thought, if only—he stifled a sigh and returned to the time when he actually was.

That same week, after the wondrous night in his hotel room, the banality of life reasserted itself. He needed money. So he reported to the address Brisson had given him. As he stood before a door in an office building near the Eiffel Tower, he wondered if he had come to the right place. The brass placard on the fine oak door declared this to be the offices of a rug importer. He checked the address a second time before he opened the door to a room with four desks and two tables. A young man worked over a ledger at the nearest desk. Through an open doorway, Henry could see an inner room filled with rolls of carpet. The clerk, a florid faced young man, looked up, squinting curiously at him.

"I was sent," Henry mumbled. "Brisson."

The clerk nodded and rose from the desk. "Just a moment," he said, then went off through the open door. Minutes later, he returned with Brisson.

"Henry," the man greeted him, smiling and offering his hand. "I'm glad you came." He led Henry through the room with its stacks of rolled carpets to a closed door in back. Henry heard voices. When Brisson opened the far door, Henry nearly gasped out loud. Claude was the first person he saw, seated at a round mahogany table. Was this a trap? Because of Eugénie? But the younger man seemed oblivious to Henry's discomfort. He nodded and smiled. Henry felt his stomach swirl. There was one other person at the table, a man Henry didn't know, an obese man with thinning hair and a thick brush of moustache. He was dressed in what appeared to Henry to be an expensive suit. They were never introduced. As soon as Brisson waved Henry to a seat and sat down himself, the three men resumed their conversation in French, as if Henry weren't even there. They were discussing an M.L.F. newspaper. Henry conjured images of Eugénie, naked on his bed, his hands stroking her soft skin, his mouth on her nipples.

"You, Henry, that's what we need you for."

"What? What did you say?"

"A liaison, Henry, between the English and French press. Such as your friend, this Yeager."

Henry wondered why these men knew Yeager. But he asked no questions.

"A strong movement needs a strong press."

"But why the English-language press?"

"Preparation," the stranger explained. "We are small now, but when Marcotte assumes power, we will need the English press."

"As I told you, Henry, we have grand ambitions for France."

Brisson smiled.

The others continued to talk among themselves. Henry glanced about the room, so incongruous to what he knew of Marcotte. The office was plushly furnished, a gleaming mahogany desk near the wall, the mahogany table at the center. The chairs were also mahogany. On the walls hung impressionist paintings, oil paintings, copies surely, not genuine Monets or Pissarros, but artists mimicking their styles. He had never seen these particular paintings before, either in museums or art books. A framed photograph sat on the desk, the head and shoulders of a man in tan ducks and safari jacket. He was possibly as old as sixty, but handsome with a broad masculine face and Roman nose. He wasn't smiling. His eyes fixed on the camera, as if daring it to take an unflattering photograph. Henry guessed he must own the company.

The three men finally seemed to remember Henry. Brisson told him to report back in the morning then dismissed him. That was all. Again the vague disappointment. Where was the romance? The tanks in the street, the Molotov cocktails? Was revolution always so bland ?

But why should he care? It was Eugénie who now filled his thoughts. He continued to meet her after work. Sometimes they went to his hotel and made love. Sometimes they made love in the back room of the *pâtisserie*, at midday, when the owners were away. They made love in other more daring, out of the way places, once in the Père Lachaise Cemetery under the cedars ringing the tombs of the French monk Abelard and his lover and wife Hélöise. Each day was a step for Henry into the unknown. Some days, he woke with a pain in his stomach or a spasm of fear in his chest. What would he do if Eugénie tired of him? When she discovered he wasn't rich? He worried about his deepening involvement with the M.L.F.

But always there was Eugénie, a light beckoning him forward. He smelled her in his dreams, tasted her, felt the heat of her skin like unguent to his soul. He had never before been in love. But now he loved, doted, craved, hungered. He would have done anything for Eugénie's touch, her body, her esteem and love. Sometimes at Marcotte rallies, his love for Eugénie flowed from his heart to embrace the crowds, the music, the shouting red-faced merchants, the smell of cheap perfume or the oily heat of a warehouse furnace. He loved Marcotte. His voice soothed his fears. The world would be better. Marcotte would make it better. Without violence or hatred and fear, and in their place would be love—and Eugénie.

The young bluebands regarded Henry now with amusement, an American M.L.F. They teased him and had their comrades take snapshots of them standing next to him, fists clinched in the air. He was their good luck charm, their mascot. Though some had seen him tossing bricks at the St. Denis rally, few thought him maliciously violent. The first nickname they'd given him "Wild Yankee" had failed to stick, and they were soon calling him "Bear," a gentle fellow, so long as no one riled him. Don't steal his honey, they joked, clapping Henry on the back. Soon, the bluebands took him with them everywhere. André, a stubby eighteen-year-old from Arles, presented Henry with a stout billy club like the other bluebands carried hidden under their coats. "An anointing, Henri," laughed André, tapping both his shoulders with the club like a king to his vassal.

These weeks, most of the M.L.F. activities seemed aimless and to little effect. They piled into dilapidated trucks and drove across Paris to parks and plazas for outdoor rallies where few people came. The indoor rallies were better attended as the weather grew colder. The job of the bluebands, Henry learned, was to remain alert for outbursts that might spark fights or riots, to scan the area around the outdoor parks for strangers, observers who could be Communists or other political enemies. There had been no further attacks, although tensions had not abated but increased. M.L.F. posters were defaced and torn down. Cars might slowly circle an outdoor square. Rocks were tossed against the sides of their truck.

Henry was spending less time in the print shop now and more hours working for Brisson. He wasn't certain what Brisson wanted from him. Most of the time he ran errands, carried posters and messages from the rug company to flats and offices in various parts of Paris. Sometimes he translated press releases into English but never knew what became of them. He saw Marcotte only from a distance at rallies. He did not see Claude. At Brisson's urging, he spoke to Bert Yeager about an article on Marcotte, an exclusive on Marcotte's political ideas. Yeager seemed bored by the suggestion, but having done little work in recent weeks, he agreed. Henry spent even less time with Yeager and his friends these days. He passed Yeager in the corridors of the hotel, where they chatted casually, usually about Yeager's frustrations with his work and lack of money. Once, he asked Henry about the novel, how it was going. Henry stared, puzzled, until he remembered his earlier lie. Nodding noncommittally, he answered, "Slowly. You know how these things are."

He waited for Yeager to ask about Eugénie, but he didn't. Whether Yeager knew about his relationship to the girl or not, Henry didn't care. He avoided Yeager and his peevish friends now, chose new cafés and restaurants away from St. Germain where he did not expect to see them. Once he spied Rice on the street, but Rice walked past quickly as if he hadn't noticed Henry. Because of Marcotte, thought Henry. He knows what I'm up to, the damn commie. He felt a stab of shame.

During the Christmas season, work for the M.L.F. slowed. Marcotte, someone said, was vacationing in the provinces. Even Eugénie was away, gone with her mother and brother to be with relatives in Arles. Henry spent Christmas by himself, his loneliness eased by knowing Eugénie would return before New Year's. They had talked about going away a few days, leaving Paris. Henry had money for that now. Brisson paid him well.

"Where do you want to go?" Henry had asked.

"To a grand hotel on the Mediterranean," she said, teasing him.

"Why not, then? I mean it may not be a *grand* grand hotel. But why not the Mediterranean?"

"To Nice? We could go to Nice?"

"We'll do that. When you return from Arles."

Christmas Day, Henry slept late, went to Notre Dame and sat in the back during a Christmas Mass. He found a Chinese restaurant open near the Sorbonne and ordered the costliest item on the menu—duck. It was the most splendid meal he had ever eaten. Americans, most likely tourists, a family of four, sat at a nearby table, husband and wife and two small children. They were well dressed and the father spoke fluent French to the waiter. Henry felt the first pangs of loneliness. Christmas had always been lonely for him. His father had usually spent the day drinking, while his mother was off to her relatives. As a boy he had never thought much about it. Christmas was not supposed to be a special day. But now, as he unobtrusively gazed at these Americans, he longed to be like them, to have a home and family and special holiday celebrations. He finished his dinner and went to the hotel and spent the rest of the day reading poetry, something he had not done in months. He felt the old urge to write but never got around to it. He stretched on the bed and slept, waking around midnight, then left the hotel and wandered along the Quai St. Michel, found a café and drank wine until he was groggy.

Brisson contacted him the next day, calling the hotel. He asked Henry to come by his flat. Henry was glad for something to do.

"I hear you are going to travel," said Brisson, when Henry was seated on his couch.

Henry nodded, startled. What had Eugénie told him?

"It will be useful for us." Brisson smiled.

Henry was in a surly mood. He had awakened with a headache from the wine. "It's a holiday."

"Of course, and a special one at that."

Henry bristled. What business to him was Henry's private life? Why did he even know about the trip? Brisson ignored Henry's annoyance, explaining that Nice was an important city for the M.L.F.

"We have strong supporters there. I would like you to take them a message from us."

Henry did not reply. He stared at the toes of his shoes.

"A letter, Henry."

Why don't you mail it? he wanted to shout.

Brisson held out a thin, brown envelope. Begrudgingly, Henry took it.

"Here is the address." He handed him a piece of paper torn from a note pad. "Please deliver it within twenty-four hours of your arrival in Nice."

Henry left Brisson's flat fuming and angry. There were times when this game of conspirator excited him, made him feel like an actor in a grand drama. But this wasn't such a time. Brisson had injected the M.L.F. into his private life—his relationship to Eugénie. How did he even know about the trip? Only Eugénie could have told him. Which made him angrier. Why had she told anyone, particularly Brisson? Sometimes he felt the M.L.F. was a monstrous octopus with tentacles that would drag him to the bottom of the sea. At least, Brisson had eased some of Henry's anger with a wad of franc notes. "Enjoy your holiday," he smiled happily as he'd walked Henry to the door.

They took the train to Nice. Except for short trips to outlying suburbs and towns with the M.L.F., Henry had not yet been out of Paris. He exulted in the excursion, reveling in the sights of French villages and farmlands beyond the train window. Though it was winter, they passed fields sown in rye, bright green against the drab earth. They rode second class in a cramped compartment with a family of six. After a while, the wiggling and crying of small children grated on Henry. He walked to the WC and back to exercise his stiff legs. Eugénie laughed and teased him. She seemed quite at home on the train. She had dressed in her best suit, a small blue hat perched on her head, cheap perfume splashed on her face and throat. Its pervasive smell threatened Henry's stomach. But Eugénie ignored his discomfort, reigning over the crowded compartment like a queen, admonishing the children to keep their feet off the seats and instructing the frustrated mother in discipline. The father, a gray young man in his early thirties like Henry, left the compartment to the women and children and spent his time between cars, his head and shoulders thrust through the open window.

The city of Nice was warmer than Paris but wasn't the sunny tropics. It was winter and the wind was chill. They found a small hotel some blocks from the sea. From the window of their room, they saw nothing but other hotels. They were on the sixth floor and peered out on rooftops where articles of clothing, odd socks, women's panties, a man's white undershirt, clung to the red tiles, having fallen apparently from balconies of the neighboring hotel. When they had unpacked, Henry went down to the street and the shops, returning with wine and bread, sausages and a hunk of Brie. They spent their first evening in Nice walking the promenade by the Mediterranean, then ate a late dinner in the small restaurant off the hotel lobby. Henry's spirits rose. He thought of the American family in the Chinese restaurant in Paris. Here in Nice, he and Eugénie were family, husband and wife. They

A Stone for Bread

might have been honeymooners or a young married couple thinking about their first child. In the soft light of the hotel restaurant, Eugénie's face glowed.

It wasn't until the next morning that he remembered Brisson's letter. He mentioned it to Eugénie. She shrugged and told him to deliver it while she washed her hair.

"How did Brisson know we were coming here?" he asked, though he knew the answer.

"I told him."

"Do you work with Brisson?" He wondered why he hadn't asked that before.

"I believe in Marcotte, Henri. You know that."

That was all she would say, but his suspicions soured Henry's mood. Did Eugénie truly care about him or did all this have to do with Marcotte? But he had been the one to suggest the trip. Eugénie had only suggested the place. Henry invited her to go with him to take the letter. She begged off and repeated she must wash her hair. He went alone, walking to save money and easily found the address, a small grocery located near the train station. He introduced himself to the grocer, who motioned him through a door into the back. He was in a storeroom, among barrels and crates of groceries. The room was dark and smelled of cured meat and an acrid odor Henry couldn't identify. He felt ridiculous, a character in a B movie. It would not have surprised him had police broken through the door to arrest him. But when the door opened, in came a short man with a gray moustache, who might have been a clerk or bureaucrat. The entire time he spoke with Henry, he fiddled with the cuffs of his shirt, twirling what appeared to be mother-of-pearl cuff links between his fingers.

"You are the American, I believe," he addressed Henry in heavily accented English.

"Yes, but I speak French," he answered in English.

"I try my English." The man grinned. Henry immediately disliked him. There was something obsequious about him and his ever-fidgety hands.

"You have the letter?"

Henry took the envelope from his coat pocket.

The man looked at it and held it to the only light in the storeroom, a single bulb on a frayed cord from the ceiling.

"Yes," he mumbled to himself.

Henry turned to leave.

"Wait, Monsieur."

"What for?"

"There is something other. M. Brisson wants this to Paris."

Henry wondered what *this* was. "Brisson didn't tell me that."

The man shrugged. "Only a package." He rummaged behind a barrel in the storeroom and came up with a square box wrapped in brown postal paper.

"It goes your suitcase, yes?"

"I suppose." Henry was furious. He had come for a holiday, to make love to Eugénie, not enter into this charade of revolutionaries among the flour barrels. He found the little man, the mother-of-pearl cuff links, the smelly storeroom with the single frayed light cord odious. Henry took the package. "What's in it?" It was heavy.

"Books."

Henry did not believe him. The M.L.F. weren't literary men. The man noticed Henry's skeptical face. "What you call bookkeepers."

"What?"

"Oh, eh, you know the word."

"Ledgers?"

"Yes, yes, leeshur. And papers."

"For Brisson?"

The man nodded and patted Henry's arm. Henry felt assaulted. He started to protest when the man reached into his pocket for his wallet. He thrust a handful of notes toward Henry.

"Bus expense, eh?"

Henry took the notes, pocketed them and stuck the package under his arm. It felt heavier than ledgers.

"Only ledgers and papers?"

"*Oui.*"

Henry left the store, grateful to be in bright sunlight. He touched the wad of franc notes in his pocket and felt prosperous. His worries eased. It was only an errand. If he was to be used as a courier for Marcotte, so be it. He was well paid. He spent a franc note for a taxi to the hotel. On the way, he studied the package in his lap. It was wrapped in paper and tied with string. He might easily untie the string, but the paper was sealed with glue. If he tried to open it, he could always reseal it. He shook it gently, but it was packed so tightly nothing inside moved or slid against the side. It *could* be ledgers. Maybe French ledgers had thicker covers. But what was so important about ledgers that they needed to be transported by courier? Unless the information recorded in them was important.

When he got back to the hotel. Eugénie was on the bed, her hair wrapped in a towel.

"What is that?" She pointed to the package that Henry set on the dresser.

"Something for Brisson."

"So they make you an errand boy?"

Henry shrugged, annoyed by the way she said this.

"So what is it?"

"I don't know. Ledgers or something."

Eugénie got up from the bed and picked up the package. "It's heavy." She shook it. "Why don't we open it?" She pulled at the string. "No!"

Henry grabbed the package. She stared astonished. He had not meant to shout.

"You think it is dynamite?" she teased, the taunt obvious in her voice.

"I don't know what it is," he snapped. "The guy said ledgers, so I suppose it's ledgers. But I'm not supposed to ask those questions."

"Because you must be a good boy and do what they tell you."

They were both angry.

"You got me into this, Eugénie," he fumed. "You told them we were coming to Nice." He was hot. Didn't she understand, he wanted to shout, that Brisson paid him for these errands? That because of Brisson he could afford this trip, afford their meals and the hotel. It wasn't a grand hotel, not grand at all, but they were here, and he wanted to be here. They were together. Brisson's money made it possible. He didn't say these things, of course. But his face must have said them for him.

"Poor boy," Eugénie said, suddenly sympathetic.

He felt stupid. He had acted like a boy, a frightened child. What had happened when Eugénie reached for the string? The silly rendezvous at the grocery, the dark storeroom. Did he believe he'd become an actual conspirator? Eugénie had laughed, asked if he expected the package to contain dynamite. Maybe it did. Dynamite or bullets, or hand grenades. But that wasn't his real fear. No, his real fear was that he would find truth in that box. The truth of what he had let himself be sucked into. Ledgers were fine. Innocuous. Benign. Even silly. This wasn't wartime. He wasn't in the Resistance. He was a flunky for a two-bit politician. But what if it wasn't ledgers? Truth, that was something else.

He went to the window. "Eugénie, I love you," he said, the first time he had admitted it aloud. "I want this to be a good time for us."

"Love is always a good time," she said, gaily. She put her hands around his waist. "My funny Henry. You must promise me one thing."

He waited, afraid what she might ask.

"You must not become serious."

"Of course not," he said and wondered how anyone kept from becoming serious. Love was serious. Life was serious. What Eugénie wanted of him was impossible.

The next two days went quickly. Henry tried to enjoy the time, enjoy Eugénie, but her warm skin and a blue sky over the Mediterranean did nothing to erase his worrisome doubts. The box tied in string sat on the dresser like a finger pointed at him. Was it a bomb? Would it explode and kill them? Henry tried not to brood, but he couldn't help it. If Eugénie noticed, she never said. She coaxed him into excellent restaurants where she ate and drank as if she had starved herself for weeks. She took great delight spending Henry's money. He was glad the obsequious little man with the gray moustache had stuffed the extra franc notes in his hand. He needed them. They went dancing in cabarets in the old city, listened to American jazz, climbed the hilltop overlooking the sea where they kissed and cuddled in broad daylight. But for all her apparent delight, Henry could not shake his growing unease. Was he being used? For Marcotte? Paid off like a snitch?

The long train ride to Paris did nothing to comfort him. An old woman across from them in the compartment snored much of the way, mouth gaping, spittle on her chin. In the next compartment, a baby cried. Henry paced the aisles of the train. Eugénie grew cross with him. She frowned and snapped when he spoke to her. Henry felt the trip to be a failure. He'd had such expectations for it. There were good moments when they made love, but these moments were fleeting, like sand through the fingers. He did not feel closer to Eugénie, instead sensed a wall had formed between them, built brick by brick. And somehow, he believed, that wall had to do with the M.L.F. He stared at the brown package beside him on the seat. Whatever its contents, they were poison, to him, to his love for Eugénie. He was Brisson's damn errand boy, a lackey. He thought of the night he had run through the streets of St. Denis. He wasn't an errand boy then. Maybe that's what was wrong with Eugénie. She didn't respect him. He was silly Henry, a boy who leaped into the Seine after a cheap hat. Even as she insisted she liked him that way, he wasn't so sure.

In Paris, Henry delivered the package to Brisson at the rug importer's. He thumped it on the desk in the back office.

"You had no difficulty?"

"Should I have?"

"No, certainly not."

"What's in it?"

"Books, papers."

"Ledgers?"

Brisson eyed him curiously. "You seem a bit ruffled today, Henry, *déphasé*."

Henry shrugged.

"Come, come now, Henry, you're much too valuable to us. What troubles you?"

"I don't want to be your goddamned errand boy!" he snapped.

Brisson fondled the string on the package. "Sit down, Henry."

Chastened by his outburst, Henry did as he was told. Brisson untied the string from the package and tore away the paper. He removed what was in the box and held it for Henry to see. Ledgers and notebooks.

A Stone for Bread

Brisson seated himself behind the desk and leaned toward him. They were alone in the office.

"Think this way, Henry. This is a battle. Politics is like that. One side will win and one will lose. It is easy, of course, to say, so be it, *c'est la vie*, yes. But if you believe in your side, believe with everything in your soul that if your side wins, millions of others will win also—insignificant people, those whom the politicians ignore, shopkeepers and clerks and farmers—if you believe this, then you must commit your whole heart to it. Your whole heart, Henry. There is no half."

Henry nodded, but without conviction.

"That means to at times be the errand boy. It is not a matter of rank. We are equals, free men. You understand that, do you not? If I have to sweep the floor for Renard Marcotte, I will sweep the floor. Because I am committed with my whole heart, Henry. My whole heart."

"Yes, I understand that."

"Think about it, my friend. Marcotte does not want weak-willed followers. And I don't believe that of you. You have courage, Henry. You are one of us, a man to be treasured, revered. We want you with us, but you must decide that for yourself."

Henry replied meekly that he needed time to think about these things. He returned to the hotel, stayed there the day and night, pacing about his room. There was a point, he understood, when one must choose to live life in capital letters. LIFE, not life. Lower case life is breathing, eating, the motions of life, Thoreau's quiet desperation. Upper case LIFE is like Brisson said, lived with the whole heart. But what did a whole-heart commitment to the M.L.F. even mean? When he stepped back from them, Marcotte and the others, he was forced to question their means and motives. Yet why had he remained with the M.L.F., paid lip service to it? Lip service was lower-case life. Like love, one either loved with the whole heart or toyed with emotions, one's own and others'. If he waited for perfection, the perfect man, the perfect political movement, the perfect woman, he would wait forever. If he chose merely to toy with a man, a movement, a woman, he was damned to a life of mediocrity. Brisson had asked him to choose Marcotte's movement with his whole heart. Perhaps Brisson was right. Perhaps only cynicism stood between Henry and LIFE. On the way back from the meeting with Brisson, he had passed an old man, a war veteran. The man had only one leg and walked with a crutch. But he held himself straight, his eyes bright and lively. Hung on his dirty uniform coat was a single silver medal, polished to a bright sheen. Henry knew nothing about French medals, why they were awarded and to whom, but he believed the man's spirit was as bright as his medal. No injury to his body had ever altered that spirit. The image lingered in Henry's mind.

That evening, Henry went with the bluebands to a rally in a town outside Paris. It was a long bumpy ride into the countryside. He began to relax and enjoy himself. The young men bantered and smoked. They were coarse, earthy fellows, yet even this, especially this, comforted him. They did not ask questions about what they were doing. They simply did it. And they accepted Henry, laughed with him and gave him cigarettes. He found he could joke with them, join in their teasing about women and drinking. As the truck bounced along, he cradled the billy-club in his lap. When they piled out into a town square, he stuck the club in his belt under his coat. Colored Christmas lights, strung in flower patterns above the street, twinkled in the frosty air. Henry took his place in the circle around the listeners. It was a small crowd, no more than fifty people and a few bystanders who had come out of curiosity. Music blared from loudspeakers. Marcotte spoke from a low platform. He seemed indifferent to cold and the sparse crowd, addressing them as if thousands were ranged before him. Henry was stirred. This night, Marcotte's words were fire and light. They warmed Henry's shivering body. People cheered and waved. Until the speech was disrupted by squealing brakes and furious shouts. Trucks and cars lurched toward the crowd and stopped. Men jumped out with sticks and bats.

"Commies!" the M.L.F. blueband nearest Henry shouted. "Goddamn commies!"

The bluebands grabbed their billy-clubs from under their coats and began to flail at the men who swarmed in among them. Smoke bombs were thrown. Henry jerked his cudgel free and charged the attackers. The crowd, hysterical and screaming, scattered, so that it was difficult to tell who was a Communist and who wasn't. Men yelled and thrashed, the thud of clubs on bodies sounding like stomps on packed dirt.

A man ran toward Henry. Did he have a weapon? Henry didn't wait to find out. He swung his club, whacking the man on the arm and staggering him from his path. A laugh rose in his throat. His hands vibrated from the impact and sent a thrill through his chest. He raced after the attackers, shouting and wielding the cudgel like a baseball bat at anyone who confronted him. He hardly felt the blows that landed on him, the fists from behind, the stone that struck his cheek. Nothing mattered, only the fight and his own fierce will. He grabbed a communist thug by the collar and shoved him into a wall, swung the club toward another who suddenly came at him. The attacker stepped away from Henry's cudgel, turned and fled, Henry shouting after him, "Run away, damn you. Run if you dare." He chased the commie into the street, catching him at the corner, and slammed his club against his back. The man fell, his barely coherent words shrieked at Henry like a curse. Henry kicked him in the ribs. The man screamed. Goaded by the scream, Henry kicked him again. The man slid from under his foot, got to his knees and tried to stand, but Henry's cudgel sent him sprawling. He curled into the gutter beneath the streetlight and rolled over, eying Henry warily as he attempted to push himself up. Henry raised the cudgel.

A shadow passed between Henry and the man on the ground. A body, insubstantial as smoke and seemingly from nowhere, emerged from the darkness. Henry, arm raised with the cudgel, moved back, startled.

The shadow spoke, in the most natural of tones, quietly, without panic or rancor.

"Please, Monsieur. He is but a boy."

Henry looked. Light sprayed from the lamp post on the figure in the gutter. Henry was astonished to see that the trembling creature trying to crawl away from him was indeed what the voice said. A boy, probably no older than sixteen.

Henry's voice trailed off. His chest tightened and he wondered he could breathe. He and Rachel had reached the road and the short path to his front porch.

"What happened, Henry?" Rachel asked.

"Nothing. And everything. I looked down and saw the kid I was about to club. I saw how young and at my mercy he was, so, of course, I couldn't hit him. I dropped the cudgel and backed off."

"And?"

"So much for innocence. When I stepped away, the boy grabbed my leg and sent me crashing to the pavement. The bastard damn near killed me." Henry paused. "I see that moment as if caught in a photograph, the shadowy man standing there, the boy on the ground. It was, you understand, a moment on which my life turned. A distortion of memory, most likely. If I could relive it, I wonder if I would discover that it happened quite differently." He sighed.

"I hardly saw the man who stepped between me and the boy. But I do know I was going to club the fellow again, possibly kill him. I was quite capable of it that night." His face darkened. "Maybe it was the conversation with Brisson about how one had to be committed. At that moment I was committed all right. Committed to what, I have no idea, not even from this vantage of forty years. My own rage, perhaps. But I would have killed a man for some image of an ideal or for no reason at all. You don't believe that, I think?"

"I'm not sure what I believe, Henry."

"Because you see me as I am now, a man in his sixties, weary of life, jaded, you could call it. But that night I was young and wild, even perhaps a little crazy. If I had struck the boy a final time, how would I have reacted? I don't know. I've often worried that I might have been thrilled. Passion is that way in us, one-third God, two-thirds devil. But the devil part can be exhilarating."

"But that man stopped you?"

"Yes, a man or providence, who knows? I hardly saw who it was, just a man in the shadows. He didn't attempt to restrain me, not physically. And it wouldn't have mattered. I might have killed him too. Except for his voice, this flat reedy voice from nowhere. 'He is but a boy.' It had the force of a thousand volts." Henry stepped onto the farmhouse porch. "I've thought about it many times, Rachel, for years. Because of what happened afterwards. My life, which had been gyrating wildly, gyrated yet again. Like a compass needle when the natural attraction has been disrupted and spins wildly." He paused, as if to end the story.

"And?"

"That was the beginning of the end for me with the M.L.F. I stayed with Marcotte a while longer, but it was never the same."

"Why?"

"The man, the man who stepped between me and the boy, was René."

NINETEEN
Nineteen

t happened so quickly. René followed the count along the row. And then the number was nine. His eyes widened. He held his breath. Before he could move, a figure stumbled in front of him and was pulled from the line. The count continued. René was confused. He took a step forward, but a hand next to him held him back. His mind reeled. He wanted to cry out for the counting to stop, there had been a mistake. No one seemed to notice. The SS officer never looked his way. René tried to see the man who had stepped in front of him. Those selected had been lined up with their backs to the others. There was no way to know. The count-off continued to its torturous end. The selected men were marched away. The prisoners remained in their ranks. Stuttering machine guns broke the silence. René's knees trembled. Why wasn't he chosen?

The stupor that had hung on him since that terrible day at the quarry worsened. He toyed with the scraps of bread and weak soup, signs his will was surrendering to the camp's horrors. He grew thinner and began to take on the appearance of what the Germans called *muselmänner*, walking dead men. He pondered other ways to die. He could run from the line at roll call and be shot by guards or throw himself against the electric fence. But he did neither of these. He had been condemned to live.

He made inquiries. Who was the man who had stepped in front of him? No one seemed to know. Possibly one of the men recently transferred from another camp, someone told him. Possibly French. Another reported him to be Dutch. Among the shaved, skeletal men, so many looked alike. No one had names, only numbers. And there were thousands of prisoners and often little camaraderie, even less small talk. A man could sleep in a bunk with three others and not know them. René grew obsessed with the man's identity. He asked everyone he met. When he passed Cooke in the yard, he asked if he knew. Cooke shook his head. One prisoner among twenty thousand. Forget it, said Cooke. But he could not forget.

One evening, a man in his Block sat on the floor beside him as René sipped at his cup of soup. René knew the man, a Swede to whom several nights ago he had given a leaf of cabbage from the watery broth. The Swede slid a tightly folded wad of paper under René's leg, then crawled away to eat beside his own bunk. René understood the man's gesture. The paper was a gift in return for the cabbage leaf, paper for the notes he sometimes scrawled and kept hidden away. René crouched over his cup of soup and slipped the wad from beneath his leg. Someone had already written on the paper, rendering it useless for his own notes. So be it. The paper could be used for his feet, although René no longer cared so meticulously about his feet. What did they matter? He wanted to die. But before he went to bed, he tucked the wad into the wall crevice where he hid his scraps of paper and cloth.

One morning, he checked his secret cache and took the square of paper from hiding. He unfolded it. Three pages, torn from a notebook, filled with words, front and back, written in a tight, small hand. French words. René was astonished. Here were vignettes of life in the prison, poems. He read the pages through several times. Tears dripped from his eyes. Who could have written them? He did not use the scraps for his feet, but kept them secure in the crevice. Whenever he could, he took out the pages and read the words again. They were bitter poems, stark images of the prisoners' torments. Yet they comforted René. Someone shared his suffering. He asked the Swede who gave him the paper wad how he got them. The Swede shrugged. Found them, was all he said.

René began to consider who the poet might be. In his despair and confusion, he wondered whether it might have been the prisoner who stepped in front of him at the selection. Such a man could surely have written them. And now left them for René to protect. To make certain the poems survived. But to do that, he too must survive. He began to eat again and take care of his feet. The weeks that followed this discovery were the calmest René had known in the camp. Krake left him alone. The work in the stables, though oppressive, could be endured. This wasn't the quarry. One day Cooke contacted him, moving unexpectedly on the path beside him as he left the stables. Cooke whispered that René should work with a man in his Block called Johann. René didn't know what Cooke meant, but that night Johann explained. René could be useful to them, to Cooke's friends. René did not resist. Cooke had helped him. He believed Cooke had brought about his transfer from the quarry.

Within days, René became Johann's courier. He carried messages to others whom he passed on his daily routines. The messages were not written down. René carried them in his head. René was good at this work. He knew two languages besides French—German and English—and could understand much of the Scandinavian tongues. He memorized messages perfectly, delivered them rote. That this job made him a resister did not concern him. He no longer thought about death. He had been selected to live, to protect three pages of poems. Left him by the man who died in his place. Although he was cautious, he no longer feared the kapos or SS. On nights when his sufferings pushed him to the edge of despair, the tiny cramped lines of poetry, the creased and dirty pieces of paper in his hands, soothed him. He began to think of home, his mother and father, his family. He remembered

Étienne. One night, these memories caused him to weep bitterly. No one paid any attention. Men wept often here. Sometimes he shared the poetry with other prisoners, reciting lines in a soft monotone. Most did not want to listen.

Some weeks after he became Johann's courier, René was again confronted by Krake demanding cigarettes. René had nothing, but Krake did not relent. He told him to find cigarettes or regret it. René spoke with Johann. After this, Johann supplied René with cigarettes and an occasional square of chocolate, but only in exchange for information, primarily lists of prisoners to be transferred or killed. René did what Johann wanted though he knew it was dangerous. Sometimes Krake complied, slipping pieces of paper into René's hand with numbers on them, prisoners' numbers. Other days, he grew furious with René, kicked or slapped him and gave him nothing. But René understood that if Krake killed him, he would lose his supply of cigarettes. René grew bolder, refusing Krake the cigarettes without something in exchange. Krake responded with blows or kicks but would then relent. This provided Johann vital information.

One day, when Krake confronted René at the latrine, he greedily snatched René's cigarettes and handed him a list of numbers. René turned to go, but Krake grabbed him, squeezing his fingers around René's neck. There is something else I want, he hissed. René did not understand. I have nothing else, he gasped, trying to breathe. Krake released him. René staggered against the side of the latrine. Krake grinned. His face came close to René's, his fetid breath like fire. Bring me the pieces of paper, he said.

René was shocked. What paper?

What the Swede gave you, bastard.

René did not reply. He skulked away as a kapo came into view.

The request desolated him. But it was his fault. He had shared the poetry with others in his block and someone told Krake. Someone who had not wanted to hear them. But why did Krake want them? The poems were René's to protect. Now they would be taken away. That night as he sipped the watery soup, he felt the black angel hovering near. He considered giving his soup to the man beside him who was slowly dying of starvation. The next day, he told Johann what had happened. He showed him the three pages with the tiny cramped handwriting. Johann seemed puzzled. René was surprised. He thought Johann, like Cooke, knew everything that happened in the prison. But Johann did not know why Krake wanted these dirty pieces of paper. Nor did he know who had written the poems. Was there some special import to them? A code of some kind? René had no answer. To him, they were poems, wrung from an unknown prisoner's anguished soul, the prisoner, he wanted to believe, who had saved his life. And they were his poems now, entrusted to him. How could he give them up?

Johann promised to make inquiries. But his contacts insisted they knew nothing about any poems. Cooke says give them to Krake, but only if he pays. Johann laughed bitterly. Who knows why anyone does anything in this hell? Sadly, René surrendered the poems, one tiny shred of paper at a time, tearing carefully between the tightly cramped verses so that no word was lost. In return, he demanded information. Krake seemed eager for the dirty scraps, as if they were gold. He gave René whatever he asked, though not without an occasional cuff to René's head to remind him of his insignificance. The exchange went on for several weeks. René prolonged it as long as he could. The information Krake provided was valuable to Johann and Cooke. But René dreaded the day the last scrap would be gone. Each torn fragment was like a piece of skin ripped from his skeletal arms. When only a single scrap remained, René pondered holding it back, refusing to give it up.

Johann reprimanded him. You have no choice. This is not for you or me but against them. It is all we have.

René wanted to shout at him. He was wrong. It was not all they had, this impossible game of resistance. René had something more, poems, the words of which burned in his heart and comforted him, gave him reason to live. That night, knowing he must do what Johann said, he cried himself to sleep. For the next week, he carried the scrap of paper in his shoe, waiting for Krake to find him and extort it from him. He would not relinquish it easily.

A Stone for Bread

TWENTY

"So René actually existed."

"Of course, he existed, Rachel. Why would you think otherwise?" Henry's face darkened as if she'd accused him of lying. He started to he door.

"I'm sorry. I wasn't doubting you. Or your story. It's just Scott told me that when *A Stone for Bread* was published, there were people who thought you wrote the poems yourself and that René was a kind of literary device."

"Yes, I haven't forgotten Scott's clumsy attempt to interrogate me." He scowled and turned, his eyes questioning her. "And do you think that?"

"I have no reason to think that, Henry. I'm just surprised to have René suddenly show up in your narrative. Like I've been lulled into thinking all this was about Paris and Renard Marcotte and your year abroad. And then René appears, which is not what I expected."

"Well, rest assured, René was quite real, more startlingly real than anyone I have ever encountered." He opened the door for her. "Come inside, Rachel. I have something to show you."

He offered her coffee, but she begged off with midterms practically on her. She stood in his living room while Henry went to a metal bookcase and removed a black three-ring binder.

"Here," he said, handing it to her.

"What is it, Henry?"

"A manuscript. For a novel."

"So you did write a novel about Paris. What you kept telling your friend Bert Yeager about."

He shook his head. "No, not that one. This is René's story, so it's not exactly a novel, although I've taken liberties here and there, filling in gaps, you might say, phrasing it in my own style. And it's unfinished. I'm not certain I'll ever finish it. But I thought you might want to read it. To help you understand."

"I'd love to read it, Henry." She opened the cover. The title page had only the single name *René* typed in all caps. She felt the binder in her hand as a precious gift, like an archaeological find, then worried if she should take it with her. "You do have a copy? I mean, in case my building catches on fire."

He nodded. "That's the copy. And I'd like your opinion about it, Rachel. Suggestions for improving it."

"You want my critique?"

"You're in American lit, aren't you?" He smiled. "And I'm an American writer."

"Yes, okay."

She was about to leave when another thought occurred to her. "Henry," she said, "I'm also in the process of casting about for a topic for my master's thesis. Now that you've brought René into the story, I'm wondering if there might be a topic to—"

"No!" he snapped, his face flushing angrily.

She physically took a step away from him, expecting the binder to be ripped from her hand. She almost offered it back to him but didn't. There came a tense moment when he bobbed his head like a disobedient schoolboy deciding whether to apologize. "No, Rachel. You'll see. It's impossible. You'll see how impossible that would be. I can't let that happen." He was again dull and defensive Henry Beam pinioned in the rocking chair by Scott's camera.

"I'm sorry, Henry. It was just a thought. I'm exploring several ideas." She hesitated. "I consider what you've told me confidential, I hope you know that. Unless you tell me otherwise, I will never violate that."

Though they had both apologized before she left, they had parted that day with the smart of her request and his response as a rift between them. She hadn't heard from him in two weeks and knew it was her fault. She should have known he might perceive the request in a way she never intended, that she was only using him, like everyone else that year in Paris had apparently used him. That same evening, she read Henry's novel about René and went to bed, sleeping fitfully, dreaming of walls and barbed wire and shadowy, suffocating places. The enigmatic René followed her through the week, distracting her from classroom lectures and required reading for her exams. And the poems—the bizarre way in which René received the poems and had them taken from him again. No wonder Henry couldn't finish the story. How did it end? And how did the poems get from the sadistic Krake to Henry in Paris? She wanted to know, had to know now. But remembering Henry's last angry outburst, she resisted calling him. He would have to call her.

But there was something else she wanted to know. On Friday, she phoned her mother and Saturday morning drove to Charlotte for the weekend. On the pretext of looking for books she had packed away, she went to the attic after the box of letters with the photograph she'd discovered years before. She couldn't find them. At dinner that evening, with no other recourse, she asked her mother about the box. Gladys Singer, once a young woman of arresting beauty, at least that's what old photos showed, was a frumpy sixtyish, hands gnarled with arthritis, face prematurely wrinkled into what Rachel considered a persistent scowl. Rachel was old enough now, matured enough, to understand how the tragedies of her mother's life had embittered her. Not even the child Rachel had compensated for her mother's grief, she knew, although at an early age she had tried to be everything her mother wanted. Until high school, when she understood that whatever her accomplishments, they would never fill the void left by the deaths of her brother and father. But she could at least feel for her mother now, understand her sorrow and try to avoid conflict.

"What box?" her mother asked. "I don't recall such a box."

"It was there when I was in high school. A box of letters from my father. No, I didn't read them. I was looking for letters from Mai, my friend from Governor's School. I found a box marked *letters*. There was a photograph with them, of a family, Rachel, Jakob and Daniel, labeled Stuttgart, 1938. I wondered who they were."

Her mother seemed to visibly shrink from her. "I don't remember any such photograph."

A familiar dodge. Her mother's memory had a way of failing when subjects arose she didn't choose to discuss.

"But I saw it, Mother. They were a Jewish family, my father's family, weren't they? I want to know. I really want to know who they were."

Her mother pushed back from the table and stood, physically distancing herself from the question. Her mouth quivered. "Your father wasn't a Jew, Rachel. How can you even think such a thing? *And neither are you!*" She fumbled with her plate, her fingers trembling as she stacked the few dishes in front of her and carried them to the kitchen. Rachel heard the splash of water in the sink. When she followed with her dishes, her mother wouldn't look at her. The subject was not broached again. Rachel drove back to Chapel Hill the next morning.

TWENTY ONE

e called her the first week of April. He hadn't meant to wait so long. But her suggestion about the thesis had deeply upset him. He was upset often these days, as if reliving his year in Paris had surfaced every humiliation and grief of his life. This wasn't Rachel's fault. He had chosen to tell her about Marcotte and René. And he trusted her, yes, he believed he could trust her. But the more of his story he'd shared, the more agitated he'd become. Would she despise him when she knew the full truth? He didn't want her to despise him. He loved her, was in love with her, like twenty-three-year old Henry had loved Eugénie, though he knew any love for Rachel was doomed to remain unrequited, at least sexually. Sometimes he felt twenty-three again with her, though the pains of body told him differently. But she had brought a rare happiness into his life, which is why he'd recoiled in anger when she mentioned her thesis. He couldn't bear to think her interest in him amounted to a Master's thesis. So he hadn't called again for several weeks. Instead, he had sat in the old house and stewed. But as the days passed, he knew he'd been unfair to be so angry and not call, though his reluctance to see her was not merely pique. There had been other matters begging his attention, letters to write, phone calls made, a house painter found to redo the outside pine siding now that the weather had warmed.

When he did finally call, he invited her to the farm the next Sunday morning for brunch and, if the weather was nice, a sprightly walk in the woods. "Dogwoods are flowering," he told her, "best time of the year out here."

Over brunch, he talked about the garden he would plant as soon as he could hire someone to plow the ground. "Not up to doing it myself this year," he said, describing the varieties of corn and tomatoes he planned to grow. "I did a lot of gardening as a boy, farming. After college, I never went near a garden. Even thinking about one repulsed me." He smiled. "I think when we get older, we discover the virtues of some of what we despised in childhood."

He was pleased by her interest in gardening, her questions about growing seasons, the effects of weather, the hours of work a garden required.

"I'd love to have space to garden," she told him. "I get tired of small apartments." She sighed. "Maybe one day. If I ever finish school."

After they'd eaten, they walked through the woods, Henry's dogs bounding ahead of them. The day was overcast but did nothing to dampen the loveliness of spring, the blooming dogwood and redbuds, daffodils scattered among the trees. He drew strength from the beauty around him, and renewed energy, walking with a brisker step until he was panting. He stopped and sat a moment on the old stump. It was then they talked about his René novel. It had deeply moved her and she asked if he planned to publish it.

He sighed. "I have to finish it first." He didn't tell her he had tried to do just that in the weeks since he'd last seen her but had found himself unable to write a word. He was cheered, however, by her response to the manuscript, that she believed it worth publishing. Perhaps now she wouldn't think him a failed old has-been.

When he had caught his breath, they resumed walking and he returned to his story: the moment after he'd backed away from the kid in the gutter and found himself slammed to the pavement. The next thing he remembered was lying between muslin sheets in the dark, under a thick down comforter. His head throbbed. Through a long night, he slept fitfully, and in his brief moments of awareness sensed someone beside the bed. Once, he aroused from confused dreams to see who it was. The eyes that returned his woozy stare were a startling blue. He came fully awake the next morning to find the eyes still there, bright agates set in the lean face of a man seated upright in a chair, gray hair thin and receding, in his early forties possibly, a grizzle of beard on his cheeks. The man helped Henry to his feet and to a bathroom down the hall. A woman brought him food. During the day, he heard children's voices in the hallway, talking about him, the American in the downstairs bedroom.

There were few words exchanged between the blue-eyed man and Henry, although the man seemed surprised by Henry's fluency in French. But by evening, Henry was greatly improved. He left the bed and joined the family's evening meal. There were three young children, their mother and the man from the street, René. They welcomed him as a guest, although conversation with them proved awkward. The woman was the man's sister, the children hers. But only the children seemed excited to have an American in their home. He spent a second night with them and returned to Paris the next morning by train. He had offered René and his sister money for his care, but the offer was refused, so he wrote his name and the hotel on a slip of paper and said if they ever needed anything to let him know.

In Paris, his life went on as before in all but one way. He no longer attended Marcotte's rallies. The blue brassard was retired to a drawer beneath clean undershirts. He was a different breed of man from Marcotte's young toughs, he decided, more important in other ways to Marcotte's movement. Brisson seemed to agree and used Henry often now, happy to pay him with wads of franc notes. Henry took the train to Marseilles with letters in a leather portfolio, returned with a small package that was obviously not ledgers. He never asked what it was, but the young café owner in Marseilles smiled and told him it was a watch, a gift to Marcotte from loyal supporters. On the train, Henry held the package to his ear to listen for ticking but heard nothing.

He continued to see Eugénie, though they frequently quarreled. She refused to go to Marseilles with him. They stood in the lobby of his hotel shouting. He accused her of an affair with Claude. She called him a bastard. He raised his hand to strike her, but she pivoted angrily away and stormed from the hotel. He went to his room and brooded. It was over. He wanted nothing more to do with her. But when he returned from Marseilles, he went directly to the *pâtisserie* with a handful of roses. She smiled and kissed his cheek. That evening, he took her to dinner at an expensive restaurant and afterwards they made love in his room.

Two weeks later, Henry moved from the hotel. Brisson was paying him well. He could afford decent quarters and rented a three-room flat down river near the Eiffel Tower. Here Eugénie could be with him away from the prying eyes of Yeager and the other hotel residents. He was proud of himself, pleased with his comfortable flat. Eugénie shopped with him for dishes and furniture. She took him to Galeries Lafayette, to an area of the store featuring American goods. Enthralled by American kitchen gadgets, she gleefully urged on him a toaster and blender, an egg slicer and long-handled dustpan. At her insistence, he bought a barbecue grill, laughing that he would burn down his apartment building.

She pouted and said, "It is for picnics."

That evening, they christened the apartment with dinner and a bottle of fine wine. She stayed the night and lingered over breakfast. Henry was definitely pleased with himself.

Two nights later, he answered a knock at the door and found a familiar figure standing in the corridor. René. How had he found him? Puzzled, Henry invited him in and asked him to sit down. But René stood in the center of his room like a lost man, nervous and fidgety, speaking in cryptic sentences.

"You have left the M.L.F., yes? You no longer attend the rallies."

Henry was startled. Why would he ask such questions? And how did he know this? "I'm not attending rallies at the moment, that's true. But no, I haven't left the M.L.F. I have other duties."

"And these duties are worthwhile?"

Was he being interrogated? Henry wanted to snap back that this was not his business, but René had been kind to him. Henry knew he should be grateful. So he nodded and again asked René to sit down. It was a strange evening, René seated on the edge of his sofa, rubbing his hands on his knees, his piercing eyes fixed on Henry's face. He asked the same questions a second time.

"Look, I'm here as a student, that's all," explained Henry. "The M.L.F. has interest for me as a writer. I'm considering a novel."

That seemed to mollify him. He said nothing for a few moments as if expecting Henry to elaborate. But Henry didn't know what to say, so he asked him if he would like coffee. René refused. But he accepted a cigarette, smoking in silence, then stood and moved to the door.

"A writer," he said, and smiled. "You write truth?"

"Of course."

He offered Henry a quick and inscrutable nod and left.

A week later, Henry came in late after a day of travel to Senlis with letters for Brisson and found René outside his door. He didn't want to invite him in but felt awkward asking him to leave, so he opened the door for him. René again sat on the uncomfortable sofa, smoking Henry's cigarettes.

"I knew a writer," he said.

"I imagine there are many writers in France."

"A few years ago."

"Okay. What did he write? He—or she?"

"Important words."

Silence.

"I write poetry," Henry cheerfully volunteered.

"Yes. Poetry too."

"You write poetry? Or your writer friend?"

René didn't answer but asked another question. "You know Renard Marcotte?"

"Is Marcotte a writer?"

"Do you know him?"

"I've met him, although I work very little with him. He's always surrounded by his own people. I see him at rallies."

"You don't attend rallies now."

"Not the last few weeks. I've been busy with other things."

"You see Marcotte?"

"See him, what do you mean, see him?" Henry was ready for this ridiculous conversation to end.

"You see him when there are no rallies?"

"Not lately. Why?"

"You know Mauthausen?"

"What is Mauthausen?"

"Not what, where."

"Okay, where is Mauthausen?"

"In hell."

Henry got up. "Look, what can I do for you? Is there something—"

"The Americans came to Mauthausen. Golden warriors, every American a hero, like Achilles. Beautiful, the most beautiful warriors ever."

"What are you talking about?"

"Are you army?"

"I've never been in the military."

"Too bad."

"Well, I missed the draft for Korea. I was in school. I mean I really don't think I'm cut out for the army. Wouldn't you agree?"

"Why are you in France?"

Henry wanted to grab the man and shove him out the door. But the bland voice and intense eyes immobilized him.

"I told you. I'm a student," he snapped.

"A student where?"

"Nowhere at the moment."

"Ah."

"Well, I intend to take classes at the Sorbonne. Well, maybe not, I mean, I've used the time here in other ways. I'm working on a novel."

"About M.L.F.?"

"Yes. Well, no not really. I don't know what I'm doing. I needed a break that's all. I've worked all my life. You have no idea about that."

"They pay you well, M.L.F.?"

"Excuse me, that isn't your business. Look, what's this about? Why all these questions? Why do you want to know about me?"

"I want to understand." He said these words so softly Henry barely heard them. He was about to ask what it was he wanted to understand, when René stood up.

"I have bothered you, I'm afraid."

"No, I mean, it's just I've had a long day."

"Forgive me."

He seemed so sincerely contrite, Henry felt shamed by his anger. René walked to the door. "There is something you must do for me," he said with a shy smile.

"Yes, of course," Henry blurted stupidly, before he realized he'd agreed without knowing what René wanted.

"As a writer."

"I'm not really that good a writer."

René waved his hand as if this didn't matter and said simply, "I will come back."

Henry closed the door behind him. His heart thumped wildly. Was the man insane? Would he follow him forever, track him down to pester him with more of his inane questions? Henry didn't sleep that night. What did René want? He seemed to have some kind of obsession with him, but why? He'd asked about Marcotte. Perhaps he was a Communist, but he didn't talk like a Communist. The truth was, he seemed oddly harmless, innocent, like the retarded child kept years in the back room—guileless, trusting, simple. But perhaps those blue eyes masked something sinister. But what? Henry didn't think he wanted to know.

The next day, he called Yeager. They met for lunch at a café near Henry's old hotel.

"Mauthausen. Where or what is Mauthausen?" Henry eventually asked, trying to make it seem like a casual question.

"Who wants to know?"

"I do."

"It was a Nazi concentration camp in Austria, one of the more infamous ones."

Henry was surprised. "I know so little about those things."

"You and much of the rest of the world. The truth is, what the Nazis did is only now beginning to come out, at least, the horrendous extent of their atrocities."

"I've heard some about it." Henry didn't want to seem too naïve.

He knew about the Rue des Rosiers in the Jewish quarter of Paris, where thousands of Jews had been rounded up and deported after the Nazis occupied the city. "But these prisons weren't only for Jews?"

"Hell no, though Jews were a priority for the butchers. They sent all kinds of people to the camps. Here in Paris, the Germans were ably assisted by collobos, collaborators. Of course no one wants to say that. The French want you to believe everyone joined the Resistance, but that won't wash. Hell, the Nazis occupied Paris with barely a quiver from the populace. And some weren't just collobos but goddamn allies. Many of them actually welcomed Hitler to France, completely threw in their lot with National Socialism."

Henry could still be shocked by Yeager's cynicism. "But Mauthausen, that was a concentration camp?"

"Yeah, why do you want to know?"

"Just curious."

"So who's been telling you about Mauthausen? The M.L.F.? That bunch of neo-fascists. Like the collobos, the kind I'm talking about."

Henry experienced an icy spasm in his gut. It was one thing to call Marcotte's movement neo-fascist, another to link it to Nazis. That war seemed far away, in another world. "That was more than a decade ago."

"Yeah, but even if he's ineffectual and little more than a clown, Marcotte's cut from the same fascist cloth."

Henry said nothing. But his heart raced and his face warmed. Wasn't Hitler first thought to be a clown? He left Yeager at the café and walked along the quays of the Seine to his flat. He half expected to find René outside his door, but thankfully, he wasn't there. René did not return to Henry's apartment that week. But now Henry wanted him to come. He had his own questions to ask. But the man seemed to have finished with Henry. Agitated and unable to sleep, Henry caught a train to the suburb where René lived, walked the short distance to his house and knocked at the door. A child answered and went off to fetch his uncle, who greeted Henry warmly and invited him into the dim-lit parlor.

"I wanted to ask about Mauthausen," mumbled Henry. "It was a Nazi camp?"

"Yes."

The blue eyes were cold and fixed on Henry's. Did the man ever blink?

"In Austria?"

René nodded.

Henry didn't know what to ask next. He offered René a cigarette and lit one himself. They smoked in silence until René finally spoke.

"I was two years at Mauthausen."

Henry waited for him to explain further, but he merely sucked on the cigarette.

"Did you wish to talk with me about that?" asked Henry.

"I wish to talk with you about writing."

"You mentioned a friend, a writer."

"Yes. A writer."

"Would you like me to meet him?"

"No."

"Someone in Paris?"

He didn't answer.

"Has he published any works?"

"No."

"What does he write?"

"Did. Years ago. Poetry. Things."

"I would like to read what he's written."

"Yes."

"You have something of his?"

"Yes."

"A manuscript?"

"No."

"Well, what?"

"Here." When he said the word *here*, he put the fingers of his left hand to his forehead.

Henry smiled. *"Your* poetry, you're talking about yourself, right?"

René stood and walked to the window. His voice was low and barely audible. "I will come to you in Paris."

"Yes," said Henry, "I would like that."

He returned to Paris in a sour mood. The next week dragged. He felt he was marking time, waiting. But for what? He grew restless, woke often in the night, his mind on René. In the early evenings he hung around the *pâtisserie* waiting for Eugénie, hoping to talk her into dinner or coming to his flat. Most days, she couldn't. Family matters, she would say. When Henry wasn't delivering messages for Brisson, he wandered the city, as if to recapture the magic of his first weeks there. But Paris seemed gray and empty. Once, he went café hopping with Yeager and his friends but was quickly bored. On one of his errands for Brisson, he discovered an Iranian artist in a squalid flat outside Paris. He bought from the man a carved lion as a gift for Eugénie. Henry thought it a brilliant sculpture. But Eugénie detested it.

"It's so frightening, Henri. I would have awful dreams about it."

He wrapped the lion in a box and put it away in a closet. In his restlessness, he began to drink in the evenings, alone in his flat, drink himself into a stuporous sleep. Brisson noticed his fretfulness and several times attempted to soothe him with patriotic words.

"The war for freedom is a difficult war to wage," he would say with a smile, "and yes, there are valleys of despair, but we must keep our faith alive, Henry, we must keep it alive."

Henry didn't care about faith. He worked for Brisson for money. One day, Brisson invited Henry to travel with him by car to Reims. Henry was surprised. Although he carried messages for the man, they never went places together. Brisson picked Henry up at his flat and drove to a neighborhood across the Seine to the Right Bank. He stopped the car before an apartment building and got out, telling Henry to wait. Henry waited more than an hour. When Brisson returned, he was not alone. Henry was astonished to see Renard Marcotte. Under a gray topcoat, he wore a blue suit, somewhat rumpled, with a black tie. He leaned down and peered through the front window at Henry.

"Monsieur Marcotte, this is our American, Henry Beam," said Brisson, as if to introduce them.

"*Oui*, Monsieur Beam and I have met."

Marcotte did not offer Henry his hand but smiled and climbed onto the seat behind him. Henry stared through the windshield, afraid that to turn and speak to Marcotte would be a breach of etiquette. Brisson drove through Paris to the Reims highway. Nothing was said until they were well out of the city.

"Air," Marcotte sighed happily. "The air of France. A man cannot breathe in cities, do you agree?"

"Paris is stultifying," answered Brisson.

Henry wondered if he was required to agree but said nothing. They did not go directly to Reims but stopped in the town of Épernay. The grocer of Épernay, Henry knew, the epithet applied to Marcotte. This was his home. They drove past miles of vineyards, the grape vines bare stalks this time of year. Épernay lay in champagne country, one of France's finest growing areas.

"Stop, stop there," Marcotte ordered, leaning over the front seat.

Brisson parked the car before a two-story stone farmhouse. Marcotte got out and walked to the door. Before he could knock, a woman and man came from the house, followed by three children. They greeted Marcotte warmly with kisses to the cheeks. Brisson told Henry they were to follow. They climbed from the car and stood a short distance back from Marcotte and the family but were almost immediately invited in. The farmhouse, though plain, seemed roomy and comfortable. The father nodded nervously for them to sit in the parlor, while his wife scurried off, returning with a tray of pastries and a carafe of red wine. Marcotte chatted amiably, asking about various family members and last summer's grape harvest. Henry was fascinated. These people had not expected Marcotte, yet seemed overjoyed by his visit. The children hovered in the doorway, eyes wide and curious. The woman never sat down. The man took a seat away from them on the other side of the parlor but jumped up to fetch cigarettes and again to show them photographs of his large family. The visit lasted all of thirty minutes.

Through the morning, they stopped numerous times at farmhouses or in shops in the town of Épernay. At each place, Marcotte was embraced, kissed and petted. The last stop was at a winery outside the town. They drove through the gates but did not stop at the large manor house or near any of the winery buildings. Brisson turned down a dirt lane that led past vineyards to what appeared to be a small outbuilding. Henry saw smoke from a flue and realized this was a house where someone actually lived. Brisson stopped the car. Marcotte got out and strode to the door. This time he didn't knock, opening the door himself. A shriek of delight came from inside. Henry and Brisson followed. They stepped into a dark room lit by a single bulb in the low ceiling. Henry saw a table in the room and a few assorted chairs, a coal stove and in the corner a couch where an elderly woman, clad in a loose shift, half-reclined against a puffy pillow. She laughed and raised up to embrace Marcotte. He signaled they were all to sit down. Henry and Brisson pulled chairs from the table.

"*Tante* Marie," Marcotte announced to Henry and Brisson, smiling happily. "Dear *Tante* Marie."

Marcotte sat on the couch beside the woman. Henry thought her quite old, her face crosshatched with lines. When she smiled, he saw she was missing several front teeth. She grinned and grasped Marcotte's hands. A young girl entered through a door at the back, stood a few feet from Henry and shyly watched.

"We'll eat here," Marcotte announced. He motioned to Brisson, who got up and went out to the car, returning moments later with a basket from the trunk. He removed from it wine and loaves of bread, meat pies and cheeses. Brisson and Henry sat at the table. Marcotte and Aunt Marie remained on the couch. Sometimes Marcotte bent toward the old woman and offered her food, feeding her with his fingers. Henry found himself moved by the compassion in these gestures, even as he experienced an edgy discomfort. His stomach hurt. He felt dizzy from so much alcohol—they had been offered wine at every stop. Food too, which he had eaten only to be polite. The room was hot from the coal stove and smelled of urine and mold. It reminded him of a place he did not wish to remember—Jared Beam's cropper shack.

When Marcotte rose from the couch, Henry was relieved. This too would be a quick visit. But Marcotte was not ready to leave. Instead, he motioned for Henry to come and they left Brisson with Aunt Marie, exiting through a tiny kitchen and out the rear door. Marcotte didn't speak. When Henry caught up with him, he glanced furtively at the man's face. The strong peasant features appeared agitated, mouth taut and jaw clenched, as if the man struggled with tumultuous emotion.

They walked behind the house and through a vineyard. Marcotte had shed his overcoat in the house. Now he unknotted his necktie and draped it around his shoulders. The blue suit seemed bizarrely out of place here.

"Do you know about vines?" Marcotte asked in French.

Henry shook his head. "No. Not much."

Marcotte bent down to a grapevine and touched the stalks. "For the grapes to flourish, the vines must be cut back each year. All but a little of the previous year's growth," he made a cutting gesture with his hand, "slashed away!"

Henry nodded as he knew he was supposed to.

"But men now—they are not so disciplined. They believe that to flourish, they must grow large, gorge themselves on whatever they desire, wealth and prestige, fine wines and women, surrendering nothing. The leaders of France are like that, men who gorge on their power. But vines left to grow however they choose become weak and useless. I know that. The people know that, the people here in Épernay whom you saw this morning."

He faced Henry, his florid cheeks lit, eyes glistening under the heavy brows. Henry stepped back, as if the man had physically pushed him. He flushed, wanting desperately to look away, but couldn't. Marcotte held him as he held his frenzied followers at the rallies.

"I know this truth, Henri, because I was born to it. Here. I was born here. In that house. Do you understand?"

"Yes!" The word burst from Henry's throat, embarrassing him.

Marcotte's voice softened. "I cannot expect you, an American, to understand. Those born into the world with nothing know there is power in the human heart stronger than National Assemblies and armies. The longing for freedom, to hold our heads up as men."

Henry nodded. He did understand. He knew what the human heart wanted. He understood Renard Marcotte perfectly. Marcotte turned and walked through the vineyard.

"Like the vine, I come here each year. To be pruned, you might say." He smiled. "To remember where Renard Marcotte was born. And though once I despised this poverty, this rude house, I kiss the ground now as holy, because the dreams of men and our hearts were born here as well." His face reddened. "Those who dare call themselves leaders of France are ignorant fools, because they have never known these truths."

The spell was broken. He was again the familiar Renard Marcotte, blasting the Mollet government. Marcotte seemed to sense Henry's attention had drifted and glared at him. "I see you don't believe me."

Startled, Henry flinched. What had his face revealed?

Marcotte stopped walking and took off his jacket. He draped it across the stalks of a grapevine. To Henry's amazement, he unbuttoned his shirt and slipped it from his shoulders. He turned away from Henry. Henry gaped. A huge scar in the shape of a J seemed chiseled from the flesh of his back. He put on his shirt and again faced Henry.

"Before the war, when I was first a shopkeeper, an official came to my shop. There was a special tax, I was informed, a tax not written into law, a tax that went into the pockets of corrupt officials. But I refused him. I would not pay his tax. I went to the Mayor. I spoke to other shopkeepers. I organized a rally against this outrage. One night soon afterwards, I was attacked by thugs hired by these same officials. They dragged me into an alleyway and held me down and thrashed me, then took a knife to my back. J for Jew. Do you believe that? For JEW!"

His face darkened. Henry, jolted into silence, saw him reach for his belt and tug it free. His hand went into his pants and came out cupping his penis.

"I AM NOT A JEW!" he exploded. Henry saw what Marcotte wanted him to see. That he wasn't circumcised. Marcotte jerked up his pants to cover himself. He moved his face close to Henry's. "I am also not a man who can be intimidated. They can take their knives and cut my heart from my chest, if they dare. Because I am not afraid to die for the people of France. I NEVER PAID THEIR TAX!"

The breath rushed from Henry's body. Marcotte's fury was a mighty wind, blowing away his resistance. He longed to explain himself, explain how his life had been in Cleveland County, how it was since he'd come to Paris. He would pledge undying allegiance to Marcotte, make him understand, but his voice seemed stuck in his throat. Marcotte put a hand on Henry's shoulder. The touch burned through Henry's coat. With no further word, Marcotte started toward the house. Like a puppy, Henry followed.

They said their goodbyes to *Tante* Marie and drove to Reims. There, Marcotte was all business. He spent the afternoon with M.L.F. leaders in a room over a butcher shop. Henry was not invited to join them. He waited on the street, wandering two blocks to the ancient cathedral, with its equestrian statue of Joan of Arc in front. Saint Joan. Peasant woman. With a vision. And courage. They were all peasants. Joan. Marcotte. Henry. Beaten down by a world that did not care about the lives of peasants. Yet somehow, dreams and visions had germinated in their hearts. But what were these dreams? *His* dreams? What was it he had wanted so desperately those years in Cleveland County?

They drove back to Paris that evening, stopping for dinner along the way. Marcotte was in a genial mood. He chided Henry as an American who knew nothing about the jewels of French cuisine and insisted he would order for him.

"A schooling for you, Henry." He laughed, pouring him wine from a dark bottle brought by the restaurant owner.

The wine was excellent. Henry's spirits revived. The day had wearied and confused him. Who *was* Renard Marcotte? Over dinner, he met another of Marcotte's personas, charming host, epicure, a man of expansive appetites. Marcotte ate heartily. They went through two more bottles of wine. Marcotte was thoroughly enjoying himself. Brisson made them laugh with stories about the foibles of past politicians. Even Henry got in the spirit and recounted a story of the Shelby deputy caught in a compromised state with the sheriff's wife when his fly zipper caught on his penis as he climbed hastily from a window. Marcotte laughed uproariously, pointing to his crotch below the table. "Zipped out, yes!" he sputtered in English.

They dropped Henry at his flat. He was buoyant, happy. He had seen Marcotte close up and was not disillusioned. The man was crude, yes, with a peasant's manner. But sensitive too. He recalled him placing bits of cheese on *Tante* Marie's tongue, hugging adults and children at unpretentious farmhouses when he stopped to greet them. And then the scene in the vineyard, a scene that burned in Henry's mind.

This buoyancy lasted a week. On his errands for Brisson, Henry recaptured his enthusiasm for the M.L.F. He even considered returning to the rallies, although there was little time, since his other duties filled most of it. Brisson sent him with papers and packets to towns beyond Paris. What time he found, he tried to save for Eugénie. But Eugénie seemed distracted, and he feared he was losing her. He continued leaving roses for her at the *pâtisserie*, but the romance of this had long ago faded. Several weeks after the visit to Reims, René again appeared at Henry's door. Henry expected to see a manuscript under his arm, but René came empty handed. As before, he perched on the couch and smoked.

"It is important you know me," he said suddenly.

Henry was at a loss to respond, but René seemed not to care. He spoke slowly in his usual soft voice, one sentence flowing to the next far into the night until Henry ached with exhaustion.

"What he wanted me to know, Rachel," said Henry, shifting slightly away from her, "was his life story. He just began, like once upon a time, and didn't stop. Oh, not in one sitting. This went on for a month or more. Not every night. Sometimes he would show up one evening then not come for days, but when I assumed he had finished with me, there he would be again. I tell you it was an extraordinary experience. He described the horrors of Mauthausen, some of which are in my story, the man seemingly able to recall every horrendous detail, though he never raised his voice or showed the slightest emotion. To hear these things was terrible, but forgive me for saying it, it was exhilarating too. Understand, I found what happened there repulsive, the worst evil imaginable. It was René who fascinated me, even as I hated him for telling me these things. I didn't want to hear them. But I had to hear them. I was drawn into his soul, transfixed there. When he failed to appear after several nights, I would sink into a funk and panic, bang around my flat like a madman, terrified he would not come back, that I would be left without knowing."

"Without knowing?" asked Rachel.

"Yes, that's the whole point, isn't it? Without knowing what? What was there to know? One human life, but what an extraordinary life. Of course, René didn't live in ordinary times. The war, Hitler's atrocities. It was one of the ghastliest epochs in human history."

"But why was he doing this, Henry, why relating all this to you?"

"Oh, he had his reasons all right, but that would be getting ahead of myself. But I think he told me things he had never told anyone. Perhaps because I was a stranger." He smiled. "As you were to me. I mean not totally a stranger. You and I had come to know each other a little. But not as close friends. Not at first anyway. It's easier, you know, to tell one's painful truths to someone to whom we're not attached, the stranger seated beside us on a long-distance flight. Although—" He rose from the old stump. He was so tired, his mind and body weary. "But whatever the reason René chose to tell me these things, I felt privileged. Even now, I still feel privileged."

He turned toward the house. They didn't talk and Henry was glad for the silence. He felt exhausted, old. At the house, he fixed coffee and they sat on the living room sofa to drink it. He would have been content just to sit beside her, allow his gaze to linger on her lovely face and hair, but she prodded him to continue the story.

He sighed and explained that those weeks were the most tumultuous of his life, as if he were spinning wildly in a dangerous eddy. He feared for his sanity. His nights echoed with René's voice, soft, paced, the words filling the apartment until Henry feared he would drown in them. When René failed to come, Henry dreamed him there, woke frenzied in the night, rising from bed to pace the room, recalling every word René had uttered. He was glad for the days he was sent on errands for the M.L.F., for the respite they offered from René's unrelenting river of words.

He saw Marcotte more often and prided himself that he had moved into the movement's inner circle. He and Brisson now traveled together by car and on trains, often tarrying over lunch to argue politics or literature. Brisson was an educated man, a university graduate, whose promising career as a professor had been interrupted by the Nazi occupation of Paris. When Paris was liberated, he told Henry, he was a lost man, wasting his life on drink and women. Until he met Renard Marcotte.

"He gave me back my life, Henry," he said without a trace of sentiment.

Henry wondered what Marcotte was doing to *his* life.

One night, unable to sleep, Henry rose from bed to take a walk. When he opened his door, René was standing in the corridor. He brought the man inside.

"You should have knocked," said Henry. "I would have come."

René didn't answer. He refused the proffered chair and stood a few steps from the door, like a man eying escape. He lit a cigarette but never put it to his mouth, holding it between his nicotine-yellowed fingers.

"Please sit down. I am willing to listen. I couldn't sleep."

"There is something I wish to show you."

"Yes, certainly."

René opened the door and stepped back into the hall, fetching a small box. He handed it to Henry. "This."

"What it is?"

"From Mauthausen."

"Okay, but what?"

He didn't answer, just said he would come back in a few days and left.

Henry paused his narrative.

"What was in the box?" asked Rachel.

"A manuscript. Of sorts."

"The poetry?"

"No, not even close. I thought that too that night in Paris. That's what I'd been expecting or some kind of novel or story. But that's not what this was. Here, I'll show you."

"You *have* it!"

He nodded and left her, returning moments later with a cardboard box. He set it on the table beside the couch.

"But this wasn't the *Stone for Bread* poems?"

Henry didn't respond but went to his pile of books and folders by the writing table to retrieve the white three-ring binder he kept there. It felt heavy in his hands, not from weight but from the toil of years it had taken him to translate what René had given him that night. He handed it to Rachel. "It isn't poetry. It's a diary. René's diary. From Mauthausen."

TWENTY TWO
Twenty two

I am condemned to live.

Worst day yet, worse than the day at the quarry. I no longer hope. All morning in the stables, tears fall. Kapo does not care. Turns his back, does not accost me. Nothing matters. God betrays me. Black smoke a taunt—you will burn in other ways.

Terrible dreams. I hear him but cannot see him, his face. There is blood and fragments of flesh. If I open my eyes, what will I see? Everywhere the blood, tortured flesh. I drown in it. But am condemned to live. I dream of the bunker, stacks of bodies. I breathe, but cannot breathe. Stiff hands grab me and I scream. Blood fills my mouth. I vomit blood and see it congeal to stone. *Quia peccavi nimis cogitatione, verbo, opere et omissione.* If only I could die. I smell death. Smell flesh and hair in the smoke. If I were ash, I would float to the clouds.

Ticking stopped.

Man in the bunk above, shook his clock, demanded it run. Shouts from the others for quiet. The man wept. Next morning, clock in his lap, gave away his breakfast. Two prisoners fought for the piece of bread. Two days, he refused to eat. I took his clock, smuggled it to the stables, repaired it, set the time. He clasps it to his chest, smiles but does not eat.

Kommandant came to the stables to ride. His mount's hoof was sore. We were blamed. Struck my face with his crop. Bled profusely.

Krake torments me. I had no cigarettes today. He was angry,

punched me. Maybe a cracked rib. I said kill me and you get no cigarettes. Others will retaliate. Perhaps he agreed. I was not hit a second time. But he will get his revenge.

J. spoke to me today. Knows about the clock, asked, What else do you repair? I was sent to the infirmary. Dreadful place. Better to die in one's bed. We hear stories, skulls of prisoners, paperweights on SS doctors' desks. But there are no choices here. J. gave me a pass, told me who to see. I followed a man down a hallway to a door, words DANGER, TOXIC in red letters. I did not want to enter. The man laughed. Why worry, he said, we die here one way or another. He led me through a laboratory. Stank of formaldehyde. No one around. Dust on tables, on test tubes, beakers. One more door, a storeroom. A wireless there. Hidden. But doesn't work. I examined it, yes, I can fix it but need parts. Tell me which part, the man said. I am to go back when they have the parts.

Man beside me died in the night. He trembled, convulsed. Sepsis, untreated wound on his leg. He cried out. Held him until breathing stopped.

Krake belligerent. Will inform the SS, he says. I don't care, I say. What good is life? They kill me, another will take my place. And retaliate. Empty boast. Perhaps he knows this. Life here is worthless. Krake can kill me when he wants, guards or kapos too, other prisoners. Our work detail kapo drives us harder. Yesterday, man collapsed from heavy bales. Kapo beat him with pitchfork. He did not return to work. I keep my head down, work hard. Avoid kapos, I tell new prisoners. Do not try to make them friends, impress them. Do not call attention to yourself. Work and look away.

J. worries Krake may find a way to be rid of me. J. will try to arrange a new work detail that will move me from my barracks. He does not tell me what.

A Stone for Bread

Krake at the latrine. Had nothing to give me, demanded cigarettes. Refused him. Slammed his fist against my head. Dragged me to a toilet, forced me to kneel, shoved my head in filthy water. Believed I would die. Mind raced with fear. Wanted to resist but Krake too strong. My chest burned. Could not hold my breath much longer. Strangely, I felt peace. The happiness I knew one night in the barracks. Krake jerked my head from the water, slapping me. Other men, someone Krake did not want to see, entered the latrine. I was released. I still have the cigarettes.

J. says I must hide. Any day I may be called out from roll call. What once I wanted, I seek to avoid.

I have been given a new work detail. In a place I fear more than death. The infirmary. I am quartered here, have been here a week. Some kapos are criminals, cruel to patients. Some are not. J.'s network eliminates criminals when it can, puts their own in place. A risky game. There is little power against brutal guards. The network exploits guards' fear of contagion. Wards labeled TB and typhus hide prisoners, contraband like the radio. I work as an orderly, help the network because I know German and English, understand other languages and assist S., a prisoner from Romania, a doctor.

I have been several times to the laboratory to work on the radio. S. discovered I have skills with laboratory instruments. Be vigilant, he says. An SS doctor oversees the medical unit. S. gained his trust. This helps the network conceal things. The SS show up without warning, examine patient charts and numbers.

Today I learned a terrible secret. Each morning, fifteen or twenty syringes are laid on a table. Syringes of phenol. "Medicine" for prisoners with X by their prison numbers. Who administers these? I asked S. He never answered.

I learn other secrets. Who lives and who dies is decided by the SS and the prisoners themselves. I am valuable to the network now, when I cease to be, they will decide for me—a stab of the needle to the heart. S. knows I keep these notes, though he doesn't ask about them. I tell him they are research notes, that once I studied science. Sometimes he gives me paper, warns not to let the guards know. They are paranoid, he says. *They* is everyone here. I too grow more paranoid each day. Now that I am given life, I am possessive of it, see death everywhere, in shadows on the wall, outside the window in the black smoke, in the watery broth and dry sausage that comprise my breakfast. I hide my notes. I have created a cache for them under a cabinet in the surgery.

A message from J. My number showed up on the deportation list. This does not mean I will be deported. It means I will disappear. Why? One never knows why. Because of Krake? Did he tell the SS that I work for the network? A friendly kapo, also network, said today they will try to stall, wait to make an exchange. I asked what this means. It means they will list me as sick and move me to the typhus ward. I trembled, protested. I do not want that kind of death. The ward houses few with typhus, he said. Mostly men saved from execution, men important to the network. When the right prisoner dies from typhus, my number will be listed on the death notice. His number comes to me. Officially, I will die. The dead man will recover. Who will know? One walking skeleton looks like any other, though I will be moved to another section of the infirmary. I wonder what he meant by *right* prisoner.

Weeks have passed since I entered a new hell. Many on the typhus ward are men like me, in hiding, but some are sick, dying. To live, one resides amid death. And death is constant. Whatever is intended for me, I no longer believe it is death. Perhaps I have served my time in purgatory. I held a boy of 15 in my arms. He died hot with fever. His final words were to bless me. When he died, I wept like the prisoner mourning his clock. My mind and will are breaking down.

My death has been arranged. I am given a new number, moved to a different section of the infirmary, officially well and back to work. Dr. S. was moved here too. We protect each other. I live in a room with ten others. Only two to a bed, a luxury. I work as S.'s nurse, clean excrement and urine from patients' bodies, examine wounds and bandages. I am surprised there are women and children in this part of the infirmary. I learn many more are in the camp. A young girl, malnourished, legs cratered with ulcers, screamed for her mother. Today she died. Age 12.

The war goes badly for the Germans. Medical supplies dwindle. Treatment hardly exists, although each illness and injury is precisely recorded in files.

Air raid sirens. Planes overhead. Dr. S. nodded and mouthed three words: Americans and British. They bomb everywhere now in Germany. The hidden wireless tells a different story from that which blares through camp speakers. *Der Vaterland* is faltering. Allied bombers fly over our heads and no one stops them.

Conditions worsen. More patients are brought here. The infirmary fills with them. I dream of syringes side by side on the white table and wake in terror. I dare not grow fond of so many sick. A woman with a broken ankle, a kapo stomped on it, although the white card read *fell down stairs.* Worse for her is malnutrition, eyes sunken, edema. A favor, she asked. A photograph, a small smudged picture of herself. An image of beauty, dark hair to her shoulders, wide, luminous eyes. Send it, she begged. The address on the back. Yes, I said, a lie. One sends nothing from here but ashes. She smiled, kissed my hand. The next morning, a kapo carried a syringe to her room. I ran the corridor to my bunk, head on my arms to hold back sobbing.

A new terror stalks this section of the infirmary. Dr. S. is ill. His eyes sink into bruised sockets. Flesh is gray. The illness of despair. He will die of it without some spark of life to loosen its grip. I try, but there is no response. He sits by a window, staring out, speaks of the Alps, how beautiful they are in the sunlight. When I look where he points, I see stone walls.

With S. in surgery when he faltered, hands shaking. I took the scalpel. He did not protest. A ruptured spleen. Not unusual here. I finished what S. could not. S. left and went to his room. He has not come out. Word spread. Kapo accosted me in the hall. Was I a doctor? How could I answer? Truth means death. A medical student once, I said. Part lie. Kapo is worried but asks nothing further. I did not sleep, but tossed on the bed. What have I done?

S. grows worse. He turns to me for comfort. I am beside him for each surgery, make the incision, the finishing stitches. His hand trembles. He stands at my elbow, explains and corrects. He knows I am no doctor but has decided I will become one. Each day, he is thinner. This morning, I repaired a broken wrist. He tapped my arm, like a father. You will do, he said, and wandered away.

Today, S. found on the pharmacy floor, syringe beside him. The kapo woke me, frightened. What happens if the SS doctor sees him this way? We will be punished. I went with the kapo to remove the syringe, carry S. to his bed, then wrote a report. Heart attack. On the signature line, my number, the one by which I am now identified, but as a doctor. I know nothing about the man I pretend to be. For this, I may die.

The SS doctor examined S.'s body. He had been drinking, seemed hardly to care, grunted and signed the official report under my number. He never looked at me. The man's apathy protects us. He feels nothing for the patients but cares only to drink with his SS comrades in their quarters. One of the network spoke with me last night. Someone must take S.'s place, protect the network in this section of the infirmary. There is no one but me. The network will search the camp for another. The kapo asks no questions. His words are soft, friendly. He cautions that I will be watched by everyone, the SS, the network too. A misstep is death.

Radio reports the American army advances. We do not believe this. Hope is a knife in the heart. Each day, a row of syringes lies on the laboratory table. I long to smash them, fling them to the floor but try not to see them. I have made my bargain with the kapo. The syringes are his business. My business is life. The network must make the decisions of death. I am a coward. Weak. Unable to balance the use of death to save life. At night, I dream of the young woman with the broken ankle. Sometimes I take the photograph from where I have hidden it, stare at her face. No older than 20, I think.

Everything is breaking down. The war is lost. American armies approach. The prisoners are frightened. The guards grow more ruthless. Hundreds of prisoners, many women and children among them, arrive at the infirmary, terrible wounds inflicted by guards. Broken bones, crushed legs, arms. We are helpless, can only wrap them in rags, bandages made from the clothing of the dead. We have few medicines, almost no anesthetic. Only terrible choices. What does it matter to set a broken bone for the dying? To try to save what cannot be saved? I drown in guilt. Prisoners working here eat better. The network provides extra rations. Though I am walking bones, my body lives. I am one of the camp elite. The many hours of surgery require nourishment. Yesterday, I was in surgery ten hours, left only for bodily needs. When there is no anesthetic, we hold patients down, stuff wads of cloth in their mouths to stifle the screams.

There are new doctors here now. One confided he is a Jew. In Vienna, before the war, he was a psychiatrist who worked with Freud.

Now he is a surgeon. Another is a pediatrician. I sense he too is a Jew, but he tells me nothing. Both labor hours in the infirmary and surgery. They know their skills provide them survival. We rarely see the SS doctor. He sends lists by his aide of those to be executed. There is little phenol left, no benzene, so we ignore them. We are told the SS stay drunk in their quarters.

What are we to do? The prison bursts with new arrivals each day. Hundreds from the countryside and nearby towns have been herded into the compound. Where are the Americans? Everyone is dying. Will they come too late?

There are no more beds. Sick and dying are laid in hallways, on floors. To reach the surgery, I step over groaning bodies. There are no medicines, no anesthesia. Rumors fly wildly about. We will be taken from the prison, marched until we drop. Many who have swelled the prison are from other camps. The SS will never let us live, they say. They will destroy all traces of their butchery. When the Americans come near, we will be forced from the prison and murdered in the fields. Or buried alive in the quarry. Two of the doctors refuse to operate. They cannot bear the screaming. What use, they mumble, and remain in their bunks, spend the day staring at walls.

Everything is chaos. The network strives frantically for order. Some talk of insurrection, a cache of guns hidden away. There will come a signal and the prisoners will take the camp. I ignore them. Boasts of desperate men. There is too much dying. Too many who need help. I bribed an SS guard with cigarettes to get us anesthesia. Surgery continues into the night. We have no sulphonamides. Dysentery is rampant. Patients defecate where they lie. We cannot clean them. They are placed two and three to a bed, on the floor, in corridors. I go from room to room, down the corridor. There is no end to misery. No end.

Yesterday, I made my way through the many sick who lie in the corridor. Human ghosts crying for water and medicine. A face I know lifted toward me, begged my help. My heart stopped. A rosy birthmark at his hairline. The man from the quarry. I hurried past. Later I spoke to a doctor, told him nothing but asked his diagnosis. Pneumonia, he said. I learn there is still phenol in the pharmacy, syringes that can be readied, though we have long stopped using them.

Roars of shelling a short distance away. Awaken an old memory I do not want to remember. The Americans are at our doors. Everyone is terrified. Any moment, we expect to be driven down the mountain and into fields and woods and murdered. The air stinks of fear.

Last night I could not sleep. Wandered the rooms and corridor with a flashlight, speaking to the sick, finding a sip of water, holding a dying hand since there is no medicine. Lights are not allowed because of airplanes overhead. A man sobbed on my chest. He did not want to die before the Americans came. Hold on, I urged. Will yourself to live.

It was still dark when trucks and jeeps were heard in the camp. A prisoner found me. A hysterical man, coughing and cackling like a hen. They are leaving, he screamed. I believed him to mean the time had come when we would be herded from the camp to be killed. He kept shouting, shaking my arm and laughing like a madman. The SS, he cried. They are gone. In my own mad reaction, I did not move, unready to believe him. I walked away, stopped to comfort a boy, leg shattered by SS rifle butts, came on the man who had wept on my shoulder. They are gone, I said, at last understanding these words. The SS are gone. We are free. He did not hear me. He was dead.

TWENTY THREE

Rachel closed the binder and wiped her eyes, relieved Henry had gone to the kitchen to fix sandwiches. René's diary was a remarkable document, a work of history and witness, miraculously saved from that terrible place. She had skimmed the first part of the document quickly: the lists, the phrases, the disjointed descriptions. There were symptoms of diseases, inventories of the few items each man was given, a cup, plate and spoon, shoes, clothing. Apart from numbering the steps to the quarry, René numbered the barracks in camp, the prisoners in his block, in his bed. It was only when she reached the diary's first declarative sentence, "I am condemned to live," that the narrative held her rapt. Surely, someone must publish it. But she wouldn't say that, not to Henry. Not after his angry response when she'd mentioned her Master's thesis. She wondered why Henry had never published it. Perhaps he couldn't, a matter of copyright. But he had published the poetry. She looked at the cardboard box sitting on the table by the couch. Had it been in Henry's possession since René brought it to his apartment forty years ago? From its appearance, it could be that old, the cardboard worn, creased, in places cracked. She wiped her eyes a second time and went to join Henry in the kitchen.

"What happened to René after Mauthausen?" she asked, carrying two plates to the kitchen table.

"When the war was over, he returned to France."

"He just went home?"

Henry pulled out a chair for her, then poured them each a glass of iced tea and took the chair across from her. "Apparently. He showed up at his sister's door in the town outside Paris where I first encountered him. And for once, I think they were glad to see him. The sister's husband had been killed by a sniper's bullet in the last days of the war as the Allies marched on Paris. Their father was dying, so they'd moved him to the sister's house with their mother. The younger brother, Michel, who'd joined the French army prior to the German occupation, had been captured early on by the Germans. He later escaped and made his way to Switzerland. After the war, he chose not to come home. The real irony was that when René returned, he found himself head of the household. I like to believe that's when his family discovered his true value. That he could do things, fix toilets and hang shutters. He also found a job on the assembly line at the Renault plant nearby and brought home a steady income."

"Did he tell you all this too?"

"Yes. He didn't leave much out. Though he didn't tell me his family was glad to see him. But I surmised that pretty quickly."

They ate their sandwiches and she cleared the table. Neither had much to say. Rachel found herself unable to expunge the diary and René's story, as Henry had written it, from her thoughts.

"Show me what's in the box," she said, when they'd washed and put away the dishes.

He nodded, and she followed him into the living room, where he set the cardboard box on the couch between them. The first thing she noticed when he opened it was the odor. Faint, but distinct. Not merely the mustiness of age but a slight stench of decay and feculence as if the very air of Mauthausen was trapped inside. She wondered if she just imagined this, her nose conjuring the odor from what her eyes witnessed: bits of torn paper, wrappers from cigarette cartons and cigarette paper itself, scraps of cloth, even shreds of worn leather scrawled upon in a tiny, meticulous handwriting. Some of the writing looked to be in ink, some pencil markings that were no longer legible.

"He wrote with whatever he could find, pencil stubs, bits of charcoal, even at times blood," Henry explained.

"His own?"

"I don't know. He told me he started scribbling on these scraps soon after he arrived at Mauthausen. At first, mostly lists and observations, as you saw."

"Wasn't that risky?"

"Extremely risky. It would have been death had he been discovered. But, as you saw in my rendering of his story, he didn't care much about the threat of death. But what I find so curious even now is that he went to great lengths to hide these scraps, so that they would survive."

"And he brought them to you years ago in Paris," she murmured, not really a question but a restatement of what Henry had said, as if repeating it might help her understand.

"Yes, that night. He had wanted me to know and have everything about him, although I felt in that instance I was being offered pieces of his flesh. It was an uncanny moment, spiritual almost, if you understand what I mean."

She wasn't sure she did, but the plain cardboard box with its tattered scraps moved her deeply. Where had those scraps been? How had they survived?

"There was one other thing that night," Henry said.

"What?"

"I guess I had begun to worry about René, why he was telling me all this. I guess I worried about his sexual proclivities, that he might see me as an object of desire, so to speak, like the young seminarian. But that same night, I came to understand it wasn't me who obsessed him so, but Renard Marcotte. The whole time in my apartment, René never sat down. He just gave me the box, which I placed on a table, while he stood fidgeting in the middle of the room, twisting an unlit cigarette between his fingers. I waited, probed, but he still said nothing, not a word. I was about to dismiss him with an excuse that I had to go to bed, when he finally spoke. For the first time since I'd known him, I heard in his voice something that had not been there before. Passion or anger, I wasn't sure which. Understand, everything he had told me to that point had been rendered in the most dispassionate manner, like an exercise recited for school. Even when he delivered the box, his voice was barely audible. But as he turned to go, what he said was uttered in a tone so different from before—he practically barked it at me—that it truly startled me. It was one sentence only, and then he left. One sentence. 'Marcotte was at Mauthausen.' "

TWENTY FOUR

There was more he wanted to tell her, tell her then, after she had read René's Mauthausen diary. But Rachel said she needed to leave, that she had work to finish before the end of the semester.

"I won't keep you long," he said. "And it may be a while before we see each other. I'm heading out Tuesday and will be gone a couple of weeks."

When she asked where he was going, he told her, Washington, D.C. "I've been wanting to see the Holocaust Museum since it opened. Have you been there yet?"

She shook her head. "I should do that one day."

"You certainly should. What happened in that time must never be forgotten." He hesitated, then asked again, "If you could stay just a little longer, please. I promise I won't keep you. And then you'll be rid of me for awhile and have plenty of time to finish your classwork."

He was glad to see her smile.

"All right, Henry. But I need to leave by three."

He nodded.

"That spring in Paris," he began, "was one of the worst times in my life. René continued to haunt me, showing up on my doorstep with these stories of his life and then telling me Marcotte had been at Mauthausen. I felt like a crazy man."

No, not actually crazy. It was more like desperate. One morning, as Henry and Brisson drove to Reims, Henry suddenly blurted, "Tell me about Marcotte, his experiences during the war."

"What experiences, Henry?"

"At Mauthausen."

Brisson stared at him, puzzled. "What are you talking about?"

"I've heard that Marcotte was a prisoner at Mauthausen, the Nazi concentration camp."

"You heard nonsense, my friend. Renard Marcotte spent the war years in France, minding his shop and trying to survive like everyone else. Who told you these things?"

Caught off guard, Henry lied.

"A friend of Bert Yeager's. I don't know his name. It just came up one night, in a café."

"And I suppose this friend of Monsieur Yeager's told you disgusting things about Marcotte. They are always trying to discredit us, you know. They will say anything."

"No, no," Henry protested, "there was nothing meant to discredit Marcotte, just that he had been at Mauthausen."

Henry stared out the window, afraid Brisson would read the lies in his face. He changed the subject, furious at himself for mentioning Mauthausen. He returned that afternoon to Paris confused. Who was telling the truth? He tried prying information from Eugénie. He asked her about Brisson. They had just finished dinner at his apartment.

"Don't be serious, Henri." She frowned. "All this politics makes you what they say in America, a box."

Henry laughed. "Square, Eugénie, the word is square."

She obviously didn't like him laughing for she pouted and snapped, "So what do I know. I am not educated like you. I'm a shop girl, nothing."

Henry got up and stood behind her chair, reaching his hands to her breasts. "Well, shop girl, I love you."

She brushed his hands away. "Pah, how silly you are. You won't love me when you leave here."

"Then come with me."

She looked up at him, curious. "*Oui*, Henri?"

He had never suggested such a possibility. In truth, he hadn't even thought it until the moment he said it. But somehow it seemed right. Why couldn't Eugénie go to America with him?

"We'll be married. And when we get back to the States, you can go to college. Be educated if that's what you want. You won't be a shop girl in America."

She rose from the chair to face him. "Americans promise these things and never mean it." Her face clouded. "And I could not do it anyway."

"Why not?"

"Because I'm French, Henri. I will die French."

He leaned over to kiss her. "We can talk about it later, but I want you to consider it."

An image rose in his mind of home and family, Eugénie, children, in America, where a successful career as a writer awaited. He would change her mind, make her see.

The next day he was off again with Brisson. They traveled together often now, leaving Paris in the morning, returning at night. Usually they visited outlying towns, meeting with M.L.F. operatives. Henry was seldom invited to their meetings but was sent off on errands, distributing Marcotte posters or picking up letters and packages. Even so, he enjoyed these trips. They took him away from Paris, from the specter of René haunting his doorway. Henry enjoyed Brisson's spirited reflections on Greek and Roman culture, the nature of the city states, the causes for the fall of Athens. And Henry was moving closer to Marcotte. Brisson took him to meetings where Marcotte was present, leaving Henry in the next room to type English press releases or tend the coffee pot. Servile tasks, but Henry was pleased to be trusted, to be considered important enough to be there. Several times, he dined with Marcotte and his aides, these occasions much like the one on the way from Reims—convivial, pleasant, with excellent wine and food.

In June, nearly a year from the day Henry had arrived in Paris, Bert Yeager phoned.

"Need to see you, Henry. Got something."

He didn't say what he had and Henry didn't really care. He hadn't heard from Bert in over a month, so his response was a tepid, "Sure, I guess."

"How about if I come by tomorrow? Around eight?"

"Okay." Henry liked the idea of Yeager at his place. He would see how well Henry was doing. That it beat being a stringer.

Yeager arrived the next evening promptly at eight, a leather briefcase in his hand. Henry laughed. He looked like an insurance salesman. Even Yeager's somber face fit the image, faux somber, I'm-here-to-solve-all-your-problems somber, thought Henry. Yeager plopped himself on Henry's sofa and opened the briefcase, removing several brown file folders.

"Man, you have done me one hell of a favor, Henry," he said.

Henry was confused. What the hell did Yeager mean?

"I'm going to score this time. Score big."

"What are you talking about?"

"What you said back some weeks ago, about Marcotte and Mauthausen."

"I didn't say that!" Henry blurted, frightened. What *had* he said?

"Well, I got the message. You asking about Mauthausen after hanging around with the M.L.F. crowd. I'm not born yesterday, you know. Besides, remember you asked me to do some background pieces on Marcotte."

"Yes, but—"

"He was there all right. Renard Marcotte spent the war years at Mauthausen, the infamous German labor camp in Austria."

"But he didn't! Brisson said—"

"Shit! This Brisson guy is a damn liar. Been checking on him too. He's up to plenty that's no good, believe me. Haven't run it all down yet, trust me, I will, but looks like he may have been a collaborator during the war and is now trying to cover his tracks along with those of other collaborators. Maybe even organizing a hit squad, so to speak, using the M.L.F. as cover. Dead men tell no tales, you understand." Yeager grinned.

Henry was appalled to silence.

Yeager slid papers from one of his folders. "I was lucky, you see, not just because I picked up on what you said. But when I started nosing around, I met this guy, French journalist, who's been digging into Marcotte's past for over a year now. We clicked, you might say. He filled me in on a lot of the pieces. We're about ready to go public. But I thought you might be able to add some details, corroborate a few things. I'll put you on deep background. Nobody will know."

Henry's mouth went dry. Sweat formed on the palms of his clenched hands. Yeager got up and began to spread his papers across Henry's sofa.

"You might be interested in these. Monsieur Marcotte isn't, of course, who he says he is. But you probably know that already."

Henry lied with an affirming nod.

"Birth name wasn't Renard Marcotte. Tagged himself Marcotte and embellished his personal history after the war. Hell, everything was so chaotic then, so many people lost in the camps, dead or whereabouts unknown. And the guy was a wily one. Probably wasn't even born in Épernay, although he spent time there as a child with relatives. He came from Châteauneuf, bastard son of a local seamstress. There're rumors his father was a rich Jewish industrialist with relatives in Châteauneuf. Checking on that too." Yeager shuffled the papers on the couch, then looked up with a querying glance. "What you think?"

"I don't think anything. I'm not interested in your documents."

"Come on, Henry. You're involved with this man. You've got to know. And I need your help."

"I don't know. I don't know and I can't help."

Henry stopped talking. The yellow cat leaped into his lap. He let his hand aimlessly caress its soft fur. He couldn't look at Rachel.

"What happened?" she nudged.

He didn't answer immediately. He didn't want to answer. Would she despise him? He flexed his fingers, the knuckles stiff from the hours at his typewriter. "I did look at Yeager's documents, read through a few of them. I now have copies of most of them. Over the next few years, Yeager accumulated quite a dossier on the man. And he seemed delighted to keep me informed long after I'd left Paris, sending me things."

"Did he publish any of it?"

"Some things. Mostly the information that discredited Marcotte, that his last name really wasn't Marcotte and how he'd reinvented himself after the liberation. Marcotte had done a one-eighty, you see. Before the war, he'd been a Communist, part of a group of young radicals in Dijon. Which is how he'd ended up at Mauthausen. And he wasn't some rube from the provinces either. That was part of the act. As a young man, he was associated with a group of avant-garde leftists and artists. These were the things Yeager published, enough to unmask

Marcotte and ruin him as a politician. But Yeager never put the larger pieces together. At least not what I realized almost immediately from the photographs and documents he showed me that day."

Rachel said nothing, as if waiting for him to explain.

"What I saw in Yeager's documents about Marcotte and what Yeager said about Brisson had left me angry and frightened about my own complicity. But as I glanced through the documents I saw something else. Yeager had several photographs from Mauthausen, photographs reputed to be of Marcotte, although Yeager had not been able to identify them with any certainty. Among them was a photograph of a prisoner in a weird outfit, a kind of clownish imitation of the SS Death Head's uniform. The man's partially shaved head revealed an odd pigmentation, or so it appeared, like a birthmark, almost exactly as René had described it. The man in the quarry, hands on the dynamite plunger, the man René believed responsible for the death of the boy singing that day to the prisoners. So, finally I understood. Or thought I did. René's obsession with Marcotte. He knew. And now I knew. And Yeager didn't know. Sure, Yeager had proof Marcotte was a fraud, but he didn't know the rest."

"Did you tell him?"

"I told myself after Yeager left my apartment that I needed to be sure, Rachel. One more rationalization, I suppose. Certainly, I was worried about my own skin too, what might happen to me if Marcotte or Brisson learned I'd identified Marcotte as a war criminal. And, of course, there wasn't a shred of evidence to convict him. Even if René were to testify against him. Marcotte was a prisoner. He could have been forced to that act. I mean, did the man even know where the wire attached to that plunger terminated?"

"But, but in René's story," she protested, "you wrote René saw Marcotte laughing after the explosion."

Henry shrugged. "There are different reasons people laugh, Rachel. At jokes and funny situations, of course. But we also laugh when we're nervous and ill at ease. Or hysterical or terrified. I'm not a psychiatrist, but I know that people in extreme circumstances are sometimes known to laugh. A defense mechanism maybe, the laughter of the damned."

He saw from her face Rachel wanted to argue, that his defense of Marcotte had upset her, perhaps even shocked her.

"But still, Henry, he could be brought to trial. René was a witness."

"Possibly so, but I doubt René would have complied." He waited for a further protest from Rachel. When she said nothing, he continued his story, knowing he had disappointed her. But it couldn't be helped. What was done or not done so many years ago could not be altered.

"A few nights after Yeager showed me the documents," he said, "I found myself with Marcotte. Brisson and I had driven to Melun, a town not far from Paris. Marcotte had met that day with a group of shopkeepers and afterwards rode back with us to Paris. I have never forgotten that evening, Rachel. Sometimes I think it's etched on my brain cells. Through most of it, Marcotte was strangely subdued. But when we arrived at his building, he invited the two of us to come up for whiskey and a chat, as he put it.

"We'd already been drinking. We'd had dinner in Melun and I'd probably had too much wine and whiskey. I was still reeling, you see, from the conversation with Yeager. Was Marcotte a murderer? But what real proof did I have that the man in the photograph was really him? There wasn't a trace of a heart-shaped birthmark on Marcotte's scalp as I sat within a foot or two of him that evening. Of course, one couldn't truly know, you see. His thick hair was usually combed across his forehead and would hide such a mark if it existed. The man in the photograph was gaunt, emaciated. Had Yeager randomly shown me the snapshot, without René's earlier description, I would never have identified the man as Marcotte. And Brisson had insisted many times, which I knew as well, that Marcotte had enemies who would happily destroy him."

"So you still believed in him?" Rachel asked.

"Yes. No. I mean I don't think I had ever really believed in him. Not his politics anyway. It was a young man's adventure. But I had adventured too far and was terrified I had gotten myself into serious trouble."

Henry paused and swallowed. His mouth was dry. His heart raced, as surely as it had that night so many years ago.

"Brisson and I went up to Marcotte's flat. There were several of his young men there, bodyguards you might say. He brought out a bottle of whiskey and we shared it. I don't remember what was said at first, mostly small talk, I think, friendly banter, the chat he'd mentioned. I was feeling sick, a bit woozy, and was about to excuse myself, when Marcotte suddenly leaned toward me.

'Brisson tells me you consort with reporters who wish to ruin me.'

'I do what?'

'Reporters, Henri, like that bastard Yeager.'

'Bert's a friend.'

'Like a snake?'

'I don't understand. What's wrong with Bert?'

"Marcotte put his face close to mine. I smelled the whiskey and had the crazy sensation he was about to bite me. A snake himself. I wanted to draw back but was too frightened to move.

'Lies, Henri, that's what's wrong with Bert Yeager.'

'The stuff about Mauthausen?'

"Without thinking, I'd uttered the damning word. Mauthausen. I wanted him to refute it, you understand. I wanted him to go to his own files and pull out photographs, Marcotte the shopkeeper minding his grocery in 1944, Marcotte, the patriotic Frenchman, snapshots of him standing next to an Épernay air raid warden or in a French army uniform, anything, anything to prove Yeager wrong. But, of course, he didn't. He only leaned closer. I felt suffocated, about to be sucked into his strength, the man's magnetism. He put his hand on my shoulder. My shoulder burned. His eyes fixed on mine. And then, then Rachel, he smiled the sweetest, most engaging of smiles. 'Lies, Henri, all lies.'

"It was an awful moment, a moment when I saw the real man— and with unshakable certainty knew. I knew who the liar was."

Henry clutched the yellow cat to his chest. Neither he nor Rachel spoke. Finally, he moved the cat, stood, mumbling he was thirsty and went off to the kitchen after a glass of water. He set it on the table beside him when he returned and allowed himself finally to look at Rachel. Her face was placid, somber, concerned perhaps, even worried, but he saw not a trace of condemnation. As if she'd just then realized he had been nervously awaiting her response, she said only, "Well, what happened then, Henry? I mean, after you realized the truth about Marcotte?"

He sighed and the sigh quivered through his chest. "Nothing. Not then anyway. Perhaps I was a better actor or dissembler than I might have thought possible. I obviously fumbled my way through the rest of the evening. I have no memory of anything that was said after that. I only remember how I felt, horrified and sick, and like a damn fool, a young hot-headed fool with my stupid, quixotic notions of adventure. What had I done for Brisson? All those messages and packages, God knows what was in them. What kind of people were these? What kind of man was I?"

"Did you tell Yeager then?"

"I thought about going to him. I thought about it many times."

"And Marcotte?"

"I did confront him, Rachel. In the end, I did."

"But Yeager?"

"I think I may have called Yeager that night. Yes, I'm sure I did, after I left Marcotte's flat. I was going to go to him. But things—I guess you might say I panicked. I certainly wasn't thinking clearly. How could I have been? You probably believe I hadn't been thinking clearly from the day I set foot in Paris. You'd be right, of course. What is innocence but colossal ignorance? Certainly I'd been ignorant, chosen not to know, because with knowing comes one's realization of complicity. After that evening, Marcotte's smiling denial—*Lies, Henry, all lies*—I felt I stood at the edge of a chasm about to fall or possibly leap. But I didn't leap. I ran."

"You left Paris?"

"Not then, though soon afterwards. But that night, I went only a short distance. Panicked, I ran to René."

"But why René?"

"I don't know. Maybe because he'd been the one to tell me Marcotte was at Mauthausen. Or because he'd told me his secrets. Perhaps I thought it was time to tell mine. Which I did. I sat in his parlor several hours, telling him about Brisson and the M.L.F., Yeager's offhand comments about a hit squad and how worried I was that I might be involved, that I didn't know what I had done for Brisson."

"What did he say?"

Henry saw how Rachel's eyes widened. Was this surprise? Or a first trace of contempt?

"I'd come to him late that night and yes he listened, but without a word, his face like I'd seen it so many times, impassive, with no expression at all, not any. Whatever he felt about Marcotte, he seemed to care nothing about what was happening with me. Or else he despised me for it. Oh, he never said that. But I felt it in him, the cold eyes, the flat, reedy voice. He let me confess everything I'd done for Brisson and Marcotte, how deeply involved I was. But I saw not the slightest concern in his face, certainly not sympathy. After all we'd been through together, the long nights when he spilled out the stories of his life, of Mauthausen. Though he'd told me these things in the same, reedy voice, with the same dispassion, I had heard them differently, felt his terror like my own nightmare, the anguish of his imprisonment, when I'd—understand what I mean by this—felt deep love for this man, as brother, suffering brother, when I'd wanted desperately to embrace him and solace his wounded soul. Yet here I was, coming to him with my anguish and fear, and there was no response. No response at all."

"None?"

"Well, not what I wanted, I suppose, compassion, understanding, maybe even gratitude that I'd told him this. But yes, there *was* a response, an odd one—after I'd told him everything."

Henry stopped, his voice quivery from recalling that night, what he had never recounted to anyone. Rachel sat quietly, her hands serenely in her lap as if patiently waiting for him to continue.

"He said nothing about what I'd told him but left the room and came back with a handful of paper, yellowing stationery, and a pen. He then began reciting in French. Poetry. Lines of poetry. When I stared at him dumbfounded, he stopped and put the pen in my hand, directing me to a chair and table. 'Write this,' he said. I was so startled and confused I did exactly that. I wrote everything he said, everything."

"The poems you later published?"

"Yes, what became *A Stone for Bread*. It's difficult now to describe what I felt then. The words he recited to me, images of Mauthausen, its horrors, stories of prisoners, the terrible things done to them. At one point I began to weep but kept on writing, trying to keep my tears from smudging the ink on the page. Even then, René seemed oblivious to my distress. I never heard the slightest emotion in his voice. He sat in a chair opposite me while I wrote down everything he said like a scribe in a courtroom. It was dawn by the time I finished. I'd had to stop him often, ask about a word, a phrase, nuances. My French wasn't perfect. And there were moments when I wanted to lurch from the chair, stuff the paper in his mouth and make him shut up. I didn't, although I believed his whole purpose was to chastise me with the tortures of Mauthausen, to twist the knife of guilt as far into my heart as he could. For my complicity with Marcotte and Brisson. Once I leaped up and went to the door, threatening to leave his house. He didn't try to stop me. And, of course, I didn't leave. I suppose my guilt had paralyzed me. And the poems were working on me, you see, my conscience, my sense of shame. They worked on me as effectively or more so than if he'd cursed and beaten me. When he finished dictating, I handed him the pieces of stationery, but he shoved them back at me and said, 'They are yours now.' He gave them to me, Rachel. The man just gave them to me."

Henry rubbed his hands across his thighs and stared at the floor. Rachel feared to speak but finally asked, "Didn't René give up the poems to the prisoner Krake at Mauthausen?"

"What he gave up were scraps with writing on them. The poems had never left him. That incredible mind of his, Rachel. René seemed to have total recall of everything he had ever read."

"Then what was the point of his saying he was giving them to you?"

"What I thought that night was that he meant them as an indictment of me, to shame me for consorting with criminals like Marcotte and Brisson. One more twist of the knife. But that's no longer what I think. It was years before I understood him or thought I did. When I published the poems, I believed that this might somehow exonerate me in his eyes, that perhaps that was what he wanted me to do. But I was so wrong, Rachel, so wrong about René. I spent years translating those scraps from Mauthausen into a coherent diary. Many were unreadable, so much so that I took them to a forensic scientist who resorted to ultraviolet and infrared tests to illumine the handwriting. Plus nothing was dated. There was no chronology. The arrangement is mine, so of course, I took liberties, made choices for words that proved unrecoverable. But by the time I'd finished what was a monumental task—it was only six years ago—I had come to see René in a finer light, so to speak. For such a brilliant man, he was actually a very simple man, a man who had lived through horror yet retained a kind of childish innocence. Like a saint, Rachel. If such exists in this world, René is surely among them. What I came finally to understand was that he'd given me the poems for the simplest of reasons. They had consoled him at Mauthausen, restored his will to live. In my distress that night in France, he meant only to console me. It was that simple. He offered me the only consolation he had."

He lifted the yellow cat that had nestled at his feet and held it on his lap, its purr warm against his stomach.

"But that long ago night, I didn't wait around to hear his reasons. I grabbed up the pages and fled his house, as if chased by demons. All I wanted was to get away from there, from what I thought was the man's madness. I was teetering at the brink of madness myself. I caught a train to Paris and spent hours riding the Metro, clutching yellowed pages of stationery to my chest. Several times I started to throw them away, even stood on the Pont St. Michel to drop them into the Seine. But something held me back. René's eyes, the reedy voice thrumming in my brain with its images of Mauthausen, I don't know why, Rachel, but I didn't destroy them." He breathed out a long sigh. "Instead, I chose that night to let them destroy me."

TWENTY FIVE
Twenty five

She hadn't heard from Henry in three weeks. There had been times before when he didn't call for awhile but usually because he'd been angry with her. She tried his phone, but no one answered. She waited another week. The day after her last exam, on a Saturday morning, she drove to Henry's house and was startled by the black BMW parked in front. No dogs trotted from the porch to greet her as she climbed from her car. She didn't see Henry's truck. As she walked toward the porch, the front door opened. It wasn't Henry, but a young man, mid-thirtyish, in a gray pinstriped business suit. He was tall, not so much hefty as pudgy, his brown hair perfectly blow-dried and swept up slightly from his forehead. Designer eyeglasses perched on the nose of a smooth, boyish face.

They stared curiously at each other before he spoke. "Are you Rachel?" he asked. He didn't smile but stepped off the porch and held out his hand. "Matthew Baxter."

She took the fleshy palm. "Who actually are you?" she blurted. "And why are you here?" He didn't seem particularly threatening and certainly not a thief, but she felt him as a threat. Something had gone very wrong.

"I'm Henry's attorney, you might say."

Might say? "What's happened? Please tell me what's happened."

"Will you come inside?"

"Yes."

He stepped back from the door to let her pass. From the hallway, she stared into an unrecognizable space, Henry's living room stacked with crates and boxes. She spun around to face Matthew Baxter. "Please, tell me!" But he didn't have to. She saw it in his eyes. "He's dead, isn't he?" she said, her words gargled. "I know Henry's dead." She walked into the living room and somehow made it to the couch, sinking into its squirmy springs. "Please tell me," she repeated.

The young man nodded. "His heart. Just gave out. He'd had a heart attack two years ago and never fully recovered. He probably shouldn't have made the trip to D.C."

Something in his face surprised her, the crease between his eyes when he frowned, the slight twist of his mouth. "You're not his lawyer, are you?"

He pulled the chair from Henry's writing table in front of the couch and sat down. "I'm an attorney all right, and I'm here about his estate, as his executor." He hesitated, the slight cock of his head familiar as well. "Henry was my biological father."

"I see him in you." Her voice quivered. She covered her face with her hands and leaned over her knees. She was dizzy, sick. Henry dead. How could Henry be dead? She didn't want him to be dead. And this man. Henry had mentioned a son once, but that's all he'd ever said. She blinked back tears and looked up, studying Matthew Baxter.

"I was going to call you," he said. "It took some doing to find your phone number."

"Yes, okay."

He stood. "Look, there's coffee in the kitchen and some tea bags. Haven't packed a lot of his stuff. How about I get you something?"

"I'd like that. Coffee, please. Black."

Now that he'd confessed his relationship to Henry, Rachel sensed he seemed uncomfortable with her. Had she caught him raiding the place? Stripping away Henry's belongings? Yet he said he hadn't packed everything and he seemed forthright enough. Perhaps beneath the expensive suit and perfect haircut was a shyer man than he'd first appeared. Like his father.

He returned with two mugs in his hand, again sitting across from her. She asked about the funeral.

"Hasn't happened yet. The body's been cremated. I wanted to talk with you about his ashes, if you knew anyone else who needs to be consulted."

She shook her head. "No, no one like that, family or anything. But if you'd like my opinion, I think he'd want his ashes interred or scattered here. He did have a few friends who might want to be part of that. There's a spot in his woods, near an old pine stump ..." She swallowed and wondered that she could breathe. "Thank you for waiting," she said. "To have a funeral, I mean."

Matthew Baxter shifted on the chair, his hands fidgeting with his belt. "Henry came to D.C. to see me. We had dinner together. I don't know what he's told you, Rachel, but Henry and I had never met each other before this visit. We'd corresponded the last few years, even spoken on the phone. My mother left him two months after I was born. When she remarried, my stepfather was able to adopt me. Henry apparently hadn't wanted children." He kept rubbing his hands together, as if they were cold, although the house was quite warm. "I didn't even know Henry existed until six years ago when my adoptive father died. That's when my mother told me. Truthfully, I didn't give a damn. I didn't give a damn either when Henry contacted me a couple of years ago. But, as I said, there was a series of letters. Phone conversations. When he asked to visit me, I softened, I guess, and agreed to it." A slight flush tinted his cheeks.

"I liked him. To my surprise, I really liked him. There was such a sadness about him, some deep hurt. And how could I fault him? He'd never hurt me in any way, probably only my mother, although

A Stone for Bread

she'd never mentioned Henry until my father died. Their divorce had obviously been for the best. She and my father, my adoptive father, were happy together." The flush deepened and, despite what he'd just said, Rachel saw a flicker of pain in his eyes.

"I fear I caused Henry's death," he said quietly, "the emotion of the visit, the wearying drive to D.C."

"Matthew," she said, her voice sterner than she'd intended, like a third grade teacher. "Don't ever feel guilty about Henry Beam. He carried enough guilt through his life for both of us."

She stayed with Henry's son into the early afternoon. He told her he'd been at the house the last three days but had to catch a Raleigh flight to Washington at five. Henry had left him the house, he said. He'd found his will. "Henry had gotten himself to the hospital emergency room sometime after our dinner, listing me as next of kin, even though I don't think he expected to stay there."

"How was it," she asked, "his death? Was it difficult?"

"He didn't seem to be in a lot of pain. They tried to keep him sedated. But that hadn't seemed to work too well with him."

"Why not?"

"God, Rachel, the man really fought. You might say he fought his own death. Not that he hadn't known. In some of his last letters, he'd indicated his health was failing, that he wouldn't be around much longer. I guess that's why I softened toward him. But he obviously never intended to die in a D.C. hospital. When he realized he'd never leave there, he went crazy, shouting at nurses that he had to go home, that he had to see you. Nurses kept asking me who Rachel was. I had no idea. Once, he pulled out his tubes and the catheter and was halfway down the hall before someone spotted him. I wasn't able to get by the hospital until the next afternoon. By then they'd straightjacketed him. He died that night."

She let her mind imagine Henry butt-naked in a hospital gown, tubes trailing after him, as he hustled along the corridor, face set to the exit. Tears rolled down her cheeks. "I guess he didn't go gentle then," she mumbled.

"Huh?" Matthew frowned, confused.

She wiped her face with the handkerchief he handed her. "You'll have to read his poetry." She blinked back more tears that pushed against her eyelids. "I wish I'd been with him. That I could have been there. But I didn't know about his health. He never said anything about it. How was either of us to know?"

Matthew Baxter seemed relieved. She wondered if he feared she might blame him for not getting Henry back to North Carolina.

"About Henry's will," he said, "he's left you a sum of money. But I won't know an exact amount until I get a sense of his assets. There were other things too, things he wanted you to have, which he listed. You can take some of them now, at least what I've packed up." He pointed to four cardboard file boxes near the hallway door. "That's why I hadn't called you yet. I'd planned to call from the airport, leave you a key somewhere, so you could come get everything. It's mostly papers and notebooks. Most important are probably his copyrights. He left those to you. There's an envelope taped to the top box with a copy of the will and my phone numbers, if you have any questions about anything. I don't foresee problems. Everything seems to come down to you and me."

He leaned forward. "Before he died, Rachel, he rattled on about Paris, as if I knew what he was talking about, said something about you were to have any of his books you wanted. And the carved lion."

She glanced toward the mantel. The lion wasn't there.

"It's packed with the rest. It's an amazing piece. I'm envious." He smiled. "Maybe I can trade you something."

"Never," she said.

"Oh, and he also said, in one of his lucid moments, no he didn't just say it, he insisted, that his books and papers were for you to use however you wanted. He then said something I thought was odd. *Cui bono*, he said, tell her that. It's Latin and means for what good or to what end."

She smiled. "I know."

Matthew loaded the file boxes in her car. "His neighbor down the road, well, not quite down the road, but a couple of miles from here, has his pets, said he'd keep them if I couldn't find a home for them. I'll be back down in a few weeks." He hunched his shoulders in a shrug, then grinned. "You know my first thought was to sell the old house, but now that I've been here, I'm not so sure. It would make a great vacation place, don't you think? A retreat. Maybe when I get back, you can help me sort through everything. I'd like to know more about Henry."

"There's a lot to know," she said, "but it will take awhile."

TWENTY SIX

Henry's funeral was delayed until early July. Before that, Matthew returned three times to North Carolina, brief visits, his law practice keeping him tied up in D.C. Rachel had moved the boxes Matthew had packed for her to her apartment, glancing through them when she could. In this first summer school session, she was teaching two sections of freshman English and had little time to sort papers. But she had a key to Henry's house and drove there on weekends or when Matthew was in town to pack more boxes. The two of them spoke often by phone about Henry's estate and items Rachel found among his papers that she thought he should know about. What she didn't share were two letters clipped together, a carbon copy of a letter Henry had sent Bert Yeager, the other letter Yeager's response. Letters, after all, were "papers," and were hers, or would be once Henry's will and the attachment were probated.

Henry's letter, typed and dated July 3, 1957, was a rambling and distraught plea for Yeager to talk with Eugénie, find a phone number or address where he could contact her. He had left Paris earlier than he'd anticipated, Henry said in the letter, citing "problems" he didn't name. He told Yeager Eugénie had agreed to marry him, that he'd given her a ring before flying back to the States, but she'd never answered his letters. Henry had apparently enclosed a list of people who knew Eugénie, but the list wasn't clipped to the copy. Yeager's response two months later was penned in a cramped scrawl on a blue postal letter sheet. He had his own list, sixteen barely legible names, people he interviewed in his search for the girl. She no longer worked at the *pâtisserie*, he wrote Henry, and when he'd checked out her Paris address, the family had moved. "It looks like she's abandoned Marcotte too and his young pimp, the guy Claude, you mentioned," wrote Yeager. "One of your buddies in the bluebands gave me a bit of advice, which I'm passing along. Leave it be, Henry. The girl doesn't want to be found."

Rachel felt the sting of this last sentence and understood what Henry surely felt. Did he afterwards return to Paris, determined to find Eugénie himself and bring her to America? Or was the prospect of a French prison, some Devil's Island hellhole, too horrific for him to face? She wondered if Henry ever learned what happened to the girl? When Rachel thought herself in Henry's place, she easily imagined the recurring wrench in the gut, the anger boiling over into tears. Had it been his fault? Had Marcotte or Brisson harmed or threatened her? Or was this her way of walking out on him? The cruelty lay in not knowing. How many weeks or months of leads and false hopes had come and been dashed before Henry gave up on Eugénie? Rachel wondered that Henry's heart hadn't failed him years ago.

She placed the letters in a folder, labeled it and filed it in one of the cardboard file boxes she'd bought several weeks ago. Another question as yet unanswered.

The funeral was on a Friday afternoon. Rachel had tried to get word to those few she thought might want to attend. Of Henry's friends from the party, Abe Wisner and Ralph Smith came, but Wallace and Helen Martin sent regrets, intimating they would be away. The others who showed up were a surprise: Scott and Adrian from the station, even after Matthew had denied Scott's request to film the brief ceremony. The only notice appearing about Henry's death had been a short obituary in the Chapel Hill and Durham newspapers with no mention of funeral plans. Scott probably told Richard Squires, who underwrote the video, and he came with his wife. Looking to be in his late sixties, Squires was tall and lean with silver hair that distinguished him, like a senator or CEO. His wife appeared somewhat younger than he was, an attractive woman, though her pallor and the puffy flesh under her eyes suggested illness or world-weariness that make-up couldn't hide. Professor Jim Green from Chapel Hill was also there and brought along three friends whose names Rachel never caught.

The service was simple. They gathered in the woods at the stump where Henry liked to sit and think. Rachel had worn a navy skirt and silky white blouse, her legs bare, feet slipped into sandals. Matthew, stiffly proper in dark blue suit and blue tie, thanked everyone for coming. He was visibly nervous but his voice held steady. He explained he and Henry had met only a few weeks ago, that in his brief time with his biological father, he'd found him to be a brilliant and intriguing man.

"I will always be indebted to Henry for two gifts," he said, "the first, of course, my life. The second gift was Henry's willingness to let my mother's second husband adopt me, in short, to let me go. While visiting me in D.C. in late May, Henry became ill, gravely ill. I learned then how much this old farmhouse and North Carolina and some of you here meant to him. If he hadn't been restrained, I think he would have walked out of that hospital and thumbed a ride back. The least I can do for him is to scatter his ashes in a place he loved." He lifted the bronze cremation urn from the ground beside him and placed it on the stump.

Rachel was next. Clutching the thin book she'd brought along, she stepped out from the others to face them. "Henry would appreciate your being here today," she began. "You're friends and people he's known who've cared about him and stood by him, when others didn't." Her throat tightened. She needed a glass of water but none was at hand. "Like most of us, Henry wasn't perfect, but he was a good and gifted man. He overcame the poverty and abuse of a lonely childhood. As a young man, he achieved success early, won accolades as a promising poet until the publication of *A Stone for Bread* and the controversy that followed. Before he was thirty, he had lost his profession, friends and colleagues and a woman he deeply loved. I think I could also say from things he's told me, he lost confidence in himself. At least for a time. But he never stopped reading and learning, he had a successful second career, and he continued to write. It may seem he lived out his days in quiet obscurity, a man who failed to reach his true potential, but what's true is that Henry remained passionately engaged though all of his life with issues of injustice and genocide, what he called the crimes of the twentieth century." She took a breath. Above her, sparrows chirped from the trees. A squirrel sprinted into the brush.

"Henry was *not* the author of *A Stone for Bread*. Those poems were neither plagiarized nor stolen. The poems are exactly what Henry represented them to be, nothing less, nothing more. Henry rescued the *Stone for Bread* poems from oblivion, and despite what it cost him, the world is better for it. Whatever Henry's failures, the rescue and publication of those poems was more than enough achievement for anyone's lifetime."

She ended with Theodore Roethke's poem "The Waking," one of Henry's favorites. Hers too. They'd discussed the poem the night he came to dinner at her apartment. Or rather, *she* had discussed it, offering him her interpretation, citing Wordsworth and the New England Transcendentalists and Sufi mysticism until Henry shut her up with "Goddamn it, Rachel, that's just scholar's crap. You have to *read* the poem, and read it again, and again, until it breathes in you, flows through your bloodstream and beats with your heart. *That's* what you do with poetry." Remembering, she felt herself flushing. Her heart quickened as she began to read.

> I wake to sleep, and take my waking slow.
> I feel my fate in what I cannot fear.
> I learn by going where I have to go.
>
> We think by feeling. What is there to know?
> I hear my being dance from ear to ear.
> I wake to sleep, and take my waking slow.

Voice quavering, she struggled on to the poem's end and closed the book. An uncomfortable silence followed. This was everything she and Matthew had planned, hoping others would add their remembrances. Matthew shifted uneasily and glanced her way, eyes widened in a question: what next? But next came unexpectedly. From Abe Wisner. His tenor voice, graveled with age yet achingly resonant, swelled into the silence, his chant Hebrew or Yiddish, the words unintelligible, at least to Rachel. Surely a prayer for the dead, ancient and haunting, yet strangely hopeful, a candle in centuries of darkness. Wisner's chant became her prayer too, for Henry, but not only Henry, for those others, barely known and unknown, the brother lost on the stairs, the family in Stuttgart, Rachel, Jakob and Daniel. Tears streamed from her eyes and she reached for the handkerchief in her skirt pocket, embarrassed and desperate to blow her nose. But weren't funerals for weeping? But more than that, she was grateful to Abe Wisner. He had brought her home.

The ashes were scattered and Matthew invited the guests to the house for refreshments. Wisner and Ralph Smith readily accepted,

Richard Squires and his wife dutifully so. Jim Green was sorry to decline. He needed to get back to Chapel Hill for a concert. Since he was driving, his friends left with him. Adrian wandered off to his car, but Scott joined them at the house. From curiosity, thought Rachel, expecting he'd try his damnedest to wheedle from her what she knew about *A Stone for Bread*. But she wasn't going to tell him. Or anyone. Not yet.

Henry's table was covered with a new blue cloth on which rested two lighted candles, four bottles of wine, an array of soft drinks and a platter of hors d'oeuvres, prepared by a Durham caterer—more than enough for the small group. Richard Squires and his wife seemed a pleasant couple. They sipped at their wine and chatted easily with the others, especially Wisner and Ralph Smith, whom they had recognized from Scott's video. They offered Matthew warm condolences and asked Rachel if she was Henry's daughter.

"A close friend," she said. "I assisted Scott with the video."

That seemed to delight Squires. "Well then, young lady, you should feel very good about that show. I certainly do. I also liked what you said out there about Professor Beam. Whatever you need to make good his reputation, you just call me." He took a business card from his shirt pocket and handed it to her. Senior Analyst. Merrill Lynch. Squires was a stock broker. She guessed he was offering money. If she was to do what she hoped to do, she might need a few grants.

"Thank you, Mr. Squires. I will."

Scott hung around awhile, downing several glasses of wine and asking Matthew questions about his father that he couldn't answer.

"I think you knew him better than I did," said Matthew finally. "Next time I'm down here, let's get together. You can show me the video and any outtakes, if you've saved them."

"Oh, I've saved them all right."

The tone of Scott's reply, its insinuation that he *expected* to need the outtakes, appeared to baffle Matthew. But Scott grinned and shrugged off what he apparently hadn't intended to imply. "You know, in case I need to re-edit something."

"Okay. Great."

Matthew turned from Scott to pour himself another glass of wine.

Scott's final gambit was to ask Rachel to have dinner with him at a little place he knew in Durham. When she said she couldn't, he gave up and left. Only Wisner and Ralph Smith remained, sharing Henry Beam tales with Matthew, some of which Rachel had already heard.

"I have to go," she said, apologizing for interrupting. She thanked the two men for coming and for their friendship with Henry. "You made today beautiful," she told Wisner.

Matthew accompanied her to the porch. "Mr. Wisner wasn't the only one. You were splendid out there, Rachel. Henry's probably up there smiling."

"You didn't know him. It's more likely he's furious that I talked about *A Stone for Bread*."

He laughed. There seemed to be something more he wished to say, but he didn't say it, just dug his hands in his pants pockets and shuffled slightly back from her. "You can't stick around?" he asked finally.

The way he kept scuffing the toe of a spit-polished shoe against a floor board told her he was asking more than that she linger a while longer. Her resolve to leave wavered but she held to it.

"I can't, Matthew, not tonight." Not on this night. Not after the wrenching afternoon. This night, she needed space to mourn Henry and to sort through what he had meant to her, what Matthew might mean to her in time, what he'd already begun to mean, though she barely knew him. She wondered if she could truly separate the son from the father, as if to love one meant loving the other or even loving the father through the son. She hugged Matthew and leaned her head on his chest. "When you come back," she said, "I want you to call me."

On Monday, after a weekend of contemplation and tears, she returned to work, knowing she could not unpack her feelings for Matthew Baxter by long distance. So she put him out of mind to draft a proposal for Professor Schwartz for a Master's thesis. A start, at least. As part of the project, she intended to pursue publication of Henry's René novel, along with the diary. She might even find she had enough material about *A Stone for Bread* for a doctoral dissertation. Certainly for a follow-up documentary. She made a note to call Scott and ask whether he actually did save all the Henry Beam footage. She also understood the potential complications for using any of these materials: who had rights to what and fair use and which of the principals remained alive. She might need a good attorney, she thought ruefully.

Henry had told her that the last he'd heard from Yeager, both Brisson and Marcotte were alive, though Marcotte had long ago faded from view. As for René, she knew Henry had not had contact with him since the night René dictated the Mauthausen poems to him. She knew too that Henry had never told Yeager about René. "The man had suffered enough," he'd reasoned. "Suppose Yeager had tried to find René, get him to testify to what he'd witnessed at Mauthausen? If René's identity had become public, who knows how Brisson and his cronies might have responded."

She had accepted that at the time, but now she wasn't so certain.

"Why did you publish those poems, Henry?" she'd asked the day before his trip, when he walked her to her car.

He had paused before he answered, as if he needed to ponder her question carefully, weigh each word of his response, then said only,

"Because I had to."

Last words. Henry's last words to her anyway. Before she could ask what he meant, he'd turned and headed back to the porch.

Rachel sat at her kitchen table, Henry's papers spread on the tabletop and chairs, some on the floor, most of them documents Bert Yeager and the French journalist had compiled about Renard Marcotte over the last forty years. Yet little of significance was ever published, no shocking truths revealed. What did it matter that Renard Marcotte's real name was Renard Rigaud or that he'd spent four years at Mauthausen? These revelations had destroyed the man politically but beyond that, nothing. Of more interest for Rachel was a 1983 document that seemed to show Marcotte had not always been a tool of his captors. It was only after some two years' imprisonment that he was apparently turned from a communist resister into a collaborator, following a brutal beating by a prisoner on his block. Someone like Krake, she suspected. But once turned, Marcotte/Rigaud seemed to fully embrace the status this granted him at Mauthausen. He became one of the *Prominenz*, an elite prisoner group, and an SS pet. From other documents, she learned these elites weren't necessarily spared SS brutality. In fact, the SS seemed to take sadistic pleasure torturing and even killing favored prisoners, like the Jewish youth at the quarry. It's possible Marcotte had been forced to wear the bizarre parody of the SS uniform, another of the SS's peculiar way of tormenting prisoners.

But even if Marcotte's collaboration with the SS at Mauthausen could now be proved, he would not be legally charged. France's Statute of Limitations for collaboration had run before Yeager and his French colleague had assembled enough incriminating documents. Yeager could publish what he knew, although on shaky grounds. He'd written Henry, since some of it had not yet been corroborated, but Marcotte would not be brought to trial. Only for crimes against humanity that had no Statute of Limitations, and Yeager apparently did not possess that evidence. As for Brisson, Yeager and his French colleague had apparently reached a dead end years ago in their investigations and dropped their pursuit of him.

One late afternoon, Rachel discovered in a box of Henry's documents a gray loose-leaf notebook marked *Mauthausen Poems*. The notebook held glassine sleeves, each sleeve identified on the outside by a number printed in black magic marker. She leafed through the sleeves in amazement. Sealed in them were dirty and yellowed pages, scrawled on in French, in Henry's handwriting—the poems dictated to Henry forty years ago in René's parlor. She turned the pages with care, as if afraid they might disintegrate, despite the glassine protectors. Though she had taken two years of French in college, she did not try to read them, but she read Henry's state of mind, his turmoil evidenced in the jerky, uneven scrawl, some letters large and angry, whole sentences almost racing off the page or drifting aslant. On one page, the ink blurred. The stain of tears? Henry had described tears to her. She went through the pages only once, afraid even to put a finger on the sleeves.

At the back of the notebook, stuck in the pocket, were typed pages of poems, each poem also numbered. Henry's translations. She glanced through them quickly and was about to return them to the notebook when she looked a second time, then looked again through the glassine sleeves. Henry's numbering was off. There were seventeen translated poems but eighteen poems in Henry's original French. Which poem did Henry not translate? She retrieved her French dictionary from the bookcase and spent the next hour checking the first lines of each poem. Number eighteen wasn't translated. Or included in *A Stone for Bread*. Rachel hadn't used her French since college, and the old pages and Henry's scrawl were difficult to read. But once she felt she had the right vocabulary and some idea of the syntax, she worked the poem over into a passable English rendering. By the time she finished, it was dark outside. She laid the notebook on the kitchen table.

Full circle. Henry's story had come full circle.

She got up and walked to the front window of her living room. Cars passed on the street below. An older man under a streetlight unloaded luggage from a gray Honda Accord. It was beginning to rain.

I did confront him, Rachel. In the end, I did.

Those were among the last words Henry had spoken to her. But how did Henry confront Renard Marcotte? Or when? Her mind played with the possibilities. Henry and Marcotte, Henry's final frantic days in Paris, Henry trying to get himself out of there and back to the States, afraid he might be arrested, days Rachel knew nothing about. So she let her mind conjure the confrontation: Henry Beam, twenty-three-years old, having spent the last hours in a frenzy, riding the Paris metro through the night, holding in his hands tear-stained sheets of paper, pages of poetry, poems from Mauthausen.

He is certainly agitated. Most likely his clothes are rumpled, shirt stained with sweat—it's summer in Paris, after all. His cheeks are dark-stippled because he hasn't shaved since the day before. When he finally leaves the trains, he staggers up into the warm summer air. It's dawn now. So he walks. For another hour. For two hours. Still clutching the yellowing pages of stationery. He stops on the bridge, the Pont St. Michel, where he had watched Eugénie's hat spiral down to the Seine. He peers from the stone balustrade to the water and walks on, coming at last to a familiar building. He enters it and for long nervous minutes roams its corridors. When he hears footsteps or people's voices, he steps into a dark corner or down the stairs, until finally he summons courage enough to knock at a door. A stranger answers, a muscular young man who snarls in his face. Henry snarls back. From inside the flat comes a second voice, one he knows well. Marcotte can be seen through the doorway in dressing gown and slippers. Henry calls to him. Marcotte invites Henry in.

Henry blurts out what Yeager's documents have told him, but Marcotte brushes this aside with soothing words in English.

—You're drunk, Henri. You must go home and sleep it off.

—I'm not drunk.

—*Mon ami*, this unpleasantness. Put yourself together, Henri.

More accusations. Henry holds nothing back. He's shouting now. Possibly weeping. Marcotte's young tough grabs his shoulders, attempts to shove him to the door but is stopped by Marcotte.

—It is all right. My American friend is a bit overwrought this morning.

—And Mauthausen, Henry snaps. What happened to you at Mauthausen?

—I've told you, I don't know Mauthausen. Why do you ask this, Henri?

—Because you're lying.

Perhaps Marcotte slaps Henry. Or shouts back in fury. Or merely smiles his placating smile. Rachel will never know, unless she finds such an encounter described among Henry's papers or stuck away somewhere at his house. For now, the scene lives only in her imagination. Perhaps at some moment there's a threat. Incriminating documents. Or worse, bodily harm to Henry and Yeager. Or Eugénie.

But Henry can't forget Mauthausen, the horrors René has described to him night after anguished night. He talks about the deaths, the brutality, the young singer at the quarry. Marcotte assures him he's mistaken, shaking his head, perplexed. Perhaps he's even bemused with his agitated young friend.

—Someone else, not me, Henri. I do not know Mauthausen.

In the end, Henry plays the trump, waves a page of the stationery in Marcotte's face.

—This, Henry shouts, this is Mauthausen.

Does Marcotte flinch? Does he even then admit to Mauthausen? Or does he deny the poem scrawled on a single yellowed page, the one not published in *A Stone for Bread,* a poem unlike the others: the first -person voice, poetic distance incinerated in the poet's fury.

> They look at me with blank eyes,
> bastard of a hated race.
> I count for nothing here
> though they cannot know.
> Blank eyes do not lie.
> I am nothing.
>
> Seamstress whore,
> you left me to the wind
> and what bad weather
> blows my way.
> I am no one.
> My heart is nothing.
> My hand that trembles on the pen
> is nothing.
>
> Though I hate their blank eyes,
> I know how in this place
> hate drains the heart of blood,
> my eyes go white
> with blank indifference

and I become them,

though marked as other

by scalding blade,

the hated J carved in my back.

I am them,

a thing made of nothing

a thing that can kill or steal or lie

within this hell where only such virtues matter.

Rachel stared at the poem, read it through a second time. So far as she knew, Henry had never denounced Marcotte to Yeager, never told anyone what Marcotte might have done at Mauthausen. Except her. She'd understood Henry's reluctance to judge the man: Marcotte could well have been coerced. He had obviously been brutalized. As Henry rhetorically asked: *Did he even know where the wire attached to that plunger terminated?* Henry wasn't wrong to ask those questions, she believed that, or even to speculate on the cause for Marcotte's laughter. Yet when he had voiced these questions, she'd protested. She still protested. Wasn't that what trials and juries were for, to sort truth from rationalization? Henry had obviously not seen it that way. Did he fear to implicate himself? That if he told Yeager what he knew, he might have been forced to testify against Marcotte, possibly extradited once he returned home or even charged for his dealings with Brisson? Surely, there was no Statute of Limitations for that. Not then, in the 1950s.

But—and the *but* loomed large in her mind. Henry had published Marcotte's poems, put them out there for the world to see. Published them as works of an unknown prisoner at Mauthausen. Surely, this might have caused Henry similar repercussions, brought him unwanted attention in France, raised the same questions about what he'd been doing that year in Paris. And Marcotte, what about Marcotte? By the time the poems were published, Yeager's findings and their subsequent publication had discredited the man. But suppose Marcotte had then decided to acknowledge his authorship? Accuse Henry of stealing from him? Might this have led to a political resurrection, the disgraced politician hailed as a hero of the resistance? Why would Henry have risked that? For money? Yet he'd told her once that he'd given away most of the royalties from *A Stone for Bread*. Rachel pushed her hands against the sides of her face and tried to think. There were so many questions, so many *whys*. And no answers.

"Because I had to," Henry had said.

But what did that mean?

On a Saturday morning toward the end of July, Rachel was at her computer typing in notes for the thesis topic that had just been approved, "Henry Beam and *A Stone for Bread:* A Literary Mystery." The night before, she had re-read the Mauthausen poems along with Henry's own published work. She stopped typing and reached for *First Things Last*, flipping to "Going Gentle." She had missed its meaning when she'd first read the poem months ago. She hadn't known then that when Henry wrote it, he sensed he was dying. But the poem was more than an acceptance of the inevitable. It was also Henry's personal summation of a life that had disappointed him: the rural prodigy who'd never achieved what had been expected of him, what he'd expected of himself. She scanned the poem and returned to four especially poignant lines.

> Our lightning words
> fork empty skies.
> Few meteors blaze
> beyond sad heights.

She read them again and thought she finally understood. Years after he'd left Paris, Henry came to believe René had given him the Mauthausen poems for the simplest of reasons. What if Henry's reason for publishing the poems was equally simple? What if he had realized even then, in the early 1960s, that his own poetry would never blaze beyond sad heights? That his words weren't lightning and never would be. But Renard Marcotte's were. And not merely lightning. They were witness to human depravity and the murder of souls.

The simplest of reasons. *Because I had to.*

Henry would never have trusted Marcotte to preserve the poems. Surely, he believed, as she now did, that it was Marcotte who'd had the Mauthausen prisoner Krake force René to surrender the poems. More than likely René's cherished scraps of paper were destroyed well before Mauthausen was liberated. So Henry published them as they had come to him, as the work of an unknown author. And although she would never truly know, she would believe this: that whatever the consequences, and the consequences were harsh in ways he could never have imagined, Henry would not let the poems be lost.

Rachel stared at the computer, hesitant to type another word on the blank screen. The weight of history and truth was hers now, both the poems' witness to crimes committed a half century ago and the possible later crimes masked under the banner of Marcotte's *Mouvement Liberté Française*. A formidable task that might take years. And to what end? *Cui bono*? She wouldn't know until the end was reached. But one thing she did know: she would search out that truth as far as was possible, beyond theses and academic degrees and publication. For as long as it took. For the simplest of reasons. Because she had to.

Miriam Herin's first novel *Absolution* won the 2007 Novello Press Literary Award and was cited by *Publishers Weekly* as an "impressive" debut. A native of Miami, Florida, she has been a social worker, taught composition and literature at two universities and three colleges and has been on the editorial staffs of *Good Housekeeping Magazine* and the *Winston-Salem Journal*. She has also free-lanced as a writer, editor, public relations consultant and producer of films and videos. As a volunteer, she organized and directed an inner city program for teenage children of Southeast Asian refugee families. This, her second novel, was a top-ten finalist in the 2014 Faulkner-Wisdom novel competition. Miriam is the mother of two, grandmother of one and lives with her husband in Greensboro, N.C.